Beach House Vacation

by

CORA SETON

ISBN: 9781988896519

More by Cora Seton

Beach House Romance
Beach House Wedding

For my husband, Lennard.
I love you.

CHAPTER 1

"I'M NEVER LEAVING Seahaven," Ava Ingerson said, fighting down a rising panic. "Why would you ask that? Do you think I should?" She stood with two of her closest friends where the ocean met the sand, foamy waves sweeping around her feet. She held her sandals in one hand and impatiently brushed away a strand of hair from her face with the other. It was barely dawn on a day in late July, and a light breeze was blowing, making her glad that she'd grabbed a light jacket on her way out the door.

"Not forever," Penelope Rider assured her. "I meant like on a vacation." She stood in the surf, too, her thick, dark hair piled high on her head, her shorts leaving her long legs bare. Wading in the waves was a tradition they'd recently added to their morning walks as summer unfolded in Seahaven. "I know I could use a getaway for a bit. Maybe head down south. All I've done this past year is work on my house. I'm getting restless."

Ava relaxed a little. The subject was a touchy one for her. She'd been in Seahaven less than a year, and settling

1

here had cost her the man she'd thought she'd spend her life with. It was no wonder Penelope's innocent question about future travel plans had hit her wrong.

"I'm not restless at all," she asserted. "I'm staying right here. Forever, I hope."

"You have to travel sometime, though, right? I mean, you did it for years before you came here," Emma Hudson said. Her blond hair was in a ponytail, and she wore a light blue sundress, its long skirt bunched in her hands to keep it out of the water. "Don't you miss it?"

"Not at all." That was mostly true. She didn't miss moving around from place to place, but she missed having a partner—a lot. Todd's betrayal was still a fresh wound after all these months. She'd gotten over the man himself, but without the sense of purpose she'd thought they'd shared, something was lacking in her life. Of course, Todd hadn't really shared that sense of purpose after all, had he? He had traveled for the sheer adventure of it. Nature was his playground, but that was the extent of his interest in the world around him. She felt a kinship with the plants and animals, the sea and sky. She was fascinated by the tiniest details. Todd was a big-picture kind of guy, and the focus of the picture was always himself.

It had hurt a lot when he left, but it helped that she loved this small seaside town where she'd come to settle after she inherited the Blue House from her aunt Laura. She eyed the other women curiously. She'd met them after she moved in. Penelope had grown up in San Jose but spent summers with her uncle at Fisherman's Point, the beach house that sat to the right of hers. He'd offered bare-bones accommodations to the people who went on his fishing charter trips, but Penelope was aiming for a different type of customer. She wanted to provide a venue for small, boutique destination weddings. Emma had inherited Brightview, the house to the left of Ava's, from her grandmother, and ran a bed-and-breakfast out of it, showering her guests with comfort and yummy baked goods. Ava had always assumed her new friends were here to stay. Did either of them yearn for more exotic adventures?

"I was just curious," Penelope said. "Don't worry, I'm not going anywhere. Too much work to do."

Ava thought she looked discouraged. Pen always said she was grateful for inheriting her beach house from her uncle, but beneath her enthusiasm for fixing it up was a trace of discontent Ava didn't know the reason for. Maybe she was simply missing Dan and her time with him on his fishing boat.

"I need to belong someplace," Ava told her emphatically. "Todd made sure we never stayed more than a week or two anywhere, and usually less than that. I never meant to travel for that long, and now that I've got a home I plan to stay."

"I didn't realize traveling wasn't your idea." Penelope shifted her weight as the waves pulled away and spun in again. The water was only ankle deep here, but it still exerted a tremendous pull, sucking the sand away from under their feet and washing it back over them with every return.

"I was teaching when Todd and I met," Ava reminded her. "We were supposed to be gone only one year. He promised after that, we'd pick a place to settle, get married and start having kids."

"What made you keep going then?" Penelope asked.

"Pen," Emma chided her. "Maybe Ava doesn't want to talk about it." Newly married to the handsome millionaire who'd been one of her first guests at her bed-and-breakfast, Emma positively glowed these days, and Ava couldn't help being a little envious.

"I don't mind the question," Ava assured them. "Todd kept putting it off. He kept coming up with new countries we hadn't visited yet. New sights we hadn't seen. I went along with it. I thought that was what couples did—supported each other." She made a face. "I was wrong."

"That's what couples should do," Emma said. "Noah and I support each other."

"You're lucky." Ava squared her shoulders. She was tired of feeling like a victim. Shouldn't she be comfortable with the single life by now? "Anyway, here I am living my dream." If her words rang hollow, neither of her friends pointed it out.

"I wish I was living my dream," Penelope grumbled.

Ava exchanged a surprised glance with Emma. "I thought you were. Pretty soon you'll have your house fixed up, and there'll be a wedding there every week. Besides, Seahaven is your home. You have a huge extended family close by."

"But now my uncle is gone and my mom is in Costa Rica with her new husband." Penelope ticked off her sorrows on her fingers.

"You own a beach house that you're getting to fix up exactly the way you want. You live in the best place on earth." Ava didn't have an extended family at all now that Aunt Laura was gone. Her parents and brother lived outside Philadelphia, and that was the extent of the family she'd known. Her mother's parents had died young; Aunt Laura was her only sibling. Her father's family lived in Belgium. He'd come to Philadelphia to go to school and refused to go home again. He kept in touch with his family, but she'd met them only once or twice.

"I guess I saw my life going differently." Penelope shrugged. "The grass is always greener, right?"

"You're just cranky because of all the construction at your place," Ava said. "I'd offer to put you up, except I've got a big party arriving today."

"Me, too," Emma chimed in. "Tell us if there's any other way we can help, though."

"You're right," Pen said. "I am cranky, and I'm going to shake it off." She shaded her eyes to look at the surfers farther out in the water. "I'm spending too much time in my house and not enough time out here. I don't have anyone to go out fishing with anymore, so maybe I should take up surfing. Maybe I'll meet someone as nice as Noah and won't feel so out of sorts."

"That's not a bad idea," Ava agreed.

"Next time the Surf Dads and Moms have a barbecue, you two need to come along with us," Emma said. "The Surf Moms love to teach newcomers."

"Sounds good." Ava made the resolution right then and there that she would do just that. She needed to be braver about exploring her new home and all the activities that were possible here. In a few short months she'd be a science teacher to kids ranging from first grade to eighth, and she'd need to lead them on day trips all over the county to illustrate the concepts they'd be learning. This was no time to be a wimp. Besides, she'd traveled the world, climbed mountains, camped out in deserts and jungles, navigated the biggest cities, faced all sorts of dangers—with Todd by her side.

Ava bit back a groan. She didn't need Todd to try new things. In fact, she felt braver these days than she had when he was around. It wasn't until he was gone that she realized how much he'd taken over her life. He'd been the one who always made the decisions. His whims guided their travels and their activities when they reached a new place. Seahaven was all hers. She could do whatever she wanted here, which more than made up for the fact she was without a partner.

At least, that's what she told herself.

"I'm so glad I met you two," Penelope said as they trooped out of the water onto the sand. Winston, Emma and Noah's dog, who'd been roaming the beach nearby, trotted up to join them. The retriever submitted to a thorough head patting and scratching behind the ears from each of them in turn.

"I know what you mean," Ava said, taking her turn lavishing love on the dog. Ever since she'd met Emma and Pen, they'd walked at dawn every morning and saluted the sunset in the evenings from their top-floor decks with a glass of wine—or soda or chocolate—when the weather permitted. Ava wondered if Noah's constant presence in Emma's life would eventually put a stop to either of those traditions. "It's okay if you want to go on vacation now and then," she added to Penelope, straightening again, "but don't you dare ever move away. Seahaven is where I'm growing roots, and I want both of you nearby."

"I'm not going anywhere," Emma declared.

"Me, neither," Penelope said, "despite my whining. I want an adventure or two, but I love Fisherman's Point. I mean, EdgeCliff Manor," she corrected herself with a shake of her head. "I swear, it doesn't matter how much I do to my house, it's always going to be Fisherman's Point in my mind. I wonder what Uncle Dan would think if he could see the place now?"

"He'd love it," Ava told her stoutly, even though she'd never met the man, and from the sound of it he hadn't been one for fancy touches. "He obviously doted on you since he gave you the place. He had to know you'd change a few things to make it suit."

Penelope made a face. "Actually, right up to the end he thought I'd marry a fisherman who'd take over the business as it stood. He was always asking about my boyfriends. Always trying to fix me up with one of his clients. I was so sure he'd leave the place to one of my cousins since I hadn't married, you could have knocked me over with a feather when I found out he left it to me after all."

"Why didn't you take over your uncle's business, then? You still have his boat, right?" Emma asked.

Penelope kept her gaze on the sand. "Women don't run fishing charters. The customers are too rough. Too male. I'm no use in a brawl. That's what Uncle Dan always said. Given that he was in the business for over fifty years, he ought to know."

Were there a lot of brawls on fishing charters? Ava had no idea: she'd never been on one. She sensed this was a sensitive area with Penelope and skirted the conversation. "You're doing a great job with your house, and soon you'll have a booming business," she said, but in truth she had her misgivings. Pen was fun and capable, but Ava wasn't sure how well she'd get along with the fussy, high-end clientele she was targeting.

"I'd better." Penelope caught their concern. "Don't worry about me. Like I said, I'm grumpy today. And hungry. And ready for coffee. Let's get going."

Their conversation turned to the guests Emma and Ava were expecting as they made their way home, slipping on their sandals when they reached the stairs that led to the street on top of the bluffs. Winston followed dutifully behind them, investigating interesting smells now and then. It was only a few hundred yards from there to EdgeCliff Manor, the Blue House and Brightview. Ava said her goodbyes and went inside.

Once there, she spent the rest of the morning bustling around readying the first two floors for her guests, turning on music when the place began to feel too big and lonely. She told herself she'd feel better as soon as everyone arrived and meanwhile she should enjoy the quiet, but after five years of spending almost every moment with Todd, she was still adjusting to living alone. The Blue House was spacious and made the most of its ocean view, with an open-concept floor plan on the first floor, its kitchen, living room and dining area all surrounded by windows and sliding glass doors. There were several bedrooms at the back of the house and more on the second level. The guests had the full use of those two floors, along with a deck and two second-story balconies that all faced the ocean. She was able to accommodate parties up to fourteen people, but today's group had only nine.

That was plenty, to Ava's way of thinking. She was a little worried about this particular group. For one thing, Chloe Spencer, the woman who'd booked the rental, had made it clear she was the type of picky guest who was going to find fault with something. For another, they were staying for two weeks, which in Ava's experience would be about eight days too long. People thought they wanted extended vacations until they actually took them; then they got bored being away from their homes and possessions. She might not have to interact much with her clients, but living on the top floor of the house as she did, she overheard plenty of conversations—and arguments.

Usually, on the first day, people were tired from their traveling but thrilled with the house, the view and its proximity to the beach. Days two and three generally went well, too. Everyone fought on day four, however. Kids were sick of being dragged to boutiques and galleries. Adults were sick of the beach. Married couples were sick of each other. Day five could be sullen, but by day six of a weeklong trip, people realized their vacation was nearly over and they rallied, often drinking on the deck until the wee hours of the morning. On day seven there was the scramble of packing up, and by noon they were gone, leaving Ava to hurry and clean everything before a new party arrived.

Add a whole extra week to that equation, and you got chaos. Not many people attempted it, and thank goodness some who did had a strategy in place. Those were the digital nomads who worked on their laptops part of the day or the retired couples on golfing vacations who'd made a science out of traveling together.

It was the extended families and groups of friends who tended to overestimate just how much they really liked each other. Ava had a list of possible activities on hand to offer them, not that it helped much, but she hoped this time would be different. Chloe seemed extremely organized, and Ava would bet she had a plan for every day she and her friends would be in Seahaven.

Besides, it wasn't any of her business what her guests did. She was there to change lightbulbs or fix a clogged sink if necessary. Otherwise they were on their own.

When she was done with the guest floors, Ava used the separate outside staircase to reach her third-story suite. Ready for a break, she picked up the photo album her aunt had sent to her one summer when Ava was traveling with her family in West Sumatra. Knowing Ava was desperately homesick and lonely, Aunt Laura had created a compendium of photos that captured all the places and people she routinely encountered during her days in Seahaven. That way Ava could better imagine the homey stories that filled Laura's letters and emails. There were images of every room in the Blue House and the view from the back deck. The Cliff Garden and Sunset Beach were documented, as were the Santana Redwoods and Sunset Slough, two places Aunt Laura loved to explore.

There were pictures of the grocery store where she liked to shop and the farm stand she visited every Wednesday and Saturday at Heaven on Earth farm, photos of the bank, the post office, the library and more. There were images of all her friends and acquaintances, too.

Aunt Laura had sent her new photos to add over the years as people came and went from her life. Every summer, when Ava travelled with her family, Laura wrote to her often, comforting Ava with funny little stories about the town and the people in it. When Ava moved to Seahaven last December, she'd missed her aunt horribly, but she'd found herself meeting the same people whose photos she'd been staring at for years. Aunt Laura had given her a big head start in making Seahaven feel like home. She had several good friends and many acquaintances. If only she could find someone who loved the place as much as she did—a man who thought of Seahaven as his home.

Someone who loved nature. Who loved being outside and learning new things. Someone who cared about the world, who could see the beauty in a rainstorm and the way water flowed across the land. The kind of guy who could slow down and watch a spider spin a web or stop traffic while a duck ushered its ducklings across the road.

Did men like that exist? Men so at ease with themselves they had something left to give to others?

Ava wasn't sure anymore—or rather, she wasn't sure those men were attracted to her. Noah struck her as filling those criteria, but Emma was special, the kind of woman everyone loved. Noah couldn't keep his eyes off his new wife. He spent much of his day supporting her career choices, photographing the dishes for her cookbook, helping her with videos and social media. Todd had participated in Ava's videos, but he'd always been the star.

She'd been lucky to have him.

Ava shook the thought away, increasing her pace as she finished her chores and prepared to run some errands. That's what Todd had always told her. So had her brother, Oliver, who'd been Todd's friend before she'd started dating him. Ava hadn't dated much in high school. She traveled with her parents too much over every break and summer vacation to be in the popular crowd, and by the time she reached college, she'd been awkward and shy. Todd liked to tell her he'd seen the potential in her. "What would you do without me?" he always asked, then kissed her before she could answer, confident she wouldn't have one.

He was right about that much at least, Ava thought. He'd seen something no other man seemed to. She hadn't been asked out since he left, not that she'd met many single men. She'd been too busy getting her new business up and running to go out much, and her new friends, Emma and Penelope, were too busy, too, to do more than their morning walks and evening salutations to the sunset.

She needed to go to parties and clubs. Maybe download a dating app.

She didn't really feel like doing any of those things.

Ava ran errands that afternoon, catching sight of several people who figured in her photo album, then ate dinner in her suite. At seven o'clock that night she donned a pretty sundress and took a batch of cookies out of her oven. She planned to leave them on the kitchen counter downstairs, inspired by the way Emma always showered her guests with home-baked treats at her bed-and-breakfast next door, but when she took a good look at the cookies, she wondered why she'd bothered.

Who was she fooling? She wasn't a natural hostess like Emma, all warm and welcoming. She'd kept the treats in the oven a few minutes too long, and now they looked hard and crispy instead of soft and chewy. Should she still serve them or simply throw them out? Standing in her tiny kitchen, contemplating the baking sheet she'd just set on top of the stove, she felt exactly like she did when her sister-in-law, Marie, had sent photos of the family Christmas celebration in Pennsylvania last year. Surrounded by the feast she'd prepared in her lavishly decorated kitchen, she'd looked like a diminutive Martha Stewart. Ava, in Heathrow airport on her way to

Seahaven to take possession of the house she'd just inherited, had promised herself next year she'd be the one whose house looked like a magazine spread. She'd imagined her family flying out to spend the holiday in her new home, friends flocking to her place for a fabulous holiday party.

That was before Todd had left her and before she'd fought with her brother, Oliver, who'd taken Todd's side of things. She didn't care if Oliver and Todd had played together on a soccer league before she'd dated Todd, or that Oliver was the one who'd introduced them. He was her brother, and he should have backed her up. Instead, he'd told Todd he wished his parents would dump Ava and adopt him in her place. Todd had made sure Ava heard about the comment, and when Ava confronted her brother, he didn't deny it. "You're never going to meet another guy like him," he told her. "What are you thinking letting him get away?"

Ava suspected his hostility toward her stemmed less from the fact that she'd split from his old friend and more from his anger that Aunt Laura had left him only a bequest of fifty-thousand dollars. When questioned about the discrepancy—the beach house was valued at well over two million—Aunt Laura's executor had told them the money she'd given Oliver was all the cash her aunt had left. She'd bought the beach house late in life and only recently paid off the mortgage. She made only enough from her guests to live on, not enough to stack

up a new set of savings. Ava's parents were the benefi-
ciaries of a small life insurance policy she'd had, and that
was that. "Besides, Ava is the only one who had a
relationship with her, as far as I can tell," the woman had
concluded.

She was right. Her mother had never been close with
her sister, and Oliver never bothered to keep in touch
with anyone. No one had suggested Ava sell the house
and share the proceeds with her brother, but Ava had
sensed a distinct coolness from all the members of her
family, not just Oliver, in the last few months. Not that
they'd ever been what you could call close.

She shook away the ugly thoughts. She'd done without much contact with her family for years. She could
keep going without them. Still, she sighed with relief
when she heard a vehicle pull up outside and people's
voices a moment later. No time to arrange the cookies
prettily on a serving dish—or to wallow in guilt over the
uneven inheritance. She left the cookies where they were,
hurried downstairs and threw open the door to her
guests, a greeting on her lips. She nearly choked on the
words, however, when she took in the size of the
passenger van parked outside. It barely fit in the spot she
reserved for guests, and she wondered if she'd be able to
get her RAV4 out around it.

"Welcome to Seahaven," she called out when she
recovered herself. A pretty woman with straight ash-
blond hair, who was holding a clipboard, waved back

and started toward Ava.

"Hello." She stuck out her hand, and Ava shook it. "I'm Chloe Spencer. That's my fiancé, Ben Heyward." She pointed to a tall blond man with football player shoulders who was stacking luggage by the oversized van. "And these are my friends Julian and Naomi, Carter and Elena, Gabe and Hailey." Chloe pointed to each person in turn, then craned her neck. "Where's Sam?" She gave a little sigh of frustration. "Ben," she called. "Where's Sam?"

"I'm right here."

Another man got out of the van, lugging a duffel bag. He bypassed the pile Ben was amassing and came Ava's way.

"I hope you're not going to spend the entire trip keeping us waiting," Chloe said to him when he drew near.

"Give it a rest, Chloe. I've apologized five different times for being late this morning. In fact, I'll do it again. I'm sorry, I'm sorry, I'm sorry, I'm sorry, I'm sorry. Now I'm at ten apologies. Are we good?"

Ava knew she shouldn't be staring, but it was hard not to look at the man who stood in front of her. Where Chloe's fiancé was fair, Sam was dark, his hair nearly black, his eyes walnut brown. He had none of Ben's linebacker-style stockiness, but he was well built all the same. Ava figured under his urban clothing, he was ripped. He had an athlete's confidence, and despite the edge to his voice, there was a tinge of humor to his tone that Chloe clearly didn't appreciate.

"No, we're not good. Don't sabotage my pre-wedding friend-group bash," the blonde hissed at him. "I've worked for months to set up this trip. You should be grateful you're even here."

"I wish I didn't have to be—" Sam broke off, catching Ava's eye. He squared his shoulders and sidestepped Chloe. "Hello. I'm Samuel Cross."

Ava's hand tingled when he shook it, and a curl of desire woke low in her belly as she stared into his eyes. It was a darn good thing she wouldn't have anything to do with these people as soon as she'd ushered them inside. It had been too long since she'd been with a man, and this man was—

Something.

"H-hi," she managed. "I'm Ava Ingerson. I own the Blue House. Come on in. I'll give you a tour."

Too late, she remembered Chloe, but the blonde had rejoined her fiancé and was giving him directions about the luggage. The rest of the guests were milling around, talking and finding their bags. Ava led Sam inside, knowing she was playing with fire. There was no reason for her to single him out for special attention.

"Have you been friends with the happy couple long?" she asked conversationally as she showed him the main floor. She noticed Chloe had listed the other guests in couples, but no one seemed to be paired with Sam. If he was single, maybe he should take one of the smaller bedrooms on this floor. No, she decided, she'd steer him toward the bunk bedroom upstairs. It had a view, and none of the couples would want it.

He gave a low laugh. "You could say that. Ben's been my best friend since grade school. Chloe—well, she was my fiancée before she was his."

Ava stumbled but quickly caught herself. "Why on earth are you here on vacation with them?"

He shrugged. "Just keeping an eye on things." He must have seen the look of surprise on her face. "Ben isn't just my friend," he explained. "He's my business partner. And Chloe is a very ambitious employee of ours."

Ava took that in, wondering about all the details he hadn't supplied. What had happened to break up him and Chloe? Did he still love her? What did he mean when he called her ambitious? "That sounds extremely awkward for everyone," she managed to say. It was the most diplomatic way to express her thoughts.

When he smiled, Ava's breath caught at the sheer gloriousness of it. This man could get a modeling contract if he wanted one.

"It's definitely awkward, and it's my job to make sure it doesn't turn into something worse." Sam looked around. "Where should I put my things?"

She made a decision. Maybe she was crazy, but she liked this man, and she hadn't liked the way Chloe had talked to him one bit. She knew she should put the engaged couple—the people sponsoring this vacation—in her best bedroom, but she had a better idea.

"Come on. Hurry." She grabbed Sam's hand and tugged him straight to the staircase. "Move," she hissed when he didn't follow fast enough.

"Yes, ma'am," Sam drawled but continued upstairs at his own pace.

"That way." Ava pointed to the ocean end of the house. When they'd traversed the central hall, far too slowly for her liking, she pulled open the last door on the left and pushed him in. Darting around him, she quickly crossed the room to the bed, tore the comforter back and messed up the sheets, then went into the bathroom, ran water, soaked a washcloth and tossed it with a towel on the floor near the doorway.

"What are you doing?" Sam watched her curiously as she emerged again.

"Trust me." She needed to do one more thing before Chloe discovered where they'd gone. One more thing that required Sam's cooperation.

She crossed the room again to stand in front of him, put both hands on his chest and pushed.

Sam didn't move.

Ava pushed harder. She knew she didn't have much time before Chloe tracked them down. Women like her had a way of sniffing out the best of everything, and this room was by far the best in the house. Chloe didn't deserve it. Sam did.

But he still wouldn't move.

"For god's sake, get on the bed!" she ordered him.

He smiled that incredible smile again, and her insides went molten with the sheer deliciousness of it. "Look, you're pretty, but we just met," he joked.

She stared up at him, hearing his words but not comprehending their meaning, too lost in daydreams of what she could do with a man like this. What was he saying—?

Oh.

Whoops.

"I'm not trying to seduce you. I'm trying to help you. Would you just trust me, big shot?"

He gazed at her impassively, but in the end, he nodded.

She shoved him again, and this time he gave way, stepping backward with each push until the back of his legs met the edge of the bed. She pushed him over on top of it.

"Scramble up there." She pointed to the headboard.

"I don't scramble. And I've got my shoes on."

"All the better. Do it. Now."

With a long-suffering sigh, Sam pushed himself back until he was sitting square on the bed, his back against the headboard, his legs stretched before him. "Are you going to do a lap dance now?"

"No." She couldn't believe him. Did he not understand the genius of her plan?

Probably not, she realized too late. He hadn't traveled around the world with her and didn't know that the quickest way to claim the best spot in a crowded hostel required getting there early and then clearly marking your territory.

Right on cue, Chloe burst in, Ben close behind her. "What are you doing in here, Sam? This is our room!" she exclaimed when she caught sight of the two of them.

"This room has been claimed already, but there's another one down the hall," Ava said steadily when Sam didn't answer quickly enough.

"But—" Chloe began.

"The en suite bathroom is a nightmare in this one," Ava told her. "You don't want to deal with that toilet, believe me. There's a trick to getting it to flush—I already had to help Sam. Come on, I'll show you the room you'll want to take."

"I want this one!" Chloe said, refusing to budge when Ava tried to herd her back into the hall. She pointed to the view. "It's the best one, which means it's mine." She headed for the bathroom to see the problem with the toilet for herself, and Ava had no doubt she'd send Ben for a toolkit if she thought anything needed fixing. She should have known the woman would call her bluff. Before she could think of another excuse, Sam called out, "Woah, Chloe, better hold up. I kinda stunk up the place when I first got here."

Chloe recoiled and quickly retraced her steps to her fiancé's side. Ben took her hand. "Come on, babe. Let's just grab a different room."

"But this is the best one."

"You should have told me you called dibs," Sam said. He laced his hands behind his neck and moved his feet across the snowy white sheets, his running shoes leaving a streak of dirt on them. Ava winced to think of the work it would take to get them clean.

Chloe let out a disgusted noise.

"Come on," Ben said again, guiding her to the door.

Chloe shot Sam a withering look over her shoulder. "We'll talk about this later," she said venomously. When she met Ava's gaze, her smile was insincere. "I guess I should have made it clear I had a plan for who would occupy each room. I would have thought it was obvious the bridal couple should take the best one."

"I think you'll find all the rooms are charming in their own way," Ava assured her.

"There's another door right across the hall, babe," Ben announced. "That room will have ocean views, too."

The couple left, but Ava braced herself, knowing what they'd find. A moment later Chloe exclaimed, "This one has bunk beds! I'm not sleeping in a child's room." She dragged Ben away in search of a better one. As soon as they were gone, Ava realized she'd probably created a mess for herself. If Chloe left scathing reviews of her accommodation, she might lose future business.

She turned to find Sam still on the bed.

Grinning.

"That was worth the price of the flight from Chicago," he told her.

Her sense of humor came rushing back. To hell with Chloe Spencer. "Anything to satisfy a customer." She gave a little curtsy.

Sam raised an eyebrow. "Anything?"

The tendrils of desire that had been sparking to life inside her burst into full-fledged flames. She probably would do just about anything to attract the attention of a man like him, but Samuel Cross was a guest, not a possible partner.

"I'd better go. Here's a key—this room has a lock," she stammered. She pulled the key ring from her pocket, got the one she needed off with some difficulty and placed it on a nearby side table, then escaped into the hall as quickly as she could. Hurrying to avoid crossing paths with Chloe again, who was checking out another bedroom, judging by the open door and voices arguing inside it, she made it to the stairs and down to the first floor. Outside, she hurried to the far side of the house and clattered up the separate exterior staircase to her third-story suite. Only when she'd locked her door behind her did she let out a breath and fall onto her own bed.

What was she doing, letting herself be attracted to a man like Samuel Cross? Someone who'd be in and out of her life before she could catch her breath?

She was only going to get hurt again.

LEFT ALONE IN his large guest room, still chuckling at the memory of Ava's shocked—but interested— expression when he'd hinted he might want something more from her, Sam leaned back against the headboard and wondered how he'd gotten into this mess. Why on earth was he on a fourteen-day vacation with two people who'd utterly betrayed him?

It was all Chloe's fault, of course. She was the one who'd led him on a merry chase for two years, upending his life, demanding more and more and more, including a share in his company—until he'd snapped and told her she couldn't have it.

Which meant maybe it was Ben's fault. His best friend was the one who'd recruited Chloe to Scholar Central in the first place. Now Sam wondered if Ben had been after Chloe all along, only he hadn't guessed it at the time. One night, working late with her, a couple of kisses had led to a sexual encounter in the break room that had blown his mind. A few weeks and several dates after that, Chloe had suggested she move in with him— then made it clear she wanted him to trade his apartment for a downtown Chicago condo. He'd happily obliged, stretching his finances thin to make it happen but confident the condo would grow in value along with his ability to pay for it. Back then he'd found her exciting.

He'd appreciated her drive to climb the economic ladder. Unfortunately, his opinion of her had changed over time.

As soon as they'd moved, she'd declared their furniture needed upgrading to match their new surroundings. Then Sam's wardrobe came in for an overhaul. It wasn't long before Chloe was hinting about a ring.

He'd bought that for her, too.

He wasn't bitter about any of it. Most of the upgrades he'd made for her had benefited him as well. He drew the line at making her a partner in his company, though. Scholar Central was his brainchild, and he'd built it from scratch with Ben. He thrived on calling the shots, and he and Ben worked seamlessly together. He'd been willing to cede control of his home and personal style because Chloe was going to be his wife, and women cared about those things more than men did. But he wasn't going to cede control of his company, and he wasn't going to fool himself by thinking Chloe wanted anything less.

They'd fought about it several times, but after their final argument, when he made it crystal clear he wouldn't change his mind, she took off to Cabo for a long weekend to "get some space." When she came back, Ben was with her. All three of them had been very civilized over the next few months as she exchanged Sam's ring for Ben's. After all, Ben was his business partner. Chloe was an employee.

What other choice did he have?

Especially now that Ben and Chloe had bought the condo one floor up from his. They were his neighbors as well as his coworkers, as Chloe liked to remind him, as if that meant he had to behave. Even so, he'd never have come on this vacation if Ben hadn't started hinting that maybe Chloe should take on a bigger role in Scholar Central.

She was making another play for control, and Sam would be damned if he let her win.

His phone buzzed, and when he saw it was Chitra calling, he picked it up. Of his three older sisters, she was the one to whom he'd always been closest.

"Are you in California?" she asked when he said hello. "Hold on, I'm connecting everyone." There was a pause, and she was back. Sam knew his other sisters would be on the line, too. They always did this.

"I arrived half an hour ago," he told them.

"Did Chloe give you the smallest room?" Chitra asked.

"I'm sure she planned to." He glanced at the key Ava had left him. He'd better lock his door whenever he went out, or he'd probably come back to a dead fish in his bed.

"But you outsmarted her?"

"Actually, the landlady did." He told them what happened. "I'm going to have to pay her extra to buy new sheets."

Chitra laughed. "I like the sound of her. What's her

27

name?"

"Ava."

"Is she hot?"

Sam could tell by the way she asked the question Chitra thought she was being funny. No doubt she pictured Ava as a middle-aged married woman.

Was Ava married? He hadn't seen a ring on her finger. She was young, tan, athletic. Her auburn hair was arranged in a messy bun on top of her head, and she wore the kind of clothes that would work as well on a hike through the woods as they did for errands in town. On his way through the house, he'd spotted a bird's nest on one of the console tables and a pile of interesting pebbles on one of the windowsills. There were nature prints and framed maps everywhere. Ava was outdoorsy. A nature girl.

The exact opposite of Chloe.

"She is kind of hot," he admitted.

"Ooh, this gets better and better. You should ditch the rest of those idiots and spend the next two weeks with her."

If only he could. Sam shifted into a more comfortable position. "I doubt she's lacking for company." Ava had the kind of toned beauty that attracted men like him.

"Don't write her off before you even try. Just because Chloe dumped you doesn't mean you need to stay single forever. Have a little fun and figure out what you're going to do next."

Not this again. "What I'm going to do next is come back to Chicago and keep working on launching Scholar Central. It's almost ready. We just need to find some clients."

"Oh, right. It's very important that you hurry home to work with the two people who stabbed you in the back. Come on, Sam! You've got to leave that start-up and go somewhere else."

"Chitra, stop it. Sam, don't listen to her!" Another of his sisters broke in. "You are doing exactly what you should do. Spend two weeks enjoying your vacation with your friends and then come home and work hard. You are on the brink of the payday you've been waiting for. You have a home, your family and your business. That's all anyone needs."

Sam remembered it was Sunday, which meant his sisters had just had dinner at their parents' house and were probably still there, lounging around the living room in a post-meal stupor, each of them on their phone. Priya was the oldest of Sam's siblings. Always a supporter of the status quo, she'd been a tyrant when they were kids—a sterner mother figure than their real mother.

"I think you should keep an open mind, Sam," a new voice announced before Sam could answer Priya. Leena was the second oldest daughter in the family and the one who liked to keep the peace. Their mother, Divya, who grew up in Chicago but whose parents immigrated from

India in their early twenties, had taken charge of naming her daughters. Their father, Samuel Cross the Second, had put his foot down when it came to his son, which meant Sam became Samuel Cross the Third. "Pay attention to what attracts you. Examine your feelings. What do *you* want to do now? No, don't answer—just keep asking the question. And remember, your future is working as hard to find you as you are to find it."

"Thanks," he said dryly. "I've got to get going. I'm sure Chloe has some kind of get-together scheduled."

"Chin up," Leena said kindly. "You'll get through this, Sam, and someday it will be part of the story of how you got what you really wanted. Chloe wasn't the one for you—you know that, right?"

"I do know that," he said honestly. After his initial rush of fury when she had announced she intended to be with Ben, he'd been strangely... relieved. It should have helped him move forward, but somehow he was still stuck. Every part of his life was entwined with Ben and Chloe's, and he couldn't figure out how to extricate himself from any of it.

Which is how he'd ended up here.

At least he'd stolen the honeymoon suite. Or Ava Ingerson had stolen it for him. He remembered the moment she put her hands on his chest and tried to force him onto the bed. A million thoughts had raced through his mind, including the possibility of taking hold of her and pulling her with him.

Sam said his goodbyes and stood up, glancing at the ruined bed ruefully. He was going to have to sleep in that tonight if he couldn't find a replacement set of sheets. At least the view was amazing from here. As he watched, the sun dipped down to the horizon. Maybe he'd keep the curtains open and stare out at the sea as he fell to sleep. Maybe Ava would slip into his room around midnight and join him—

Hell, he needed to get a hold of himself. Fooling around with the host of this vacation rental could get awkward.

He heard a rumble above him, a sound he knew well from his condo in Chicago. That was a sliding glass door opening somewhere upstairs. Curious, Sam carefully slid the door to his balcony open, too, not wanting to give away his presence. Were Chloe and Ben up there? It would be just like home if they were.

"I may be interrupted," he heard Ava say loudly from somewhere above him. "I've got a house full of guests. They're settling in, but someone is bound to need something."

"I thought your place was supposed to be self-serve." Another woman's voice sounded from farther away. Sam poked his head out of his room and craned his neck. If he wasn't mistaken, Ava was up on the third floor, on a balcony of her own. It had to be set back from his, because the only thing above him was sky. The balcony in front of the bunkroom across the hall from his was empty. It looked like no one had chosen to stay in it despite the fact it had a view. Looking past it, he took in the house next door. The lots were narrow here, which meant the homes stood close together. Upstairs on its third-floor balcony stood a woman with dark hair and a curvy build. Was she one of Ava's friends? They looked to be about the same age.

"It is—I'm just being a good host," Ava answered her.

"You're always a good host," a third voice said. It came from the opposite direction. When Sam turned that way, he saw a blonde on the third floor of the house on that side. She was young, too. Late twenties or so.

"Thanks, Emma," Ava said to her. "That's high praise coming from you."

"I'm sending you both over a new wine to try, by the way," the dark-haired woman called to the others. "Tell me what you think." She leaned over the railing and placed two wine bottles into a large cloth bag that was hanging on a clothesline strung between the two houses. She began to tug on the line, sending the bag across to Ava.

"Thanks," Ava called to her a few moments later. "I'm sure I'll love it. I'll pass this other one on to Emma."

A couple of minutes later, Emma called out, "Got it!" She held her bottle up high. Sam was impressed with the delivery system they'd rigged up.

"Both of you be honest," the dark-haired woman called from her house. "I only want to stock the best for my guests."

"Will do. See you tomorrow, Penelope," Ava said.

"Night, Ava. Night, Emma," Penelope called.

When the other two women—Penelope and Emma—disappeared inside their houses, Sam waited a moment, figuring Ava would withdraw into her room, then he came all the way out onto his balcony to get a better view of the ocean.

"Hello," Ava said from above him.

Busted.

"Hi." Sam turned his back to the railing and leaned against it as he looked up to where Ava stood.

"Did you hear my friends and me at our nightly ritual? We salute the setting sun with a little wine—or at least a square of chocolate, if we're not in the mood for a drink."

"That doesn't look like wine." He gestured to the beer in her hand.

"Tonight felt like a beer kind of night. Want one?"

"Sure."

She disappeared for a moment, came back and leaned over the railing. He moved directly beneath her and reached up. When she dropped the bottle, he caught it. "Thanks."

"You're welcome."

He moved to where he could see her more easily.

Opened his drink and took a long drag at it. The beer felt good going down. "Have you been running this place long?"

"About seven months. I inherited the Blue House when my aunt passed away in November. Moved here at the end of December." Her expression grew wistful.

"Do you miss her?"

She nodded. "Horribly. She was my rock. My family traveled so much for my parents' work, I was always on the outskirts of my group of friends. Kids and teenagers are lousy at keeping in touch. She's the one who understood how lonely I got when we were overseas. She made a point of telling me everything that was happening in Seahaven, so I felt like I still had a home base, even if I never actually lived here. It always seemed so comfortable here."

Comfortable? That was a strange choice of words. "Compared to where?"

"Papua New Guinea, Borneo, West Sumatra… My parents are anthropologists. They both teach at the University of Pennsylvania and do field work every chance they get. We spent every break and summer vacation overseas when I was a kid."

"Sounds like an interesting childhood."

"It was." Ava picked at the label of her beer absently. Caught him watching her and stopped. "What do you do for a living?"

"I'm part of an educational start-up. Scholar Central.

We're building an online portal that will allow students anywhere to access a top-tier education competitive with the best private high schools. We're hoping to be picked up by school districts to offer to their remote students."

Ava frowned. "Online portal? You mean kids will do all their work on a computer?"

"That's right."

"What about real-world experiences? Hands-on learning?"

That was everyone's first question, and Sam was well-prepared to answer it. "Studies show that repetition is the real key to mastery. We present new concepts in each field of study and then use a proprietary algorithm to determine how often the student needs to see and manipulate that information again. Our curriculum builds on itself organically—"

"But they don't manipulate anything, right? The word *manipulate* comes from the Latin root word *manus*, meaning hand. It doesn't sound like there will be any hands-on learning in your curriculum."

"That's not exactly true." He hadn't expected this level of pushback, and he reassessed her. What did Ava Ingerson know about teaching?

"How much of the school day will your students spend outdoors?"

He shrugged. "They can spend all of it outside if they want, as long as they can get an internet connection. We're making sure our site works on tablets and phones of all sizes."

"It doesn't count as outside if you're still hunched over a screen." Ava put her beer down on the railing and braced her hands on it. "Kids and teenagers need to move their bodies. They need to learn by doing. They aren't robots."

"Our curriculum is so efficient most students will be able to complete it in less time than they'd spend in a normal classroom. They can go outside when they're done."

Ava threw her hands up in the air. "That's ridiculous."

"No, it's not. Most high-school students are using laptops or tablets at school. How is what we're doing any different?"

"It's not. That's the problem," Ava said. "That's why I'm teaching at Seahaven Outdoor Adventure Academy this fall. At least they understand that students have been oppressed for far too long."

"Outdoor Adventure Academy?" Sam had never heard of such a thing. "What does that mean?"

"Just what it sounds like. Our students learn everything by doing. Except during truly inclement weather, we're outside moving in the world, doing hands-on activities that teach concepts intrinsically."

Sam rubbed his jaw. He had to admit that sounded pretty nice—especially in California. "That wouldn't work in most places," he pointed out. It wouldn't work for all subjects, either.

"It would work in plenty of places," she retorted. "You can't really think it's good for kids to sit at desks all the time."

"Not all the time. We do incorporate a gym program, you know."

"Twenty minutes, three times a week?" she guessed.

Put like that, it sounded pretty lame. "There are a lot of students who deserve a top-notch education but don't have access to it now," he said. "You're not going to make me feel guilty about what I do."

She sighed. "I don't want to make you feel guilty. You're right—there are a lot of kids who don't get the education they deserve." She was quiet a moment, staring out at the ocean behind him. "I used to try to reach kids like that."

"Oh yeah? How?"

"When I was traveling, I made videos for the online science channel my boyfriend and I had. Teachers used them in the classroom and parents showed them to kids at home. Other kids found me themselves. We had a ton of regular viewers."

"That's pretty cool. Why'd you stop?"

"I inherited the Blue House." She lifted her shoulders. "Seemed like a good time to settle down and grow some roots. Start a family. I thought—" She broke off. Stared at ocean behind him again. "Well, anyway, it doesn't matter what I thought."

"Your boyfriend didn't stick around?" Sam guessed.

She shook her head. "When we got to Seahaven, he stayed for one night. When I woke up, he was gone."

"You're kidding." Who would leave a woman like Ava? He was already feeling prickles of interest throughout his body every time she looked his way.

"He took all our camping gear with him. Took the RAV4 I inherited with the house as far as the nearest used car sales lot and left it for me to pick up. He said he wasn't the settling-down type."

"I guess some people are born to roam."

Ava snorted. "Oh, he roamed, all right. He bought himself an old car. Made it as far as Oregon, where he met a woman with a dairy farm. Now they're married with a kid on the way."

"He did all that in seven months?"

"Yep."

That had to sting. There was no mistaking the bitterness in her voice. "I'm sorry," he said honestly. He knew what it was like to be left behind when you no longer suited. "You'd wanted to start a family, huh?" He'd thought he wanted that, too, when he proposed to Chloe, but he'd never been able to get her to commit to a solid plan on that front.

Somehow, she'd always put him off, something Chitra liked to remind him of when the subject of his ex-fiancée came up. *Find a girl who wants kids as much as you do,* she always said. *You can't change people, Sam.*

"Yeah." Ava picked up her beer but didn't take a drink. "Why does it seem strange to admit that?" she asked. "It's like you have to be embarrassed if you want domestic things these days."

"I hear you."

She looked down at him, raising an eyebrow. "You do?"

"I thought I'd be starting a family by now."

"With Chloe?"

He nodded.

"I'm sorry that didn't work out."

"I'm sorry things didn't work out for you, either."

"You know, right now I'm okay with it," Ava mused. "I don't think Todd was the one. You know what I mean?"

Sam let his gaze run over her. He knew exactly what she meant.

CHAPTER 2

ARE YOU STILL up?

The text came as Ava was getting ready for bed. She'd said good-night to Sam reluctantly, wishing she could stay and chat with him longer. A little male attention felt good, especially when he looked at her with those serious brown eyes of his, as if she was the only one in the world at that moment.

She wondered if she'd be able to sleep. If her dreams would be crowded with thoughts of Sam.

Yes, she texted back to Penelope.

Her phone chirped a moment later, and she answered it. "What's up?"

"What's up with you? I saw you talking to some guy. Was that one of your guests?"

"Yes. His name is Sam. Get this—he's here with his best friend and ex-fiancée, who are now engaged to each other."

"Ouch! What's he doing with them?"

"Apparently they all work together." Ava filled her in.

"So he's single," Penelope mused. "It looked like the two of you were hitting it off."

"We were just talking." Ava knew what she meant, though. Sam had seemed... interested. "He's leaving in two weeks," she added, reminding herself of that fact as much as telling Penelope.

"So what? You could have a fling. He's really handsome."

"He is," Ava agreed, but she didn't like the idea of a fling.

"Let me guess. When you fall for a guy, you really fall for him?" Penelope asked.

"Nailed it," Ava admitted. "I got burned badly by Todd.... I don't need any more heartache."

"I guess."

"How did your day go? Get any renovations done?" She was ready for a new topic. Ava moved around her apartment, cleaning up, setting out an outfit for the next day and getting ready for bed.

"Today was a drag," Penelope said with a sigh. "I bought the wrong color grout for the downstairs bathroom tile, and I made a huge mistake with the trim around the windows in one of the bedrooms. I got the angles all wrong. I can't decide on what furniture to order, either. I'm so sure I'm going to make a mistake. Why on earth did I think I could cater to a high-end clientele? I don't know what rich people want."

"You're doing fine," Ava assured her. "You know

I'm willing to help anytime, right?"

"I know." Penelope sighed. "I'm really afraid I've bitten off more than I can chew. Now that I'm getting close to opening, the thought of actually hosting people makes me feel nauseous. Just because I helped Mom with her wedding last year doesn't make me an expert. What was I thinking?"

Ava wished she could soothe Penelope's nerves. She was glad she'd never need to have the level of interaction with her guests that Pen would have when she was ready to open. It seemed like she was trying to be a cross between a wedding planner and a bed-and-breakfast owner, with little experience in either role.

"Starting to wish you'd stuck to fishing charter clients?" she teased. "Did you ever try to run a charter by yourself?"

"Not exactly. Like I said earlier, my uncle thought women couldn't handle the job. He wouldn't let me take the boat out by myself, but there were times when he was so hungover I ended up doing everything myself anyway. He'd just sit there in the shade of the awning while I handled the clients and the boat, but according to him, his presence was still necessary."

"Was he hungover a lot?" Ava ventured to ask.

"Now and then. The point is, I know that boat backward and forward. I can fix every part of it, I know the feel of it in different weather and waters." She cut off with a sigh. "And yet I haven't taken it out once since I inherited it. Can you believe that?"

"Sounds like your uncle undercut your confidence."

"I guess. I feel like I need someone's permission before I can take it out, but whose?" She shook her head. "I can't bring it up with my cousins. I think one or two of them still think they should have gotten the boat instead of me. I'm too busy to fish, anyway. This house isn't going to fix itself."

"Your house is going to be wonderful when its done," Ava assured her. Surely running a wedding venue would be easier than fishing charters. Far less blood and guts, for one thing, she thought with a shudder. She didn't enjoy fishing.

"I hope so. I'd better get some sleep. See you in the morning?"

"Of course. See you then."

"YOU TALKED TO her?" Chitra demanded. "What happened?"

Sam didn't know why he'd texted his sister to tell her about his conversation with Ava. Maybe because he was too restless to sleep. He'd been pacing his room and knew Chitra was always up late.

"It was for only a few minutes." He picked up and put down each of the decorative carved wooden fish that sat on the dresser. "She was out on her balcony talking to her friends." He told her about the women in the neighboring houses and the way one of them had sent the other two bottles of wine via the clothesline pulley system.

"I love it," Chitra said. "I wish I had friends living next door to me. What did you find out about her?"

"She's a teacher. And she doesn't like online education. She thinks kids ought to spend their days outside."

"A teacher, huh? Does she want kids of her own?"

Trust Chitra to focus on that. "She says she does." He paced the room again, coming to a stop in front of a small bookcase.

"Hm."

"Don't start." He scanned the titles, old hardcovers from the past century. Mysteries, adventure stories. That kind of thing.

"She sounds smart," Chitra pointed out. "She shares a common interest with you—and she wants a family."

"So?" Sam pulled a book from the shelf. A copy of *War and Peace*.

"You said she's pretty."

"She is."

"So why are you talking to me? Why aren't you wooing this woman? You've got only two weeks."

Sam sighed and replaced the book, turning on his heel to pace again. "You're getting way ahead of yourself."

"I'm just pointing out the possibilities."

"Why are you so invested in my love life?" He stood in front of the sliding glass doors, staring into the darkness at the ocean.

"Because I don't have one, and you're thirty. You want a family. Your biological clock is ticking."

"I'm going to hang up," he warned her. He might be used to his sisters bossing him around, but he drew the line when they tried to treat him like he was one of the girls. A man had to keep his self-respect.

"Sorry. I shouldn't tease you about it. You do want a family, though, and you're not dating anyone seriously. Why shouldn't you fall in love with Ava?"

"A mutual desire to settle down doesn't mean we're right for each other. It's not convenient to try for anything long term with someone who doesn't live in Chicago."

"It wasn't convenient for our grandparents to move from India to the United States, and yet they did. When did you get so lazy?"

"I'm not lazy." He'd brought a start-up almost to fruition. If Scholar Central could get a school district to buy into its idea, others would follow, and the sky was the limit.

"Then act like a go-getter. Go get her."

"I'm going to bed."

"At least think about it," Chitra said.

"Believe me, I am."

ONLY HER SISTER-IN-LAW, Marie, would call her before sunup, Ava thought the next morning when her phone buzzed as she walked out the door. She was on her way to meet Emma and Penelope for their sunrise walk and hesitated as she looked at her screen. Marie was difficult at the best of times, but she was also persistent, and Ava had the feeling if she didn't pick up, Marie would keep calling.

Besides, someday she and Oliver needed to patch up their feud. He couldn't stay angry forever.

Could he?

Ava accepted the call. "Hello?"

"Hi, Ava." Marie was relentlessly cheerful. "Just calling to remind you it's Mom's birthday in three days."

Ava bit back the first reply that sprang to her mind, which was definitely unkind. The "mom" in question was *her* mother, not Marie's, but Marie had begun calling her that the moment she became engaged to Ava's brother. Ava knew lots of people called their in-laws Mom and Dad, and she understood that Marie missed her own mother, who had died when she was eleven. By all accounts her father was an introvert. It must have been frustrating for Marie, who loved large gatherings, especially around the holidays, to put up with his quiet ways. That didn't give her the right to try to take over Ava's family, however. She got so little of her parents at the best of times it grated on her to share them.

"I know when Mom's birthday is," she said, keeping her tone even. She wondered what Marie's real purpose for calling was. Marie liked to manage people. She wasn't exactly passive aggressive, but she wasn't exactly forthright, either.

"Want to go in on a present with us? I have my eye on this gorgeous throw blanket from Malaysia I saw at a shop downtown. It's authentic."

Ava's suspicions increased. Why would Marie want her to go in on a gift? So she could take all the credit for it and make Ava look worse in her parents' eyes than she already did? They already disapproved of just about everything she did these days. "I've already got a present for Mom, but thanks." A blanket from Malaysia wasn't going to impress Ellen Ingerson, anyway, she thought. Her parents' home was filled with artifacts from around the world given to them by the artisans themselves after they spent time in their villages. She thought about warning Marie but knew her good intentions would be misinterpreted as criticism. Marie could be as prickly as Ellen was.

"What did you get her?" Marie asked.

"A gift certificate to the Leaping Dolphin." It was a high-end sushi restaurant in Philadelphia, one of the few her mother actually seemed to enjoy.

"Again? You gave her that last year."

And you gave her a bracelet that was supposed to be imported from Borneo. How did that go? Ava thought the question but didn't ask it. It had taken her an entire childhood to learn how hard it was to please her mother. She couldn't blame Marie for taking a few years to do the same.

"It's my signature gift," she said lightly.

"How is the Blue House? Did you replace those bedspreads you were talking about?"

How on earth did Marie remember details like that? Every time Ava talked to her, she felt like she was being interrogated. "I did."

"Text me a photo," Marie said. "That room definitely needed refreshing, and I suppose bedding is the simplest choice."

"I will." She didn't say when, however. Marie had an annoying way of expecting you to meet your deadlines, no matter how trivial.

"How are your bookings? A house like that must generate a solid income."

Ava wasn't going to talk about the Blue House's income. Sometimes she wished Marie would follow Oliver's example and stop talking to her altogether. She didn't appreciate the constant reminders she should feel guilty that Aunt Laura hadn't given anything to her brother.

"I've got to run. I'm heading out for my morning walk," she said quickly to Marie.

"With your friends Emma and Penelope? They inherited beach houses, too, didn't they? You three are so lucky." Marie always remembered everyone's names, which annoyed Ava since she struggled with names herself.

"We are," Ava admitted. "I've really got to go."

"Talk soon," Marie chirped.

"Sure. Talk soon."

Marie was right about one thing, Ava thought as she entered the gate to the Cliff Garden. She was lucky to have such good friends close by; their morning ritual started her days on the right note. Today the marine layer was already thinning. It would burn off much earlier than usual, leaving a cloudless blue sky for most of the day. She spotted Emma's sister, Ashley, at work weeding a flower bed at the other end of the garden and waved.

Ashley waved back and kept on working.

"Hello," a masculine voice said in Ava's ear, making her shriek and jump away. A man caught her arm and kept her from falling.

"It's just me—Sam. I didn't mean to scare you."

Her heart was beating wildly, and Ava put a hand to her chest, willing it to slow down. At the far end of the garden, Ashley had stood up and was looking their way. Ava waved again to let her know everything was okay. "I didn't hear you coming."

"I wasn't being quiet. You were lost in thought."

"I guess I was." Ava wasn't sure what else to say to Sam. He'd taken her by surprise, and now she couldn't collect her thoughts. She was grateful Ashley hadn't come to see what the matter was. That would have made things only more embarrassing.

When the garden gate opened again and Penelope came through, Ava sighed with relief.

"Morning, Ava," Pen called out.

"Morning."

Penelope reached them, waited a beat, then asked, "Who's your *friend*?"

Ava wanted to roll her eyes at the way Penelope emphasized the final word, but instead she said, "This is one of my guests. Samuel Cross."

Penelope raised her eyebrows, and Ava nodded, sending a silent message. *Yes, the man from the balcony. The one I was telling you about.* Pen looked suitably impressed now that she could see him up close.

"Hi, Samuel."

"You can call me Sam." He shook Penelope's hand.

Emma arrived, and they did it all over again. "Too bad Noah isn't along today," she told them. "He's surfing again. Are you coming on our walk, Sam?"

"Sure."

They set off, Sam keeping pace as if it was natural for him to be there. Ava wasn't sure how to behave toward him. Was he simply a guest at loose ends, up too early in the morning, or had he deliberately kept watch for her?

Did he… like her?

Ava told herself to get a grip. Sam was from Chicago. Any interest he might be feeling was in the vacation-fling direction, and she wasn't the sort for short, torrid affairs.

"Let's head straight down to the beach today," Emma said. "I want to see Noah surfing, and maybe some of the Surf Moms will be around and we can ask about lessons."

They had made it only a dozen yards down the street, however, when a truck pulled up behind them and slowed to match their pace.

"Hi, Emma! Hi, Ava! Hi, Pen," a woman called out the window.

It was Kate Lindsey, one of Emma's first guests last spring at Brightview. She'd fallen in love with Seahaven and decided to stay and open a landscaping business with a friend she'd made in town, Aurora Bentley. Aurora was in the passenger seat. She leaned forward and waved at them.

"How's business?" Ava asked them.

"It's great. We've already got more work than we can handle, especially since Aurora really needs to slow down soon."

Aurora was four months pregnant. She'd be taking over the office jobs until her baby was born and she was cleared for physical labor again.

"I'm glad to hear you're so busy," Ava told them.

"We need to hire someone to help," Kate said. "I want to talk to you about that, Emma. I know Connor just finished his stay at Westside Recovery. Do you think he might want a job?"

Emma brightened. "I'm sure he would. Call me later, and we'll talk."

"How is Connor doing?" Penelope asked Emma when Kate and Aurora drove away. Ava waited for the answer, curious. She hadn't heard any news during the time Emma was on her honeymoon. She turned to Sam.

"Connor is a young man Emma helped a few months ago, when he was struggling." She wasn't sure how much she should say. Connor had been in the throes of addiction when Emma found him on the Trouble Bench in the Cliff Garden one day. She'd called the Surf Moms for help. Through their network of connections, they'd been able to get Connor into a detox-and-recovery program. Emma had kept in touch with him ever since and updated them when she got news. Even though Ava had never met him in person, she felt invested in his progress.

"He's doing really well," Emma said. "I think he could be a good addition to Kate and Aurora's team, as long as they've got a contingency plan in place. It's one thing to stay sober when you're in a treatment program and another thing altogether to do so out in the world. They'll have to be realistic about his temptations and make sure they know someone they can call to take his place if he ever falls off the wagon."

They took the stairs down the bluffs to Sunset Beach, the one closest to their homes, and struck out across the sand to where surfers dotted the waves. Winston, who must have come to the beach earlier with Emma's husband, noticed them and came loping over to greet them. As the sun rose over the horizon, the last of the fog burned off, making the early morning gloriously warm. Ava kicked off her sandals and led the way to the water's edge where they could walk along in the surf. Winston resumed his spot on the sand, his nose pointed toward the ocean.

"There's Noah." Emma pointed to a man straddling a surfboard taking photographs of some of the other surfers as they rode waves. "He's just playing today. These waves aren't big enough for him to get any really great shots."

"Is he a professional photographer?" Sam asked.

"Yes. He just got the cover of *SurfWorld*," she said proudly.

Noah must have spotted them because he waved suddenly and began to paddle their way. A minute later he was on shore, setting his board on the sand and shaking the water out of his hair. Winston's tail thumped on the sand as Noah approached. Noah gave him a good petting before he came to meet them.

"There's the love of my life." He and Emma exchanged a long kiss that had Ava turning away. She didn't begrudge them the love they had for each other, just wished she could find it, too. She caught Sam watching them, and when he lifted his gaze to hers, a zing of interest shot through her. His mouth curved into a smile, and something tugged inside her in answer. She remembered what he'd said about wanting to settle down and have a family soon. Did he go through life as aware of all the happy couples as she was? She always wondered when it would finally be her turn.

"This is Sam Cross," Emma said, introducing Sam to her husband when they'd broken apart. "He's one of Ava's guests."

"Just got here last night," Sam said as he shook Noah's hand. "Looks fun out there."

"Do you surf?"

"Never tried it."

"Want to try now?"

"Sure." Sam looked surprised, but he jumped at the suggestion. "I don't have a wetsuit, though."

"You'll be okay for a couple of runs. In the middle of summer like this, the water is tolerable. You'd need a suit if you wanted to stay in for hours."

"Sounds good. See you back at the house," Sam told Ava.

"Let me show you a few things on land," Noah was saying to him when Ava went back to walking with her friends.

She had no reason to feel disappointed, Ava told herself as they trailed down the beach, but somehow she was. She'd hoped to spend more time with Sam and find out who he was.

"He's pretty cute," Penelope said.

"He is," Emma agreed. "Did you invite him on the walk?"

"No. He just showed up. Nearly scared me to death." She told them what had happened at the Cliff

Garden. When they reached the end of the beach, they put on their shoes and went up the steps to the street, continuing on. "He's here for only two weeks," she concluded.

"So what?" Emma asked.

"So I don't want to fall for someone who's just going to leave again."

"Why not just enjoy yourself and see what happens?"

"That's what I told her," Penelope said.

Ava shrugged. "And I told you I get too attached to people. No sense getting hurt." Even if her body reacted the way it did every time she saw Sam.

She was grateful when Penelope changed the subject. "Have you heard about the owls roosting in the eucalyptus grove at Two Arches State Beach?" she asked Ava.

Ava shook her head. "What kind of owls?"

"Great horned owls. Someone told me they've been there for months."

"I'd love to see them." Ava perked up. Maybe she could show them to her students this fall if they stuck around that long. "Do you want to come with me? Maybe we could all go tonight."

"Sunset wine with the owls?" Emma suggested, laughing.

"Something like that. Maybe we should bring bin-oculars instead of wine."

"I can't tonight," Penelope said. "I've got my exercise class."

"I can't, either," Emma said. "Noah and I are going out." They reached the end of Cliff Street, turned around and headed for home.

"You could invite Sam," Penelope suggested to Ava.

"Sam will be busy," she said confidently. "Chloe Spencer will make sure of that."

"Who's Chloe Spencer?" Emma asked.

"His ex-fiancée and the one in charge of his vacation. Did I tell you how he got the best room in the house?"

Penelope nodded. "But Emma doesn't know."

"And I have a feeling there's a lot to tell," Emma said. "So get talking."

Ava did, keeping her friends laughing all the way back to their homes.

"THERE HE IS," Ben exclaimed the moment Sam walked in the door. Sam recognized immediately his business partner was stressed out. Whenever something was bothering him, he got very cheerful. It was maddening.

"Where the hell have you been?" Chloe demanded. "We were about to leave without you." No cheerfulness there. You always knew where you stood with Chloe, and it was clear he was in the doghouse. She was dressed up, obviously ready for an excursion. Sam had found an itinerary slid under his door when he woke up this morning, but he'd made it only to the line that said, "Art galleries," before he'd tossed it aside, losing interest. He figured he'd simply show up and get in the van each morning and go along with whatever was planned. He didn't need to know what that was ahead of time.

"It's still early," he pointed out. "I've been surfing." He'd even managed to catch a wave—for a few seconds, although most of the experience involved paddling out into the surf, trying to stand up and pitching right back into the water. He couldn't wait to try it again when he was dressed for the sport. The shorts he'd worn this morning were made from a quick-drying material that was close enough to what swimsuits were made of, so he hadn't been too uncomfortable, but he really needed a wetsuit if he was going to spend any real time in the ocean.

"Surfing? We're supposed to leave in fifteen minutes. Everyone else is ready." Chloe gestured to the rest of the group, who were clustered around the entryway. "We're all waiting for you!"

"I'll be ready in fifteen." He went to push past her, but Chloe stepped in his way.

"I hope you can be a team player. We've got a lot of ground to cover today. Ben and I need art for our condo, so we're covering five galleries before lunch. Afterward, we're driving up to wine country for some tastings. It's going to be an amazing day."

It sounded boring as hell to Sam. He didn't much care what art hung on his condo walls since the place barely felt like home to him. It would be different if he was planning a life with a woman, someone like Ava—

Where had that thought come from? Sam stared at Chloe, the woman he'd thought he'd marry until she jumped ship last year. Shouldn't she have come to mind just now instead of Ava, whom he'd only just met?

"I'll be a team player." He edged past Chloe, refusing to meet Ben's pleading gaze. Ever since he'd hooked up with Chloe, Ben had become a shadow of his former self. Always seeking to please the woman he wanted so desperately, he hovered around her, leaping to fulfill her every desire. Right now he was silently begging Sam to go along with Chloe's itinerary. Sam knew as well as anyone how Chloe got when her precious plans were upset, but it still bothered him to see Ben so afraid to annoy her. Sometimes Sam felt like he barely recognized his best friend anymore. What had happened to the go-getter he'd started Scholar Central with? It was like they were in grade school, when Ben's home life had him dragging through his days with his head bowed.

Sam took the stairs two at a time and unlocked the door of his bedroom, grateful he hadn't lost his key during his surfing adventure. In minutes flat he showered and changed and made his way downstairs.

"All right, everyone, load up the van," Ben called in that overly bright voice when he spotted Sam. Chloe was deep in conversation with Elena, one of the other women in the party, about a possible change in itinerary, both of them peering at the screen of a phone.

"I'm sure we can fit in another gallery," Chloe was saying. "I don't know how I missed this one before. It sounds so interesting."

"I know, right? When I found it I was so surprised it wasn't on your list already," Elena said.

Six galleries in one morning? Just shoot him now, Sam thought. Did he really have to go on this outing? It wasn't like Chloe was going to make her move to take over Scholar Central in between gazing at paintings.

Usually Sam thought of himself as up for anything. Ben used to be the kind of friend who made any task bearable, and Sam would bet his life Ava would be just the same way if her antics last night were anything to go by. Chloe was a different breed. She would discuss the merits of every piece of art she saw as if she were a professional critic, trying to decide if it was worthy to be featured on her walls.

He couldn't imagine anything less interesting.

Sam was the first out the door, followed by Gabe and Hailey, who were discussing whether they could afford to buy some artwork themselves on this trip. His heart sank when he saw the passenger van. The ridiculously large vehicle would make them conspicuous everywhere they went, and although Ben was a good driver, he'd had trouble parking the thing when they arrived here last night. Backing it out was going to be a nightmare. Sam could just see Chloe, clipboard in hand, shouting directions as Ben maneuvered the beast.

And then doing it over and over again, all day long.

Sam shuddered. Despite his determination to keep an eye on Chloe, he wanted no part of this day's excursion. But how could he get out of it now? He scanned the parking area. Caught sight of Ava's vehicle, a reasonable Toyota RAV4. Moving closer to it, he saw the back seat was piled with odds and ends, including a rough-looking blanket. He didn't see any light that would indicate a security system was on. Sam tried the door. It opened readily, and no alarm went off.

He waited until Gabe and Hailey climbed into the van before ducking into Ava's back seat and throwing the blanket over him. He knew there'd be a fuss when he was discovered missing, and Chloe would lead a search for him, but he also knew she wouldn't break her schedule. They were due to leave in six minutes, and in six minutes she'd be gone.

So when the RAV4's front door opened suddenly a few moments later, Sam went rigid. How had Chloe found him already? He hadn't even heard her come outside.

"See you all later," Ava called out. The car door shut again, the RAV4's engine turned on, and before he could figure out what to do, Ava was backing out around the passenger van.

"Do I have room?" he heard her say to someone.

"You're good." That was Ben. He must be helping her.

"Where the hell is Sam?" he heard Chloe yell from farther away, and he suppressed a grin. He hadn't considered the possibility that Ava would go for a morning drive, but in some ways this was even better. Chloe couldn't catch him now.

A minute later they were speeding down a road. Ava turned the radio on and was humming along to a pop song Sam didn't know. He waited a few more minutes before he sat up.

"Hi, Ava."

Ava screamed.

CHAPTER 3

"I NEARLY WENT off the road," Ava said again when she'd recovered from her surprise and stopped to let Sam get in the front seat.

"I'm sorry."

He didn't look sorry, Ava thought. In fact, Sam looked entirely unrepentant for someone who'd hid in her car and scared the daylights out of her. It was a good thing he'd popped up while she was driving through town and not on the winding highway she would have turned onto in a minute or two.

"I couldn't face the thought of touring six art galleries with Chloe," he went on. "Where are we going?"

"*I'm* going to the Santana Redwood State Park. I don't know where you're going. I should let you out on the side of the road and make you walk home."

"You're too nice for that."

"I'm too something." Ava didn't feel nearly as irritated as she was making herself out to be, though. Now that she was over her surprise, it was kind of nice having Sam in her passenger seat, and the idea of bringing him on a hike was appealing. It was always more fun sharing outdoor experiences with other people, and she was curious about the handsome man. Why had he chosen her car to hide in? He could just as easily have escaped to the beach.

"I'm definitely down to see some redwoods," Sam said. "Chloe doesn't even have them on her itinerary." He filled the passenger seat in a way only a man could, his presence larger than life in the small space. Normally she thought of her RAV4 as roomy, but not with Sam in it.

"That's crazy. They should be the first thing people visit after the beach." Chloe struck Ava as a person who preferred safe, clean, indoor environments. She probably thought forests were messy.

"That's what I think."

There was that smile again, the one that turned her insides molten with wanting. Ava imagined pulling over and parking on the side of the street, climbing into Sam's lap and kissing him.

With some effort, she shifted her attention back to the road.

"Can I come along?" he asked when she didn't issue an invitation. "We can split up, if you like, once we're there. I won't bother you."

"You're no bother," she assured him, then wondered if that had sounded too eager. She made a right into the parking lot of Cups & Waves, her favorite coffee shop.

"You don't mind a quick stop first, do you? I need my caffeine."

"Not at all. I'll grab something, too." When she'd parked, he followed her inside. The little shop had a wide plank floor with soothing cream walls and seafoam accents. Large windows let light in. Ava loved to linger and people watch while she drank her coffee, but today they'd get it to go. "My plan is to scout out the Santana redwoods so I can figure out what activities I could do with my students there. Things they won't have done before."

"Sounds like fun. Have you taught for a long time?"

"No," she admitted. "I did for a few years straight out of college, then started traveling with Todd. Now that I'm settled in Seahaven, I thought it was time to get back to it." When she inherited the Blue House, Todd had said he'd find a teaching position in Seahaven, too, but he'd kept putting off applying for any, claiming he wanted to focus on the last couple of months of their travel adventure. When the time to fly to California drew near, he said he couldn't find the right situation, even though there'd been a second position open at the Seahaven adventure school Ava thought would have suited him perfectly. Somehow she found herself telling Sam that. "It was a position that combined two part-time postings. He would have taught kids all kinds of tech-related skills half the time and math the other half. I thought we could do some team teaching, and I came up with a number of activities that crossed over between our specialties. The adventure school encourages that kind of thing."

"Too bad it didn't work out."

She remembered she was talking to a man who was on a two-week vacation with his two-timing ex and the best friend who'd betrayed him. He probably wasn't all that interested in talking about old flames.

Luckily, it was their turn to order.

"Hi, Kamirah," she said to the young woman at the till. She was enough of a regular she knew most of the baristas by name, and it was hard to forget Kamirah, with her dozens of braids twisted and looped in a spectacular updo.

"Hi, Ava, how's it going?"

"Good." She placed her order. "This is Sam," she added when Kamirah had entered it into the system. "He's a guest at the Blue House."

"Hi, Sam," Kamirah said. "Welcome to Seahaven. Are you enjoying your stay so far?"

"Definitely," Sam said. "Ava made sure I got the best room at her place. The view of the Pacific is amazing— and I got to try surfing this morning."

"That's fantastic!"

"When does school start again?" Ava asked her after Sam had placed his order. She knew Kamirah drove to Santa Cruz several days a week to take classes at UCSC, but she was a little vague on what she was studying.

"First week in September. It's been nice to have a break, but I've got to keep slogging along if I'm ever going to graduate."

"What do you want to do then?" Sam asked.

"Go into politics," Kamirah said, not missing a beat. "I hope to be on Seahaven's city council within the decade. After that, who knows? Maybe run for a state office."

Ava braced herself, hoping Sam wouldn't say something patronizing. Kamirah was young and she was a barista, but she was whip smart. Ava had a feeling she'd be governor someday.

"Have you been volunteering for any particular candidate?" he asked.

"Of course. Several of them, actually. There is a coalition of women running for offices in the state who are working together to try to help each other succeed. I've been working with them for several years."

"That sounds like a brilliant place to start. I work for an educational software start-up. Right now we're focused on teaching the basics, so we're in line with curriculums you'd find in other K-12 programs, but I'd love to offer special-interest classes to our students as well, especially one about navigating the political system."

"That's a great idea." Kamirah brightened. "What's your URL? I want to check out your company."

They exchanged information, Ava looking on with

gratification. All the baristas at Cups & Waves were nice, but she always looked forward to seeing Kamirah when she got her coffee. The young woman was full of interesting information and had her finger on the pulse of the town.

"Thanks," she said to Sam when they left the coffee shop and got back into the car.

"For what?"

"For taking Kamirah seriously."

"Why wouldn't I?" He seemed genuinely baffled, which made Ava question why she'd assumed he'd be judgmental. Because she'd never felt taken seriously when she was young?

"I'm not sure." Ava shrugged and changed the subject, keeping things light until they reached the redwoods. Once there, they were too busy craning their necks looking at the tall trees to talk much. The flat, wide loop through the big trees was set up to be accessible to as many people as possible and would be the easiest place in the park to keep an eye on a group of kids. Besides, the trees here were wonderful, huge old giants that seemed impervious to everything.

"I wish I had a better camera with me." Sam snapped photos with his phone. "I'd love some high-quality footage I could add to our curriculum."

"It's better when students come here in person, anyway," Ava said. "Kids need hands-on experiences, not just video clips."

"Video is better than nothing," he pointed out. "What percentage of students in this country live near enough to take a field trip to the redwoods?"

"They can go to their own nearest forest. All trees are valuable to study if you want to learn about the world."

"I'm sure that's true, but some kids can't get to any forest."

"Come on."

Sam's eyebrows rose. "Not every parent can send their kids to a place like the Seahaven Outdoor Adventure Academy," he said. "How much does it cost to go there?"

"The tuition is reasonable, and there are scholarships," she said. "Besides, public schools have field trips, too."

"Not as many as you might think." Sam stalked onward, leaving her behind.

IF AVA DIDN'T realize the future of education was online, then she was short-sighted as well as deliberately obtuse, Sam thought. When every student had access to the best materials produced by start-ups like Scholar Central, the world would be fairer. Schools like the Seahaven Outdoor Adventure Academy kept the best experiences for an elite group of students. He thought that was wrong.

Ava caught up to him again. "All I'm saying is seeing

photos of nature and being in nature are two different things."

"I'd like to get a 3D camera here and create an online walk-through experience of this trail. Students all around the world could navigate it and get a feel for what it's like."

"It wouldn't be the same."

"It would be better than nothing."

"I want all students to have the best childhoods they can possibly have," she argued.

Sam stopped in his tracks and turned to face her. "I want all students to have the best chance at surviving a future in which they're competing not only against each other but also against a growing set of technologies that can do jobs better and faster than them, without ever taking breaks." In a perfect world every child would go to an adventure school, but this world was far from perfect. Hadn't Ava said she'd traveled extensively? She must have seen kids left behind by their school systems.

She stared at him. "Well, that took a turn into a bleak, dystopian future."

"That dystopian future is happening right now."

Ava waved that off. "Can you at least admit that viewing a forest on a computer screen isn't the same as touching the bark of a redwood tree, smelling the scent of the decaying leaves on the ground and hearing the birds singing and animals rustling through the under-growth? It's like going on a dating app, chatting with someone for hours but never meeting face to face. You can't know what they kiss like—or if they stink—until you meet in person."

Sam made a face. Sniffed in the general vicinity of his armpit. "Do I stink?"

A smile quirked Ava's lips. "You definitely don't stink," she told him.

"Definitely?"

"You smell good," she admitted.

"Glad to hear it." He bumped his shoulder against hers. "Know what?"

"What?"

"I'm good at kissing, too."

"Race you to the big tree." Ava took off running, leaving him to gape after her. He guessed she didn't care about his kissing prowess.

"Which big tree?" Sam yelled after her, his competitive juices kicking in despite the snub she'd just given him. He took off running, as well, and soon passed her, but since he didn't know where they were going, and there were big trees everywhere you looked in this forest, it was hard to press his advantage. He slowed down until she caught up. "Which tree?" he demanded again.

"That one!" Ava sprinted past him, ducked around a group of tourists and headed for an enormous red-wood—the biggest he'd seen so far.

Sam put on a burst of speed, caught up, surged ahead and beat her handily to it.

"No fair. You cheated," Ava gasped when she caught up with him.

"How did I cheat?" Sam laughed at the outrageousness of her accusation.

"You've got longer legs."

"I think that's my parents' fault. Not mine."

She tucked a tendril of her hair behind her ear. She didn't seem angry at him for flirting with her, even if she'd literally run when he'd started. She was smiling, glowing from her exertions, and something inside him dipped and tilted when she lifted her gaze to his. His body came alive as he thought about reaching for her, but he held back, aware of the throng of other tourists around them. He needed to take this one step at a time.

"What are your parents like?" Ava asked.

"Mom's a lawyer. Dad's a surgeon." He was glad to talk about anything she wanted, as long as they kept talking. It was far too soon to flirt, he decided. Served him right she'd felt the need to make that clear. He took a breath, savoring the fresh, loamy smell of the forest, and tried to relax.

Ava laughed. "No pressure on you, huh?"

He nodded. "Wait until you hear what my sisters do."

"Tell me."

"Priya is the oldest. She's an obstetrician, specializing in infertility. Leena is dean of Global Studies at the University of Chicago. Chitra, the one closest in age to me, is a structural engineer, employed by one of the biggest architectural firms in the city."

"Wow."

"Yeah. Wow."

"Are you all close?"

He nodded. "We eat dinner at my parents' place every Sunday. Report on our accomplishments, make fun of each other, that kind of thing. My sisters call me all the time—together. They set up a multi-party call, plot their next line of attack and then add me in."

"Who's the cook in the family?"

"We all are," he told her as they started walking again. "Leena picks a different theme each week, so we don't get in a rut, but I love it when we make the recipes my grandmother handed down to my mother. My grandparents came from India to study in Chicago when they were in their twenties and decided to stay. Mom was born in the same hospital where my sister practices now."

"That's really cool. What about your dad?"

"His folks have lived in Chicago since there was a Chicago, practically." Sam thought they'd discussed his family enough. "What about you? Did you grow up here?"

"I'm from the Philadelphia area," she told him. "Bryn Mawr, actually. It's a suburb."

A swanky one, Sam thought. "And your parents are anthropologists?" he prompted.

"Yes. They're both professors at the University of Pennsylvania. I have one brother—Oliver. He's a professor there, too."

Ah. Talk about pressure. "You chose elementary education instead of following in their footsteps? How did that go over?"

"Not well. We're a little snobbish in my family."

"You don't say," he said dryly. Ava slugged him in the arm.

"They understood me better when I was traveling, since that's something they adore," she told him. "They simply can't fathom why I'm more interested in trees and stones and weather formations than I am in people."

"You don't like people?"

She scrunched up her face. "Not grown-up people for the most part. Present company excepted."

"Of course." Sam was enjoying himself. Ava was obviously passionate about what she did, but she didn't take herself as seriously as Chloe did.

"Actually, I do like people," Ava confessed. "I'm just fascinated by the way the whole world works together in one big system. If you focus on only one part of the system, like human interactions, you miss the big picture."

Sam could understand that.

"Come on." Ava grabbed his hand and tugged him off the path through the forest.

"Are we supposed to come this way?" The path was

clearly marked, and they had definitely left it.

"Not really, but it's a shortcut to one of my favorite places." She kept going, and Sam kept following. He didn't want to let go. He knew Ava had taken his hand without a second thought about it, the way she would take the hand of one of her young students, but her touch sent ripples of interest through his body. When they reached a small creek and she tried to let go, he held on.

They stood like that a moment, watching the water make its way among fallen logs and sandbars. It was quiet here, far from the tourists who'd walked the path with them among the big redwoods. Sam squeezed her hand and released it.

"Thanks for bringing me here."

"You're welcome." She bent down. "I love the way the water looks reddish gold here.

He crouched down next to her, pressing close to see what she meant. Sunlight fell through the high canopy of the trees, dappling the surface of the creek. She was right; the shallow water looked russet here, a trick of the light and iron in the water, maybe.

"It's beautiful."

"It is." She turned her face to his, and suddenly her mouth was within inches of his. Sam didn't think. Instead, instinct took over, making him lean forward to brush a kiss across her lips.

When she pulled back with an intake of breath, he

came to his senses.

"Shit. Sorry about that."

"No—it's all right." She blushed. Ducked her head. "I mean, it was a special moment. Anyone could get carried away."

Sam studied her. She'd given him an easy out, but he didn't want one. "I didn't get carried away," he told her, lifting a hand to touch her chin. "I've wanted to do that since you pushed me into bed yesterday."

He'd meant the joke to lighten the mood, but Ava's blush intensified. "I'm sorry about that. I really crossed a line," she said.

He kissed her again to stop her explanation. Pulled back. "Now I've crossed a line, too. We're even." He stood up and offered her his hand. When she took it, gratification filled him. He didn't let go during their amble back to the path and around the rest of the loop. They took their time, Ava chatting about possible activities she could do here with her students and him adding an idea now and then. When they reached the start of the trail again, she stopped to look up at him.

"Now what?" she asked.

"LUNCH," SAM SAID firmly in answer to her question. "Where do the locals eat?"

"I've been a local for only seven months." Ava chided herself for being disappointed at his response. What had she expected him to do—declare his undying admiration for her? She wasn't sure what they were doing. Why was Sam holding her hand? Why was she letting him?

"You know more than I do about the area," Sam pointed out.

"Let's go to Reggie's Pizza, then." She'd been there a couple of times on the way home from outings like these in the redwoods. It was a casual place, but the pizzas were wood-fired and delicious. Filling, too.

"Sounds good."

It wasn't far to go, and soon they were sitting at an outdoor table spread with a red-and-white-checked cloth, reading huge, laminated menus. They decided to split a pepperoni pizza, and Sam ordered a beer. Ava stuck with water.

While they waited for their food, she amused herself by scouting out the other customers. There was the usual mixture of tradesmen, professionals, and families at the restaurant. At the table next to theirs, a young mother fed tiny bites of cheese pizza to her toddler, who was tightly constrained in a highchair but seemed determined to make a break for it if the possibility presented itself.

She looked up to find Sam watching her.

"What?"

"Nothing. You seem at home here."

"I am," she said frankly. "I love it here in the redwoods as much as I love it down by the beach. I always knew I wanted to settle down and be a real part of a community. I still can't believe I get to do that here in Seahaven."

"You want to stay here?"

"Definitely. This is my home now. When I have kids someday, they'll go to my school. When I retire, I'll still have the income from my vacation rental to sustain me. I've got the beach, the redwoods, my friends. What more could I want?"

She knew she was almost daring him to say, "a man," but she didn't care. If he was interested in her, he needed to know these things.

Something flickered in his eyes, an emotion Ava couldn't quite read. Disappointment? Determination? Sam's phone buzzed, and it was gone. He took the call.

"Hello? Yeah. I'm at lunch." A pause. "With… Ava. Yes, the woman who owns the rental. Hang on." He stood up. "I'm sorry, I have to take this."

Sam moved away, still talking into his phone, and Ava watched him go. He paced the far side of the deck, gesturing now and then even though the person on the end of the line couldn't see his movements.

Whoever he was talking to knew about her. Was it a friend? One of his sisters?

It didn't matter, she told herself. The only type of relationship she could have with Sam was a short-lived one, and she didn't think she was made for those. She didn't want to fall for Sam only to have him head home in a couple of weeks.

Saying goodbye to him was already going to be hard.

"YOU DITCHED CHLOE and Ben, and you're hanging out with the hot vacation rental owner?" Chitra asked.

"Something like that." Sam decided he wouldn't tell her about hiding in Ava's SUV. "We went to Santana Redwood State Park. Walked around a little. Had a nice morning. Now we're eating pizza."

"A friend date," Chitra said. "That's the best kind. That means she's already comfortable around you. She doesn't feel like she has to impress you."

"It's not a date at all," he corrected her. It wasn't— even if they had kissed. "Ava had already planned to visit the redwoods. I just came along." Uninvited, he reminded himself. He needed to keep a clear head. He might be thinking lecherous thoughts about Ava, but she knew he was here only temporarily. He doubted she'd taken their kisses all that seriously.

"I think you should go for it," Chitra said. "Fall for her head over heels. You need to experience love."

"I have experienced it. I had a fiancée, remember?"

"You thought you had a fiancée, but that was just practice. You need the real thing. Fall in love with Ava," she said again. "Try something completely new. Forget the past and—"

"Don't you dare listen to Chitra," Priya broke in. Just like he'd thought, this was one of their conference calls. "Don't you dare fall in love with the woman who owns that vacation rental."

"Why not?" Sam asked since it was clear she was going to tell him anyway. He stopped pacing and shoved his free hand in his pocket, running his gaze over the outdoor tables until it landed on Ava. She was smiling as their waitress set a large pizza down on the table. When the waitress left, Ava looked his way, pointed at the pizza and beckoned him to come back. He held up one finger. "Make it fast, my meal just arrived."

"No woman is going to leave California for you. Is that fast enough?" Priya snapped. "Don't get your heart broken again. It isn't worth it, and you're smarter than that. There are plenty of women in Chicago who would love to date you. Enjoy your vacation, come home and we'll find you the perfect—"

Leena broke in. "You don't need anyone's advice, Samuel. Follow your heart. It won't lead you astray."

"It did last time," Sam pointed out.

"That wasn't your heart. That was your fear."

"I need to go. I'll call you later." Sam hung up, pocketed his phone and stalked back to the table. Why all his sisters felt qualified to analyze his love life when they had none of their own was a mystery to him.

"Everything all right at home?" Ava asked as he slipped into his seat.

"How'd you know it was a call from home?"

"In my experience, there's a certain expression people get when they're being lectured by family members."

Sam laughed. "That's exactly what was happening. My sisters all think they know best, and they gang up on me."

"They care about you. That's sweet." Ava's tone was wistful.

"You don't get along with your brother?" Sam's stomach growled, and helped himself to a slice of pizza. He hadn't had any breakfast.

"No. He thinks I'm still his dumb younger sister, and he's pissed I messed things up with Todd. They were friends before Todd and I started dating, but I think Todd dropped him when he dropped me. My sister-in-law, on the other hand, wants me to move back to Bryn Mawr. As if."

"You're not interested in that?"

"What's the point? My family might live there, but being around them is pretty much the same thing as being alone." She snapped her mouth shut, as if surprised by what she'd said. Sam gave her a minute. He had a feeling she needed it. When he was done with his slice of pizza, he took another.

"What are you doing the rest of the day?" he asked casually.

"Hmm? Oh. I was thinking of going kayaking." She hesitated. Glanced his way. "Want to come?"

CHAPTER 4

SAM SEEMED TO take a long time answering, and when he finally said yes, Ava let out a relieved breath. Not that she should be inviting him to do anything. It was crossing some sort of line between hostess and guest, a line she should honor if she didn't want to lose her heart.

She took a bite of pizza to cover her confusion, wishing Sam was a local. They could explore Seahaven together. Go on all kinds of adventures.

Could she fall for Sam? She looked at him again, trying not to be too obvious. Luckily, he was engrossed in preventing the cheese on his slice of pizza from sliding off it all at once. From what she'd seen, he was kind and attentive. He was interesting. Athletic. For all his talk of online education, he seemed to enjoy being outdoors.

"What are you thinking?" Sam asked.

Whoops. He'd caught her staring. She couldn't tell him what was on her mind, so she deflected his question.

"Is there hiking near Chicago?" she ventured. He looked like an outdoorsy guy, despite making a living with his computer.

He shrugged. "You have to drive a little, but then there are plenty of places. Of course, our winters are pretty brutal."

"But there's skiing?"

"Plenty of cross-country around. If you want real slopes, you have to drive a few hours."

She nodded. "So you're able to be active and outdoors quite a lot, even though you live in the city."

He took a drink of his beer. "In theory, yes. In practice, I'm part of a start-up. I don't have time for anything."

"You look like you're in shape."

"I'm in the kind of shape you get from working out in the gym downstairs in the condo where you live, not from getting out in the great outdoors. I wish I were able to be more active. Hopefully in a year or two when we hit our goals."

Ava couldn't imagine waiting a year or two to get outdoors and play. She'd had a whole lifetime of that so far, and it hadn't occurred to her that might ever change. She wondered if she'd have a hard time transitioning to her teaching job. Would she end up inside too much, even if it was an adventure school? After all, the kids had to learn as much as their peers.

No, she decided. The school was run by people like her who valued movement and exploration as much as she did. Even when she'd taught at a regular school before, she'd never allowed herself to be cooped up indoors for too long.

"I hope things go the way you want them to and you're able to get back outside," she said.

"Me, too." He raised his beer and took another drink.

An hour and a half later, they were paddling their kayaks in Sunset Slough, Ava's favorite place to go when she wanted to look for birds and other wildlife. The slough was full of activity if you were quiet and patient enough to listen and watch for it.

Sam seemed to understand the situation called for silence. Ever since they'd slipped their kayaks into the water, he'd held his tongue, pointing now and then to an interesting plant, a duck gliding by or something else he wanted her to see.

He was a better companion than Todd had been in similar circumstances, she admitted to herself when they'd nearly traversed the slough. Todd was wonderful when it came to tricky situations that called for action—rigging up a rappelling system for a steep part of a climb, fixing a broken sail on a boat, carrying her to camp once when she'd badly twisted an ankle on a remote hike.

He wasn't as suited to situations like this, though, in which you had to exert restraint if you wanted the kind of wildlife encounters Ava lived for. She hadn't been lying when she said she was interested in the whole web of life. Out here, she could see for herself all the ways every living thing depended on another. Even the non-living elements came into play. Sunshine, wind, rocks—they were all part of a system. A system she was a part of, too.

Sam glided close in his kayak and pointed to where a great blue heron was fishing in the shallow water. They watched the bird wait motionlessly for several minutes before it spiked into the water with its long beak and swallowed a small fish.

"Are you getting tired?" she asked, then bit her lip. That's what she used to ask Todd whenever he got bored. Phrasing it that way meant if he agreed, he had to admit a physical failing, which he never wanted to do. Invariably, he said no, and she got another half hour to enjoy her time in nature while he got more and more impatient. She always tried to make up for it later by pushing herself past her comfort level to accompany him on some extreme adventure that scared her to death. Now she wondered why she'd bothered. Her efforts hadn't made up for the way she'd bored him most of the time.

"I'm not tired at all. I could stay here for weeks," Sam said. "There's so much to see. Did you notice those dragonflies back there? They're like little dinosaurs."

A rush of some emotion—surely not desire—swept through Ava as she realized Sam wasn't teasing her. He wasn't bored at all. In fact, his whole face was lit up with enjoyment. He understood that tiny discoveries could be just as joyful as rousing activities.

"I did see them."

Sam set his paddle on his kayak, stripped off his shirt and stowed it away.

"I love stuff like that. I love being outside," he said and laughed. "Sounds ridiculous, I know, but these days I sit all the time…" He trailed off, his expression closing. Was he worried she'd pounce on what he'd just said? Point out that he intended the customers for his educational software—his students—to do just that?

Ava didn't say that. For one thing, she was too absorbed in the sight of his muscular arms and torso. However he worked out, he was in peak physical condition. For another, let him come to his own conclusions. He was right, after all: plenty of kids didn't have a shot at attending a school like the Seahaven Outdoor Adventure Academy.

She realized she was staring again, so for lack of anything better to do, she pulled out her phone and started filming the slough, the way she'd done when she was on an adventure with Todd. It had been so long since she'd done this, she felt like a novice as she focused on one of the dragonflies Sam had commented on. She took a panoramic shot next and then turned the phone to face herself, trying to recapture her old comfort with the process. "This is Ava Ingerson, and I'm coming to you from Seahaven's lovely Sunset Slough, accompanied today by Samuel Cross, dedicated educational software developer. Sam, say hello to the kids."

Sam grinned. "Hello, kids!" He waved at her phone, playing along.

"Today I want to talk to you about great blue herons." She focused on the bird still silently fishing some meters away and went through her spiel, outlining its life and habits. Sam paddled in and out of view in his kayak, doing his best to illustrate the concepts she was outlining with hand gestures and facial expressions that sometimes had her in stitches. "And that, kids, is what it would be like to be a great blue heron. What do you think? Would you want to be one?"

She wrapped up the video with a plug for her channel before she remembered it wasn't live anymore. Todd might have something to say if she tried to revive it, since he considered himself the star of their old series. If she wanted to upload this video to the internet, she'd have to start all over. Ava stopped filming and slipped her phone into a pocket, remembering how much time it took to get a video ready for public consumption.

"That was cool. Are you going to post it?" Sam asked, paddling close to her.

"Would you mind if I did?" She was torn about doing so. On the one hand she missed the interaction with her viewers. On the other hand, she didn't really miss the hours of work it took to get the videos viewer-ready. She had a feeling it was going to be far more fun this fall to simply teach the children in her class than to continue to try to connect with people online.

"Not at all. As long as I can plug my software in the comments," he added with a wicked grin.

"Hey!" Ava splashed him with her paddle. The great blue heron lurched up into the air and flew clumsily away.

Sam splashed her back, but she was good at this game. She'd done a lot of kayaking in her life. She angled her paddle just right and hit him with a sheet of water. Gasping and coughing, he lunged for her kayak. Instinctively, Ava jerked away. When Sam landed in the water, she shrieked, then outright screamed when he surfaced right next to her, reached up and pulled her in, too.

By the time they pulled their kayaks onto shore, they were soaking wet and out of breath from exertion and laughing. Ava pulled out her phone. Still working. Thank goodness for the waterproof cover she'd bought long ago. "I hope I still have my keys," she said accusingly.

"I've got my wallet." He produced a dripping leather mass.

She'd left her purse in the car, and she always attached her keys to a belt loop when she kayaked, just in case. They were still there when she checked.

"Hey, I'm sorry about dunking you." He caught her wrist as she went to move past him. "Did I go too far?"

"Not at all. Everything's fair in a water fight," she assured him.

"Good." He leaned forward and kissed her.

"WHAT WAS THAT for?" Ava asked when Sam finally pulled away.

"An apology kiss," he said lightly. He didn't want her to suspect how badly he'd wanted to touch her again ever since they'd shared that moment at the stream in the redwoods. All day he'd watched her emotions play over her face. He'd witnessed curiosity, joy, humor—and interest in him, if he wasn't mistaken. His body was making it clear it wanted to get a whole lot closer to Ava. Her dripping clothes were molded to her figure, and her curves begged to be touched.

"We should dry off." She opened the door to her vehicle and pulled a couple of towels out of the back seat. "I come prepared for anything," she told him.

"I'm impressed." He did his best with the towel she gave him, but his shorts were still dripping water.

Ava bent down, flipped her hair over her head and squeezed the excess moisture out of it before straightening again. Something about the movement revved up his already too-active libido. When she spread her towel over the ground and lay down on it, it took him a moment to realize it wasn't an invitation.

"The sun will have us dry in no time," she said.

"Good thinking." He joined her, spreading his towel close to hers, lying down and closing his eyes because that was the only way to stand the brightness of the day from this angle. He moved his hand until it found hers, twined his fingers through hers and gave them a light squeeze. "You're a fantastic tour guide, Ava Ingerson."

"That's my job."

By the time they left for home, Sam was logy from the sunshine, hungry from a day's exertion—and thoroughly confused.

He was having a hard time remembering why he'd ever wanted to buy a condo in downtown Chicago. Why he'd signed on to do an educational software start-up— and why he'd stuck with the company after his best friend and business partner stole his fiancée. Every decision had made sense at the time, but now they added up to a life he didn't recognize as his. He remembered how good it used to feel when he camped and hiked and pushed his body to the limits, then went to bed thoroughly exhausted—a feeling he hadn't had in years. He'd definitely sleep tonight. When was the last time he'd played all day?

Sam thought about that. When had he stopped camping and hiking—and all the other outdoor pursuits he used to make time for? He'd done a lot of it during high school and college, and even after they started Scholar Central, he and Ben used to go on adventures several times a year. Then Chloe came along.

Sam sighed. Chloe had changed everything. First she'd taken over his life and then she'd taken over Ben's. He'd never even considered how Ben must have felt when he began to cancel the activities that used to be their lifeblood. Before they let Chloe derail everything, they'd worked and played together, shooting for a shared dream.

Did Ben miss the old days, too? If Chloe were gone, would they get back to the kind of easy friendship they'd once had?

Probably not. Too much water under the bridge. Besides, he didn't want to go backward in life. He wanted to move forward.

Sam couldn't help looking at Ava, who was driving them home. Why had he never met someone like her in Chicago? He'd had more fun today than he'd had in years, and when he tried to picture going home and re-creating the adventure with someone else there, he couldn't imagine it.

"Here we are," Ava said, pulling into the parking area behind her house. "Uh oh. I think you're in trouble."

Chloe was standing by the door in a tan skirt and wine-red blouse, an outfit more suitable for the office than the beach. Her arms were folded across her chest. Ava was right; she looked pissed.

Sam opened his door as soon as Ava parked and climbed out. "What?" he said to Chloe. He wasn't interested in drawing this out.

"Where the hell have you been all day? Do you have any idea what you've put us through? Ben couldn't focus on anything because he was so worried. We didn't buy a single thing. And did you forget about dinner? We have reservations at one of the best restaurants in town. You're going to make us late."

Sam didn't bother explaining himself. "I'll be ready in ten minutes." He nodded at Ava. "Thanks for everything."

She nodded back and made her way around the house to the stairs to her place. Sam hoped she understood he didn't want to drag her into this drama. He'd talk to her later and let her know what a great time he'd had today.

"That's all you've got to say for yourself?" Chloe followed Sam inside. "I knew it was a mistake to let you come on this trip, but I had no idea you'd be such a child about it. I can tell you're doing this to get back at me. Well, it's time to grow up. Go get ready."

Sam, who was already halfway up the stairs, had intended to ignore her, but when Ben appeared at the top of the stairs, he found himself trapped between them. Ben, in khakis and a polo shirt, squared his shoulders. "I think you owe Chloe an explanation for disappearing on us today," he said quietly.

Anger, pure and clear, welled up in Sam's chest. "Really? You think I'm the one who owes someone an explanation?" He held Ben's gaze until Ben looked away. They'd never actually talked about the fact that Ben had jumped at the chance to hook up with Chloe before Sam's engagement to her was officially over. Evidently, he was surprised Sam would bring it up now.

"Chloe set up a nice dinner for everyone—you in-cluded," Ben went on doggedly, still not looking at Sam. "The least you can do—"

"The thing is, I don't want to be included," Sam said angrily. "In fact, it's entirely inappropriate for me to be included. I don't know why you even invited me." He wondered if everyone in the house was listening to this argument. Standing in the stairwell like this, their voices would carry.

"Ben invited you because you're supposed to be friends. I told him you'd be spiteful," Chloe said from the downstairs hall. "You want to ruin this for me."

"No, I don't." He'd had enough. "I'm here, which I admit was a mistake on my part. I will try to accompany you on some of the activities you've lined up." He said this to Ben. He didn't give a damn about Chloe's feelings, but once upon a time, Ben had been a good buddy of his. If they were going to keep working together, they had to try to get along. Besides, he did need to keep an eye on Chloe, even if spending time with the two of them was beginning to feel like torture.

Ben swallowed hard. "I can live with that."

"Enjoy your meal." He clapped Ben on the shoulder as he passed him and kept moving, feeling better than he had in weeks now that he had a free night ahead of him.

AVA HOPED THINGS would go okay for Sam when he

went inside, but she heard the sound of raised voices, so she wasn't optimistic. The way Chloe had followed him suggested she wasn't ready to drop the argument they'd started in the parking area. Ava considered going after them to try to keep the peace, but it wasn't her place to interfere in the lives of her guests. She made her way around the house to the stairway to her suite instead, but once there she found it difficult to settle down.

When she heard the passenger van's doors shut a few minutes later, she waited until she figured her guests were gone and retraced her steps. As she'd suspected, the parking area only contained her RAV4. The door to the lower unit was shut, and the place was quiet. Chloe must have strong-armed Sam into attending her dinner.

Upstairs again, she changed, showered and stepped out onto her deck, eager to breathe in the ocean air and let the view soothe her. She'd had such a wonderful day with Sam; it was a shame it had ended so abruptly.

Ava leaned on the wide railing.

"Hi," Sam said from the deck below hers.

"Oh!" She laughed at her own surprise. "I thought you went with the others."

He shook his head. "I made it clear I'm going to pick and choose what events to join them at."

"And Chloe accepted that?"

"Ben did, which is what matters. Chloe wishes I'd just disappear."

Ava wondered if he was really as dispassionate as he

pretended when it came to his ex-fiancée. If Todd and his wife were here in the house, she'd struggle to keep her composure. She tried to picture it and winced, glad the two of them were miles away.

"You all right?" Sam asked.

"Fine."

"Hi, Ava!"

When Emma called a greeting from the house next door, she startled Ava all over again. It wasn't time for sunset yet.

"Just wanted to say hi now, since you're going to see the owls later," Emma reminded her.

"Right." She'd forgotten all about the owls.

Emma craned her neck. "Hi, Sam," she called. "Having a good time here in Seahaven?"

"I'm having a great time."

"Well, I've got a few things to do. See you two in the morning."

"See you!" Ava said.

Emma disappeared inside, and Ava wondered if Sam would join them on their sunrise walk again in the morning.

"Want to get some dinner?" Sam asked.

"Yes," she said slowly. "If you're game to visit some owls afterward." She told herself it was okay to spend more time with Sam if they were doing something educational. Maybe he'd go home with some ideas to add to his curriculum.

"I'm down for that."

They stopped on the way for a leisurely dinner at a Mexican restaurant, so it was dusk by the time they reached the eucalyptus grove at Two Arches State Beach where the owls were reported to be nesting. No one else was around, and Ava wondered if the rumor Penelope had heard was just that—a rumor. They approached the trees through a picnic area that was probably packed during the daytime. This late in the evening she spotted one couple walking some distance away and could hear the voices of teenagers down at the beach. Other than that, the place was empty.

"Would owls really hang out this close to where people congregate?" Ava whispered.

"I don't know," Sam said. "Why don't we sit here and see if we notice anything moving in the trees?"

"They're supposed to sleep pretty high up," Ava said. She sat on top of a picnic table. Sam joined her, his shoulder pressed against hers. She welcomed the friendly contact. It was quiet here, a light breeze playing through her hair, the sound of the surf in the distance an ever-present ebb and flow.

A minute passed and then another as the sky grew darker. The trees were shadowy, and Ava saw no signs of life among their branches. She was beginning to wonder if Pen had been pulling her leg. Maybe Emma was in on the joke.

Sam sucked in a breath. "There."

She followed his pointed finger and at first didn't see anything. Then there was a shifting in the shadows among the branches of a tree. Was that—?

It was. An owl swiveled its head. Ruffled its feathers. Preened a little, then went still again. She could barely make it out in the dusk, but when it moved, it was easier to see.

"It's so big," she whispered, terrified any noise she made would scare it away.

"Imagine it up close."

She shivered a little. Sam put an arm around her shoulders, and she leaned against him, still watching the trees. The owl preened some more, using its beak to bring its feathers into proper alignment. Ava appreciated having the place all to themselves. If there had been a crowd watching its performance, it wouldn't have been so special.

A flash of shadow through the trees made her sit up straight again, her heart beating hard. Another owl. The first one's mate? It settled in a separate tree, and Ava waited, barely breathing. A few minutes later, it hooted, a low, compelling sound that made the tiny hairs at the back of her neck stand on end.

Sam's arm tightened around her. The owl hooted again, paused and then sounded a third time. Its soft calls echoed through the growing darkness for several minutes before the first owl answered. Her call was slightly higher, and it was a joy to hear them talking back and forth. Ava wondered what their conversation meant.

When the owls lifted off from their perches several minutes later, almost as one, her heart soared with them for a moment, until they were gone and she was left alone with Sam. She turned to him, already knowing what would happen next. His arm tightened around her as he gathered her close, and he kissed her.

WAS THERE EVER a more perfect time for a kiss? Sam mentally thanked the owls for favoring them with their presence. He knew Ava was feeling as blessed as he was to have been given a glimpse into the lives of two such wild, independent creatures. Now she was in his arms, kissing him back, melting against him, and his body was reacting to the soft feel of her in his arms.

He'd kissed her before, but this was different. He explored her mouth with his own, brushing his lips softly over hers, but soon grew more urgent, his arms tightening around Ava, wanting to feel more of her.

When Ava pulled back, it was almost painful to let her go. He knew she wanted him as badly as he wanted her, but he recognized her hesitation. She'd been hurt—badly—by a man not so long ago. Sam controlled himself with difficulty, knowing a few more kisses would end up with her in his bed. He wasn't going to push this woman, though. If they were together, he didn't want her to regret it.

"It's early," she said, having a hard time meeting his

eye.

He searched her face in the growing dark, although he couldn't see much. Coming to a decision, he stood up and took her hand again. "What do people do for fun in Seahaven?" he asked.

Ava thought about that and hesitated so long he was afraid she was going to say she was ready to call it a night. "Live music," she finally answered. "The Pelican's Nest is a restaurant and bar on the wharf that also has a dance floor."

"Then let's go there."

"I guess we could do that."

Back at the car, she drove them to the wharf. On the bar's rooftop deck, he ordered drinks for both of them. They'd secured a small table where they sat across from each other. Ava still seemed happy to let him hold her hand while they listened to the music play and waited for their drinks. She liked him.

Maybe too much.

Sam considered that thought as the band began a new song and people filled the small dance floor. Was Ava afraid she could lose her heart to him? He could see why she wanted to avoid that. So much disruption came with a long-distance relationship. He wasn't sure he was ready for one. Yet here he was, pursuing her. If he was a gentleman, maybe he'd bring her home right now.

He didn't want to be a gentleman, though.

He moved his chair to the same side of the table she

was sitting at and entwined his hand with hers. When their drinks came, he toasted her, but as soon as he could, he pulled her to her feet.

"Let's dance."

She followed him onto the floor. The music was a fast-paced, upbeat tune, but Sam pulled Ava close into a slow dance.

"I don't think this is what we're supposed to be doing," she said in his ear, laughing.

"I don't care." He held her close and swayed slowly, keeping them on the outskirts of the crowd so they wouldn't get bumped by the other, more vigorous dancers.

Every fiber in his body wanted to take Ava home right now and make love to her. He let himself enjoy being turned on, aware of every place where her body pressed close to his. This is what being alive felt like, he told himself. He'd been sleepwalking his way through life since Chloe dumped him. He didn't want to go back, but he'd lost track of where he was headed, except for focusing on Scholar Central.

Sam told himself he could worry about the future another time. Right now all he wanted was to dance with Ava. Song after song, they swayed that way, going back to enjoy their drinks now and then, until Sam felt more intoxicated by Ava's proximity and his own desire for her than from the alcohol.

"Sam," she sighed when he kissed her for the dozenth time. It was a helpless plea. Did she feel like he felt? Was she buzzing with anticipation of the moment they came together? He—

"Oh." Ava pulled back suddenly and clapped a hand to her hip. Withdrawing her phone from her pocket, she pressed it to her ear. "I have to take this," she said. "Hold on."

CHAPTER 5

*A*VA DIDN'T KNOW whether to be grateful or annoyed by Marie's timing. She hurried to the stairs that led to the main part of the restaurant where she could hear better, away from the sound of the band.

"Marie? What's up?" It had to be late in Bryn Mawr.

"Just calling to remind you about Mom's birthday."

Sam joined her in the stairwell and ushered her down the steps as she spoke. "Again? We already talked about this."

"I know, but it's almost here. Did you put that gift certificate in the mail?"

"I didn't have to mail it. I'll forward the email on her birthday, and she can print it out."

"That's kind of tacky, don't you think?" Marie asked. "I mean, you're sending a card, right?"

"Marie, look," Ava said in irritation. They were on the first floor now, threading through the restaurant. "I've got things under control. Okay?" Sam opened the door and led her out to their parking spot on the wharf.

"Okay. Didn't mean to overstep." Marie sounded

offended.

"I'm actually out with a friend. I'll call you tomorrow." Ava hung up, not sure if she was more irritated with Marie or Sam. "What are you doing?" she asked him.

"Heading back to the Blue House."

Ava swallowed her disappointment. She'd been enjoying the music and dancing with him. Liked the sensation of being close to him in a situation where there was no danger of things going any further. She drove home in silence. She parked behind the house, grateful to see the passenger van wasn't there. Chloe and the other guests were still out.

When Sam took her hand, she pulled it away quickly.

"Can I come up?" He indicated the walkway that led to the stairs to her top-floor suite.

"No."

Sam looked surprised. "No?"

Trepidation filled her as she wondered how to say what she needed to express to him. This was probably the end of their wonderful flirtation, and she couldn't lie to herself—she was going to miss it. "You live in Chicago. You're leaving in less than two weeks, and I don't do flings. If I sleep with you, I'm going to fall for you, and then you'll be gone. It's too much."

After a long moment, Sam heaved a sigh. "I want to argue with you, but I can't. You're right—I am leaving, and there's not much time for us to get to know each other. I've had a great time with you so far, though. The hike, the kayaking, the owls, the dancing. Today was the best day I've had in a long time." He hesitated, as if he was searching for something else to say, something that would put off the end of their good time together. "Are you sure?" he finally asked. "Maybe a short time together is better than nothing?"

"That's not the way I'm made," she told him reluctantly. God knew she wished it was different. Her body was aching to lead him upstairs and take him to bed. She knew she was going to regret sticking to her principles.

He sighed. "Guess it's time for me to say good-night, then." He leaned in for one last kiss, and she allowed it, nearly moaning as their mouths met a final time and her fingers clutched the fabric of his shirt. She wanted him so badly.

All she had to do was say so. She was a big girl. She could have a fling if she wanted to.

Ava waited a beat too long, though. When the kiss ended, Sam got out of the car and made his way into the first-floor entrance. Ava gathered her things, rounded the house and walked up the two flights of stairs, which tonight seemed endless. She let herself into her suite, kicked off her shoes, padded to her deck and slid open the doors. Maybe the ocean breeze could soothe her tortured soul—

"Guess great minds think alike," Sam said, from the deck below her.

Ava groaned. She couldn't get away from this man.

Sam chuckled, a low, heady sound in the dark. She wished she could climb over the railing and jump right into his arms.

"You know, when it was clear things were over with Chloe and me, I was sure I'd never find another woman I could fall for," he said. His back was against the railing, his arms crossed over his chest. "I was wrong."

Ava swallowed. Nodded. "When Todd left, it was like my life was over. I kept going through the motions but couldn't seem to catch my breath. It got easier over time, but I thought I'd had my one chance at love. That I'd never feel anything like the way I felt when I first met him, but…" She wasn't brave enough to finish the sentence, but she figured it was obvious what she meant to say. Sam made her breath catch every time she saw him. His touch made her crave him. "Sam—"

A car door slammed. And then another.

Sam swore under his breath. "They're home."

Ava stared down at him helplessly. "They'll go to sleep." But it was only half a minute before someone was knocking at Sam's bedroom door. She could hear the pounding from where she stood.

"I'll see you tomorrow, Ava." And he was gone.

"IT'S LATE," SAM said to Ben after he'd closed the sliding glass door to his balcony and opened the one to the hall to let Ben into his room. He was struggling to suppress the desire he felt for Ava and his disappointment that she was holding back. "You've been drinking. Why don't we talk tomorrow?" He didn't have patience for another confrontation.

"Let's talk now." Ben closed the door behind him and moved farther into the room. Sam wondered if he'd fortified himself with alcohol before coming to find him. The Ben he'd known before Chloe came onto the scene would never have needed to do such a thing. Once upon a time they'd thought of themselves as brothers.

"You've had a problem with me and Chloe since the start," Ben said.

"Gee, I wonder why?" Sam bit off the rest of what he wanted to say. Sarcasm wasn't going to help anything.

Ben pulled back. "Okay. You're right—the way I got together with Chloe wasn't cool, but the thing is I always loved her and you never did."

"I got engaged to her, didn't I?" Sam pointed out.

"That doesn't mean anything. You were going through the motions. You never really listened to her. She came to work and told me about it day after day. Do you know how hard it was to listen to that, knowing she'd chosen you over me?"

"You and Chloe talked about me while I was still with her?" That made things even worse. Ben was supposed to have his back. Why hadn't he mentioned Chloe was bringing their personal business to him?

Any sympathy he'd felt for his old friend was slipping away fast.

Ben dropped his gaze. "We worked together on projects all the time. We had business issues to discuss, but yeah, life came up—the way it does with people you care about."

"So you were angling for her right from the start."

"No, I wasn't," Ben said. "I was being her friend. You weren't there for her. You never even helped with the wedding. You wouldn't pick colors or talk about flowers or table settings, the things that matter to a woman. After a while, she started coming to me for advice."

Sam couldn't believe what he was hearing. "She never once asked me my opinion about any of those things. She was Chloe the conqueror. She had everything figured out. When I printed out a playlist for the reception, she balled it up and threw it at my head."

Ben scrunched up his face. "Why was she asking me about china patterns all the time, then?"

"Because she was making sure she had a backup plan in case I refused to give her shares in Scholar Central." Chloe had dropped hints for months about becoming an equal partner in the company before they had their blowout fight. He'd rebuffed every one of them. She must have known there was a good chance she wouldn't manage to convince him.

Had she been playing them both for fools?

He stared at Ben as the truth sank in. All this time

he'd thought Chloe had changed her mind about him after their big fight. That wasn't how it had happened, though, was it? She'd been hedging her bets all along, making sure that no matter what, she'd still have a pathway to becoming a partner.

"She set both of us up," he told Ben. "She kept you on hold until she was done with me."

Ben shook his head emphatically. "You're way off base. Chloe's not a player. Besides, that's not what I'm here to talk about."

"What are you here to talk about?" Sam wanted him to see what was right in front of his nose, but he knew if he tried to force it, Ben might refuse to talk about it at all.

"Respect. We all have to work together, which means you need to be okay with Chloe and me being a couple. You have to get over her."

Sam nearly laughed, remembering how hard he'd been trying to get Ava into bed fifteen minutes ago. "I am over her," he assured Ben.

"Good. Because Chloe is integral to the future of Scholar Central."

Sam stilled. *Integral.* That was a loaded word. "In what way?" he asked cautiously.

"What do you mean, in what way?" Ben sounded exasperated that he had to spell it out. "She's the one putting feelers out to get us customers."

"She hasn't got us any yet." Maybe he shouldn't feel

happy about that, but right now he did. As far as he was concerned, it was time for Chloe to move on from Scholar Central.

"She will soon. She's ambitious, Sam. I don't think you appreciate that about her."

Ben was right. Sam knew all about Chloe's ambition, and he didn't appreciate the way she wielded it like a club. "She's replaceable."

"No, she's not," Ben said sharply. "She's going to be the making of us."

Something was off here. Why did Ben sound so sure about that? Chloe hadn't produced any deals yet. She was young, like the rest of them. Untested. "Is that your assessment of the situation or Chloe's?"

Ben dropped his gaze again, and Sam's gut tightened.

"Come on, Ben," he said. "We had a hundred applications for the position you hired Chloe to fill. She's not that special."

"Yes, she is."

Couldn't Ben see how toxic this all was? Sam paced a few steps before facing Ben again. "This is my fault. I should have asked Chloe to quit when I proposed to her. I screwed up, but that doesn't mean you have to." He figured he was going to regret saying what he needed to say next, but this trouble had been brewing for months. "You should tell Chloe she can't work for Scholar Central anymore, and you should do it before the wedding."

"No way." Ben straightened. For once he looked like the man he was before he got tangled up with her. "I'm not asking Chloe to quit. Not when she's so valuable to the company."

Was Ben going to ask him to make Chloe a partner right now? Sam steeled himself against the possibility. There was no way he'd do that. It was bad enough Chloe was still an employee of the firm, given their circumstances. There were a dozen other people they employed who deserved to become partner more than she did. People who'd joined Scholar Central long before Chloe.

"Can you really not see how uncomfortable it is for me to work with her?" Sam asked evenly. He knew he needed to keep his anger in check. Ben loved Chloe, for better or for worse. He wouldn't stand for Sam attacking her.

Ben pulled back. "Yeah, I can," he said quietly.

Sam wasn't going to let him off the hook. "Don't you see how awkward it is for everyone in the company?"

Ben frowned. "It isn't any of their business."

"Of course it is. I kept things professional at work when Chloe and I were together, but the two of you are all over each other. She's by your side half the day. Everyone thinks she's running the show now. They think she's getting favorable treatment."

"No, they don't," Ben said. "Everyone loves Chloe. That's why everyone she invited jumped at the chance to come on this trip. And when they find out—" He cut off. Turned away as if transfixed by the view out the sliding glass doors.

"When they find out what?" Sam's anger turned to alarm. What had Chloe cooked up with Ben?

Ben took a deep breath. Met his gaze again. "When they find out she's going to take this company to the next level, they'll love her even more."

Sam laughed. "I won't hold my breath."

Ben leaned toward him. "I know you think I'm a big joke for picking up what you put down, but you're underestimating Chloe, and you're going to be sorry when you find out what she's capable of."

"Is that a threat?" Sam asked. "Is she going to kill me in my sleep?"

"She's going to show you who really deserves to run Scholar Central," Ben said and walked out the door.

"ARE YOU SURE everything is okay?" Ava asked Sam when they stood on the Blue House's stoop early the next morning. He'd appeared silently in the Cliff Garden when she'd come to walk with her friends and had accompanied them, but he hadn't taken part in their conversation, which had faltered after a while in the face of his preoccupation. She'd told her friends she'd talk to them later and ushered Sam back to the house.

Sam kissed her cheek absently. "It's fine," he said.

"Sam."

He glanced her way and then seemed to come back to himself. Ava thought he hadn't heard two words she'd said to him so far today.

"Sorry. I've got a lot on my mind. Ben gave me a bit of a dressing down last night about—" He broke off and shrugged. "About everything. Chloe. Our business. I haven't decided what to do about it."

"Sounds like a lot to process," Ava said.

He stepped closer. "Look, could we get out of here?"

"Here he is." Ben stepped out of the door, calling over his shoulder to someone inside. "You're not trying to slip away, are you? We're driving down to Monterey to go to the aquarium and spend the day. We'll eat lunch and dinner there, too. I'm counting on you to come along. Understand?"

Ava held her breath. Sam didn't say a word. He just stared at Ben until the other man nodded and ducked back inside.

"Guess you've got a full day." Ava asked.

Sam shook his head slowly. "The last thing I want to do is see a bunch of fish."

"The Monterey Aquarium is actually pretty great. I'm sure you'd like it."

"Not with Ben and Chloe along."

"It's that bad?"

"Yep."

"I'm going to Shelbridge Heights," she heard herself saying. "It's an area in the hills that was burned by a wildfire a few years back. I'm going to use it to teach my students about succession growth."

"I'm in. Let's go."

She tossed him the keys to her car. "I'll be right there."

She raced upstairs to her suite, rummaged in her refrigerator for the sandwiches she'd packed earlier, grabbed some extra fruit and drinks and then went to the pantry, where her picnic basket was stored. Luckily, she kept it stocked with utensils, a blanket, paper towels and more, so it wasn't long before she was ready. All the while she told herself she was doing Sam a favor, but she wasn't sure that was true. After hanging out with him yesterday, the idea of exploring Shelbridge Heights alone hadn't sounded like that much fun. It was too easy to lure him along with her instead of encouraging him to stay with his coworkers.

"Where do you think you're going?" Ben erupted from the downstairs door just as Ava made it to the parking area, basket in hand. Sam, who was sitting in her car, got out.

"I think I'm going to study succession growth with Ava." He pushed past Ben, took the picnic basket from her and stored it in the trunk of her RAV4.

"You're making a mistake," Ben told him. "Every time you leave, our employees think something is wrong with the company. We need to present a united front—especially now."

"Now that you're giving your fiancée perks they aren't getting?" Sam asked.

"Now that my fiancée is poised to take this company from being theoretically valuable to having real worth."

"Sure. Whatever." Sam returned to the passenger side of the car. Ava got in the driver's seat, eager to leave.

"Sam." Ben came to peer in the window.

"Drive," Sam told her. Ava didn't need to hear it twice. She started the engine and revved it. Ben stepped back. "See you later," Sam called to him as she pulled out. "Much later," he added more quietly.

Ava left him alone for the first few minutes. "I bet visiting a bunch of burned trees will take your mind off your problems," she joked to ease the tension.

"I bet it will." He took her hand for a moment, squeezed it and then released it to let her drive. "It's a little weird always being the passenger," he remarked a few minutes later. "Nice to be able to watch the scenery, but I'm used to being the driver."

"You're on vacation," she pointed out. "Think of me as a tour guide."

"I think of you as a lot more than that." Sam looked away, as if surprised by the words he'd said. Ava wasn't sure how to reply to that. She'd tried to make it clear last night she didn't want a fling, but she'd nearly caved when they talked on their balconies, and she couldn't pretend she wasn't attracted to him. If Ben, Chloe and the others hadn't come home when they did, who knew what would have happened?

She studied Sam out of the corner of her eye when she thought he wasn't looking. He looked comfortable enough, filling the passenger side of the car. His hands rested on his thighs, his fingers tapping out a tune only he could hear. She knew he would spring into motion when they reached their destination, ready to join in whatever she wanted to do. It was nice to have someone around who was unfazed by her capability and interests.

When they reached Shelbridge Heights, she parked the RAV4 in a pullout by the side of the road and got out. A trail wound into the hills to what once had been a lookout with a pretty vista of a wooded valley but now was more like a disaster area. The charred remains of the fire were grim, but enough time had passed they should be able to spot signs of life springing back.

"You take me to the nicest places," Sam quipped when he got out and surveyed the blackened forest.

"You're going to love this, believe me." She handed him the picnic basket, locked the car and led the way to the trailhead. "The point of this lesson is to teach kids about the ways fires and forests interact naturally and unnaturally when people get involved. Fire was suppressed around here so long that when it did burn, the damage was far more destructive than it might have been, and a number of people lost their homes. Now the forest is renewing itself—and so are the people. They're rebuilding in the same places, even if it might not be the best idea."

As they walked, she pointed out how some trees had fully burned and others had resisted the flames. There were places where new growth was charging back and others that looked lifeless. When they reached the vista forty-five minutes later, they could see the extent of the damage.

"It must have been a hell of a fire," Sam said, whistling.

"It was, from what I've heard. Makes me grateful I live right near the coast," she admitted. "Everyone got out, at least."

"Good."

He helped her lay out the picnic blanket, and they both sat down.

"Is it weird having a picnic in the middle of a forest fire disaster area?" Sam asked.

"All in a day's work for an adventure scientist," Ava told him. She handed him a sandwich. "Better than sitting at a computer screen all day, don't you think?"

SAM ATE HALF his sandwich and washed it down with water from the container Ava handed him, before acknowledging her question. He set the rest of it aside, wiped his hands and then pulled Ava into a kiss. "I'm not going to talk about the relative merits of our occupations," he told her.

"You aren't?"

"Nope. In fact, every time you try to get a rise out of me about my online education company, I'm going to kiss you." He released her and went back to eating.

"Is that a fact?" Ava took another bite of her own sandwich.

"That's a fact."

She chewed and swallowed. "So, for example, I shouldn't say that I don't think little kids should sit for hours at a desk?"

"Not if you don't want me to do this." He set down his sandwich again, edged over to her, cupped her chin in his hands and kissed her thoroughly. All of his senses were buzzing nicely by the time he pulled back.

"Huh. So I shouldn't say that education can't be one size fits all, and teachers need to tailor their curriculum constantly to the students in their classes?"

He kissed her again, taking even longer before they came up for air. It was hard to stop, like weaning himself from oxygen when he was desperate to take a deep breath.

Ava smiled at him. "And I shouldn't say I think kids need to be taught how the lessons on their screens translate to the world around them?"

It was pretty clear to him she was enjoying this as much as he was. This time he bowled her over onto her back, careful to cradle her on the way down, and quickly moved on top of her, pressing the length of him against her, kissing her until both of them were breathless. She felt so good underneath him, and his body wanted more, something he was sure was apparent.

Kisses weren't enough. He slid his hand under her shirt.

"Sam!" Ava's swift reaction surprised him. She couldn't shove him off her, but the minute she tried, he rolled away.

"What's wrong?" His first reaction was that she'd been stung by a bee or wasp, but Ava only sat up, set her shirt to rights and glared at him.

"I'm not doing anything more than kissing. You're leaving in two weeks. I'm not getting involved with you."

"Could have fooled me," Sam said a little more gruffly than he meant. He was aching for her, and it took every ounce of self-control not to reach for her again. He'd spent hours in bed last night picturing everything the two of them could get up to together, and now he wanted to make those dreams a reality. He knew she wanted him, too, and it frustrated him she was holding back. There was real chemistry between them, even if they'd known each other only a couple of days.

"I don't want to get hurt," she said stiffly. "I know I'm acting like a teenager on her first date, but I know myself, Sam. This isn't going to end well for me."

"I don't want to hurt you," he growled. "It's the last thing I want to do." He sat up and shoved the rest of his sandwich into the picnic basket along with the remnants of their meal. When he was done, he stood up and waited. Ava got to her feet slowly and stepped off the blanket, watching him silently while he folded it. He knew he shouldn't be angry with her, and he wasn't. Not really. He was just—Hell, he *was* mad. At Chloe for ever bringing him here. At Ben for ranking Chloe above their years of friendship, and at fate in general for arranging for him to find the perfect woman in California instead of Chicago.

"We'd better get going," he said.

"I guess so."

It was a long, silent hike to the car and a silent drive home to the beach house. Sam knew he should try to tell Ava what he was thinking. It wasn't fair to make her feel he was angry with her.

He couldn't find the words, though, and the truth was he didn't want to *talk* to her. He wanted to be inside her. To finish what they'd started in the burnt-out forest. His body was craving that release, and it didn't help he could picture every part of it. He knew just how she'd feel in his arms. Knew how it would feel to explore her body. Didn't she want that, too?

When they pulled into the parking area, the passenger van was still absent. Sam helped carry the picnic basket to Ava's third-story suite. When she tried to take it from him in the doorway once she'd unlocked her door, he lifted it out of her reach and walked right in. After he'd set the basket on her kitchen table, he faced her.

"I know you think this can't work between us. I know you don't want a fling. The thing is, I want you as badly as I've ever wanted anyone, and I'm willing to take anything I can get. I'll play by your rules, but, Ava—" He lifted his hands in a gesture of defeat. "I'm human. I'm going to keep trying."

CHAPTER 6

"*I* WANT YOU, too," Ava said, then put a hand up to stop him when Sam crossed the distance between them in a few short strides. She was still frustrated at him for pushing her too far and frustrated at herself for not simply telling him to leave her alone if she wasn't going to pursue anything with him. It wasn't fair to either of them to keep hanging out with Sam and kissing him, then pretending she didn't want more. She wanted to be angry at the way he'd cut short their picnic, but she wasn't sure if he deserved it. He was the one being honest about what he wanted. She was saying one thing and doing something else altogether.

"I don't know what to do," she told him truthfully. "What I do know is I need to think it over. You've been honest with me, so let me be the same."

He nodded, his body tense and ready as if he was merely waiting for her to give him permission before he picked her up, carried her to the bed and made love to her for the rest of the day.

Maybe that was exactly what he was doing. There

was an intensity in Sam's gaze that told her he wasn't playing games anymore. He wasn't interested in her in a casual way. He'd crossed the line in the way men did to wanting to possess her.

Heady stuff. Dangerous, too—for her heart.

Ava was beginning to wonder if that even mattered anymore. One way or another, she was going to be hurt when Sam left. Why was she wasting precious time?

Because she'd told herself she wasn't giving herself or her heart to just anyone after what happened with Todd. She'd meant to take her next relationship—if there was one—slowly enough to ensure that she chose someone more suited to her. She had criteria, one of which was that the next man she dated would be someone who lived here in Seahaven.

Sam failed to meet that test.

"I'm going to take tonight to make a decision whether to be with you for the rest of the time you're here or whether to end this now," she said, telling herself it was the responsible thing to do. "I want you to spend tonight with your friends." When he blew out an angry breath, she raised her hand again. "I need you out of the house so I can think straight." She got a grudging smile at that. "In the morning, I'll give you my answer."

Sam heaved a gusty sigh. "Guess I can go along with that."

"Good."

He moved closer.

"Hey, you're supposed to give me until the morning." Ava lifted her hands to ward him off.

Sam drew her close until her palms rested on his chest. "Just giving you some evidence to weigh while you're thinking your options over." He bent down, brushed his mouth over hers once, twice, before claiming hers for a kiss that went on and on and on. She felt it down to her toes, a flush of desire surging through her like a wave.

"See you in the morning." He left so quickly she had to steady herself with a hand on the kitchen counter.

When she'd caught her breath, Ava texted Emma and Penelope. *Emergency meeting. Can I come to one of your houses?*

Within ten minutes she was seated at the counter that surrounded two sides of Emma's kitchen at Brightview. Emma was whipping up a batch of blueberry scones. Penelope sat beside Ava.

"So he's cute, he's built, he's smart, has a good career and he's a great kisser, but he isn't a local?" Penelope ticked off Sam's attributes on her fingers.

"Exactly. I want him. Bad. But he's going to leave in a matter of days. Then what?"

"You could follow him," Emma suggested.

"No, she can't!" Penelope exclaimed. "We need her here."

Ava smiled at her. "I don't want to live in Chicago," she told Penelope. "I love it here. I love my home. I can't wait to start my teaching job. I don't want to give all that up."

"Maybe he could relocate," Emma said. "From everything you've told us, it seems possible. He's struggling with his business partners, right?"

"Sam doesn't strike me as the kind of guy who walks away from a project," Ava told them. "I think he finishes what he starts."

"So you'll wait until he's finished, then he'll move here. You could do a long-distance thing for a while, couldn't you?" Penelope asked.

"You're such a romantic. What about his family? His condo?" Ava asked.

"What do you want to do?" Emma put in.

"I want to be with him for as long as I get." As she said the words, Ava realized they were true. "I just never thought of myself as the kind of person who got involved with someone when there was no possibility of a future."

"You don't know there isn't a possibility," Emma said.

"She's right," Penelope said. "Have your fling with him. Neither of you are being dishonest with the other person about the situation. This isn't at all like Todd pretending he'd settle here and then running away. Sam has been clear with you this whole time."

"I guess you have a point."

"Enjoy him for the time you have with him," Emma

said. "Face it, you're going to be unhappy either way. If you don't sleep with him, you'll be just as broken up about it as you will if you do. Maybe more."

"Who knows? He could be lousy in bed and then you'll be happy to get rid of him," Penelope joked.

"He could be lousy in bed," Ava agreed. But somehow she knew he wouldn't be.

"Want to dance?"

Sam looked up, surprised to find Hailey standing before him, holding out a hand. He'd done his best to be inconspicuous during dinner and the night out on the town Chloe had planned, but he was counting the minutes until he could go back to the Blue House. Hailey was one of the group that had come on this vacation, a friend of Chloe's who'd come to work for Scholar Central within the last year. She was a little younger than him, polished and glossy like all of Chloe's friends. Sometimes he wondered if she'd recruited them from a talent agency: must fit the role of smart, young professional—female.

That wasn't entirely fair to Hailey, though, who had a business degree from Purdue and who was coolly efficient at work, but it was true she fit a certain mold, like everyone Chloe cultivated. Chloe believed in upward mobility and believed that certain people buoyed you, while others weighed you down. While they were together, he'd watched her sever the ties of several of her friendships, and those women had sunk away into oblivion as Chloe kept moving up. When he'd turned from a helium balloon to dead weight in her opinion—when he'd refused to make her a partner in Scholar Central—she'd cut his tether, too.

"Uh… sure." Sam looked around the club, wondering where Gabe had gotten to. Hailey's boyfriend owned a couple of gyms in the metro area and was usually draped over Hailey's shoulder possessively. Had something happened?

He followed Hailey onto the dance floor and started to move half-heartedly, realizing too late saying yes had put him in a compromising position. He was Hailey's boss, after all.

"We're not in the office now," Hailey said, as if reading his mind. "I wanted to talk to you."

"Okay." Sam wondered if he should make a quick escape. He must have betrayed himself in some way because Hailey put a hand on his arm to prevent him from leaving.

"I think what you're doing is a mistake," she said loudly enough that several other people dancing near them turned their way.

"What I'm doing?" Sam didn't know if she meant dancing with her or the fact that he'd thought about running away.

"Keeping Chloe down. It's obvious she's the one who's going to put Scholar Central on the map. Don't get me wrong; you and Ben designed a great service, but neither of you can do what Chloe does. She's a dealmaker."

"She hasn't made any deals that I know of." Had Chloe put Hailey up to this?

"Not yet. But she will, and when she does, you're going to feel pretty small."

Sam stopped dancing and peered at her. Was Hailey drunk? He was still her boss, whatever she thought of him. He opened his mouth to say so, but she didn't give him the chance. She stopped dancing and faced him.

"You should make her a partner. We all feel that way."

"What's in it for you?" The words left his mouth before he thought them through, but they seemed to hit home nonetheless. Hailey backed off.

"No more than I deserve." She turned and darted through the crowd of dancers, leaving him standing there looking after her, trying to process what had just happened. Had Chloe bribed people to back her in this endeavor of hers to take over his company?

As he made his own way off the dance floor, he reminded himself she'd spent a mint on this trip. He'd thought she'd done it to soften the blow to her work friends if she got promoted to partner, but maybe she was being far more proactive than he thought.

What had she promised Hailey and the others? Had she told them there'd be bonuses if she got the shares in the company she wanted? Perks? Promotions? After all, she was pretty sure she'd be running the place soon.

The knowledge she was outmaneuvering him didn't sit well. Sam didn't bother to let the others know he was leaving. He'd find his own way to the Blue House.

And then he'd figure out what to do next.

AVA WAS SITTING on her balcony when she heard a sliding glass door rumble open below her and knew Sam was home. She hadn't heard the passenger van park outside, nor were there sounds of anyone else in the house. Either the others were tiptoeing to their bedrooms, or Sam had come back alone.

"Ava?" his voice asked.

Should she answer him or pretend she hadn't heard? "I told you I'd give you my answer in the morning."

"It's past midnight," he pointed out.

"That's cheating."

"I know." There was a long silence. "What if we call a timeout for the rest of the night? I'll come join you, and we'll be two strangers looking at the stars having a chat. I could use the company."

Was this a ploy to lull her into a false sense of security? Ava stood up from the deck chair she was sitting on and came to the railing. "No touching?"

"No touching," he agreed.

She turned the idea over in her mind, pretending she hadn't decided yet.

"Okay, you can come up." She turned to let him in her door, knowing he'd have to get through the house, outside and around to her stairs, but when she heard a chair scrape across the balcony below hers, she retraced her steps to find Sam clinging to the railing. Before she could protest, he swung one leg over the edge, levered himself up and dropped to stand in front of her.

"What are you doing?" she squeaked.

"Coming to join you." He plopped down in a chair. After a moment, shaking her head, she took the other one.

"And here I thought I was safe from intruders on the third floor. I'm going to have nightmares now."

"I could stay with you. Keep you safe." He stopped himself and made a face. "Sorry. Can't help myself."

"We're supposed to be strangers," she reminded him. "Strangers don't proposition each other."

"You'd be surprised. People do all kinds of unexpected things."

She wondered what had happened tonight. Sam was a little disheveled, like he'd run his hands through his hair a hundred times. "Want a beer?" she asked him.

"I've had enough to drink."

She fetched them both tall glasses of water and sat again. "Want to talk about it?"

He grunted. "Is it that obvious I've got something to talk about?"

"Something's wrong." She took a sip of her water,

set it on the ground and leaned back in her chair. Above them the stars were clear, but fog was moving in. She knew in an hour the little pinpricks of light would be obscured.

"Hailey gave me a talking-to tonight—at the club we went to."

Ava remembered her, a glossy blonde who seemed like she'd be far more comfortable in a suit than in the sundress she'd worn when she arrived. "Isn't she one of your employees?"

"Exactly. She's also one of Chloe's good friends. She let me know I was messing up. She thinks Chloe should be in charge. I wouldn't be surprised if Chloe has told everyone she'll give them a kickback when she secures shares in the company."

"Wow," Ava said. "Do you think they're all going to take her side?"

He nodded glumly.

"There's nothing they can do to force your hand, though, right? You're the boss."

"So is Ben. And he's siding with Chloe."

"I'm sorry to hear that."

"I wish I'd been here with you instead. All night I was thinking of holding you in my arms like when we danced before." He took a long drink, then drained the rest of his glass. "I wish you lived in Chicago," he said, setting it down.

"I wish you lived in Seahaven."

Their words hung in the air, pregnant with all the things they weren't saying. She hadn't asked him to think about moving to join her here.

And he hadn't asked her to come to Chicago, either.

Which made sense, given they'd known each other only a few days.

"I can't figure out why this is happening," Sam burst out. At first Ava thought he was talking about Chloe's machinations, but then he added, "Why would I meet someone I can't even be with?"

"Fate?" Ava hazarded.

"I don't even know if I believe in that. My sister Leena, does. She's always talking about it. *Follow your heart. You're being guided to your best life.* So if this"—he gestured from her to him—"is fate, what's the point? Is our time together supposed to motivate us to keep looking for the right person close to home? Or drive us crazy with the knowledge that the right person is out there, but we can't have them?"

Maybe Fate is telling you to move to California, she thought but didn't say it out loud.

"I don't know," she finally said when it was clear he'd run out of possibilities. She wished she could urge him to move to Seahaven permanently, but he'd told her about his family, and she could picture him at Sunday dinners at his folks'. Three sisters bossing him around lovingly. Parents doting on him. Surely it would be wrong to try to tempt him away from all that. It made no difference if she was physically close or far away from her family. They probably barely noticed her absence.

Marie was the only one who ever called her.

"I'm kind of tired," she heard herself say, even though every fiber of her being immediately protested the idea of losing any time with Sam. "I should get some sleep."

"Let me guess. You don't want me to stay and guard you from intruders," he asked glumly.

"Not tonight. Seems like you have some thinking to do, anyway."

"I guess." Sam stood up. Took her hand and pulled her to her feet, then gently into his arms. She stiffened, but he only said, "Good night, Ava," kissed her on her cheek and then walked through her suite and let himself out the door.

Ava watched him go, her heart aching to follow him and call him back. She'd done the right thing, she told herself.

Even if it felt so wrong.

THE NEXT MORNING Sam meant to join Ava for her daily walk again, but when he heard a quiet knock, he opened his door to find Hailey outside.

"I'm just here to say I was drinking last night, and I don't want you to misconstrue anything," she said stiffly. "Chloe hasn't made me or anyone else any promises. I stood up for her because I know she's going to do great things for Scholar Central. You need her. We all do." She slipped away down the hall before he could answer.

Had Chloe coached her about what to say? It seemed likely. Sam considered retreating to his room and locking the door until everyone else left for the day, but he decided he needed to show he wouldn't be cowed by a mutiny.

He met Chloe and Ben on the stairs.

"Everyone's up early," he said a little gruffly. He still wanted to catch Ava and her friends before they left for their walk. Ben and Chloe blocked his way, though.

"Don't you ever look at the itinerary?" Chloe asked. She wore a stylish dress and heels today. Something upscale and name brand, he figured. "We're going to San Francisco. We're leaving in half an hour. Everyone needs to eat first."

"I hope you're coming with us today," Ben said. "I think it's important everyone sees us together. People were talking about the way you ditched us last night."

Sam just bet they were. Had Hailey told them all what she'd said to him? Had she been triumphant about the way she'd set him down a peg?

He wished he could walk out the door, but he needed to know what Chloe was up to. He had a feeling she was expecting him to duck out again and that she would welcome it. Despite Hailey's muttered protests to the contrary, he was confident he'd guessed the truth last night. Chloe was paying people to take her side. What was her next move?

"I'll be ready to go when you are," he said and got the satisfaction of seeing Chloe's frustration. He'd keep an eye on her today, but he was frustrated himself; he'd much rather spend time with Ava. He followed the couple downstairs, grabbed a couple of pieces of toast and a cup of coffee and hurried back to his room, hoping to catch Ava on her balcony when she returned.

When Chitra called, he was grateful for the distraction. There was no sign of Ava yet, so he filled her in on everything that had happened since their last conversation.

"Invite Ava along to San Francisco," Chitra suggested. He could hear the sound of people talking in the background. She must be at work, heading from one meeting to another.

"I can't ask her to an event I didn't plan."

"Sure you can. There's room in the van, right?"

"Definitely." Sam had no idea why Chloe had gotten one that seated so many more people than were in their party.

"Ask Ben. I bet he'll say yes. Anything to distract you from the fact he's shacking up with your ex-fiancée."

"I'm not sure Ava will go along with it," he pointed out. "She sent me to bed pretty early last night."

"She told you she wasn't going to decide until today. You were pushing her. She was setting healthy boundaries. I'm telling you, Sam, you have to go after her—"

Priya interrupted her. Her line was full of noise, too, and he could picture her hurrying through the halls of the hospital. "Haven't you given up this foolishness yet? This girl isn't for you. When you get home, I'll find you someone local. Someone you can settle down with."

Sam was beginning to wonder how his sisters found time to work when they spent so much of it ganging up on him. "What if Ava is the woman I want to settle down with?"

"You've known her three days! Three days!"

"Nearly four," Sam broke in.

"And you want to uproot your life for her? What about your business? What about your condo? What about Mom and Dad—and us?"

"I'm just saying—"

"You're saying nonsense, that's what you're saying. All that sunshine has gone to your head!"

"Have you seen any signs?" Leena asked. Her line was quiet. She was probably in her office at the university.

"Signs?"

"There are always signs to tell you what to do if you look for them. Does the sun come out every time you see Ava? Is there a shooting star when you're out together at night?"

"It's California. The sun is almost always out."

"Keep looking. You'll be guided by what you see."

Every time he saw Ava his whole body sprang to life

with desire. Wasn't that sign enough?

"Invite her to San Francisco," Chitra said. "Spend the day with her and just have fun. You need to lighten up."

He supposed that was good advice. "Okay. Talk to you all later." Ava still wasn't home from her walk as far as Sam could tell when he ended the call, so he went downstairs and found Ben in the kitchen, pouring himself a second cup of coffee. He looked tired; Sam wondered if he and Chloe had been fighting. "Hey, I want to bring Ava along today if she's game to go."

Ben set his cup on the counter. "Chloe doesn't like last-minute alterations to her plans," he said carefully.

Sam's anger flared. "At this point I don't care much what Chloe likes and doesn't like. I've got a limited amount of time to spend with Ava, and I want her to come with us." He met Ben's gaze, holding it until his friend backed down.

"Fine. You settle it with Chloe, though."

Sam thought it didn't bode well for Ben's marriage if he couldn't talk to his wife-to-be about such a small matter, but he didn't say so. Instead of searching out Chloe, Sam went outside, spotted Ava's car in the parking area and continued around the house to the stairs to her apartment.

Ava opened her door when he knocked. She wore a sundress that set off her figure nicely, and he stifled the urge to reach for her, remembering he was still awaiting her verdict. "I was wondering if you'd come with us to San Francisco today? I think we're going to some garden and shopping, and we'll get lunch and dinner somewhere."

"I'm not sure." She wouldn't meet his gaze. Sam's gut twisted. She'd decided against being with him, hadn't she?

He wasn't ready to face that reality, so he pushed on. "We'll just be two adults spending a day together touring a culturally rich city."

"But—"

Sam stopped her. "Come on, Ava—it's a day trip. There will be people around us at all times. I won't try anything." He was stalling, and he was sure she knew it. He braced himself, expecting her to turn him down.

"Fine, I'll come to San Francisco, as an adult touring a culturally rich city with a friend," she said, making clear she knew just how far from his real intentions that was, "but what about Chloe? Are you sure she wants me along?"

He let out the breath he'd been holding. "I'm not sure about that at all," he admitted. "But it's not going to stop me from bringing you. Can you be ready in fifteen minutes?"

Ava sighed. "I'll be there."

"Good."

Fifteen minutes later they were in their seats when Chloe climbed aboard the van, spotted Ava and frowned,

just as each of the other passengers had done when
they'd entered it. It was clear everyone thought Sam was
deliberately trying to rock the boat. The other couples
whispered among themselves or closed their eyes and
feigned sleep. Were all of them anticipating a confrontation the way he was?

"I didn't know you were bringing a friend." Chloe
looked down at her clipboard as if trying to find Ava's
name on her list.

"I didn't know either until just a few minutes ago.
You're so good at rolling with the punches, I knew you
wouldn't mind." He brazened it out, wondering what
Chloe would do. Chloe did not as a general practice roll
with punches. She struck back at anyone or anything
interfering with her game plan hard enough there
wouldn't be a second attempt.

It was clear she was unhappy with Ava's presence
but equally evident she couldn't say so without causing a
scene. She pinched her lips together, nodded and took
her seat up front, just behind Ben, who always drove the
oversized vehicle. Sam could almost feel the relief of the
other couples sitting around them.

"So, Ava, have you always lived in California?" Naomi asked when they were underway and the silence
grew too long. She was the director of marketing at
Scholar Central, a heavyset woman with an auburn bob
who was always ahead of the social media curve. Sam
appreciated her dry sense of humor, especially when she

used it to cut the tension in difficult meetings. Maybe she could relieve the tension in the van.

"No." Ava explained how she'd traveled for years, had settled down only recently, and would be teaching this fall.

"What about family? Where are they?"

"Near Philadelphia. Bryn Mawr, actually. My parents and brother all teach at the University of Pennsylvania."

Naomi's partner, Julian, leaned forward in his seat. "Why don't you teach there?"

"I prefer the elementary-school level," Ava said.

"Doesn't being a professor pay better?"

Ava shrugged. "It's not about the money for me. Is it for you?"

"It's a little bit about the money." Julian hammed it up, eliciting a chuckle from several of the others. Chloe kept her head turned decidedly away.

"I looked you up when Chloe booked this place," Naomi said. "The Blue House doesn't have a very large online presence. Are you doing all your marketing yourself?"

Ava nodded, and soon the two were chatting about different social media channels and how she could maximize exposure on them. Other people chimed in from time to time as the conversation broadened.

Sam was pleased to see how well Ava fit in with the group, and as time passed and her comfort level with the rest of them increased, he wondered if he'd been making all of this too complicated. Chloe was the only one shunning her. Everyone else was doing their best to be friendly. Maybe Chloe didn't have the influence she thought she had. Maybe there was a possibility his relationship with Ava could extend beyond this trip. What if they did things long distance for a while? If all went well, he could ask her to consider moving closer to him. She obviously meshed with his crowd.

Maybe this was the sign Leena had talked about.

Maybe Ava was meant to be his.

CHAPTER 7

*A*VA COULDN'T WAIT to get home.

It wasn't that she disliked San Francisco. She just didn't care for the activities Chloe had planned—or the way Chloe bossed them all around. When she'd heard they were including a trip to the botanical gardens in their itinerary, Ava had perked up, but it turned out more like a forced march than an enjoyable outing, in and out of the enormous grounds in less than an hour.

Next they toured the San Francisco Zoo at a similar breakneck speed, then stopped at a restaurant for a mere half hour for lunch, barely time to wolf down their meals before they boarded the van again. Ava's stomach hurt, her feet ached and she was overwhelmed by all the sights they'd taken in. Now they were in the Union Square shopping district.

"We have two hours to shop before we'll head to Fisherman's Wharf," Chloe announced. "We need to stick together. Remember our plan of action from the other day? Ava, you weren't there, so I'll reiterate it. We all go into a store and take five minutes to find the clothes that interest us. When I blow the whistle, we head for the changing rooms. When I blow the whistle again, it's time to get to the cash register. Then we wait outside the store for everyone to be done. Got it?"

"Got it." She turned to Sam and whispered, "Have I been extraordinarily evil without realizing it? Am I actually in hell?"

Naomi, sitting near them, tittered.

"What?" Chloe called over everyone else's heads. "Did you have something to say, Ava?"

Whoops. Ava ducked her head, thinking Chloe had to have supersonic hearing. "No," she murmured.

"Then let's go." Chloe led the way into a high-end boutique, and Ava saw at a glance she wouldn't want anything from this store. It was the kind of place where items of clothing on the racks were spaced six inches apart, created with models or anorexics in mind. None of it would fit her, and she couldn't afford it, anyway. When her phone buzzed, she pulled it out gratefully.

"I have to take this," she said to Sam and retreated to a quiet corner of the store, near the front window. "Hi, Marie. What's up?" She'd never thought she'd be happy to hear from her sister-in-law.

"Hi, Ava. Glad I caught you. I've got a question for you about Mom's birthday."

Was she still on that topic?

"What about it?" Ava knew she sounded unfriendly, but she also knew Marie probably had an ulterior motive for the call. She probably wanted Ava to know how hard she was working to make Ava's mother's party special. The implication being that Ava wasn't working hard enough on it.

Unfortunately, she'd learned a long time ago that the only way to make anyone in her family happy was to conform to their ideas of who she should be. She remembered a day when she was eight years old and they were spending the summer in West Sumatra, her mother's primary spot for field research. They'd been there for weeks already, living among a set of villagers so her mother could more easily complete her observations and interviews, and the days stretched endlessly before Ava. At fourteen, Oliver was already assisting his parents with research tasks, and Ava was sick of being shunted off to play with local kids who didn't want her around. Now she could see her parents thought they were giving her a wonderful opportunity, but back then it hadn't seemed that way. She was easily overwhelmed by new things, often got headaches from the glaring sun. Wanted to be with her friends at home.

"Oliver gets to be with you all the time," she'd whined, lonely and hot and miserable. "Why can't I?"

"You want to be helpful like Oliver?" Her mother had handed her a pad of paper and a pen. "Go ask those children about their lives and record their answers."

"They don't speak English!"

"Then learn to speak their language. That's what

Oliver did."

Oliver always shone in her parents' eyes, and she was always in the way, as excluded from her family group as she was from the gang of village children her mother wanted her to befriend. Knowing there was no use expecting any actual comfort from her parents, she'd trailed away again. Avoiding the village children, she'd taken the pen and paper into the shade of the nearest tree, lain down on her belly and drawn what she saw from that angle—tiny plants barely poking out of the ground, the rugged terrain of the dirt seen from a nose-length away, insects that loomed as large as automobiles if you imagined you were less than an inch tall. Over the course of that summer, she drew hundreds of pictures like that, recording the smallest details of the smallest objects she could find, feeling a kinship with them.

She was as invisible as they were to most people's eyes.

Her total indifference to them and utter concentration while drawing attracted the other children in the village in a way her previous overtures hadn't, and in the end she did become friends with them. Soon all of them wanted paper and pens, too.

"You're supposed to observe the people we're studying, not influence their behavior," her mother had said in exasperation one morning when she came across a dozen village kids lying on their bellies like Ava was, drawing the same outsized versions of the tiny objects and insects they found in the dirt.

"I'm just being me," Ava said.

"A little less of that would be a good thing."

"I don't know what to do about the cake." Marie broke into her memories. "I can get a lovely layer cake from my favorite bakery, but I don't know if Mom will like that. Do you think she'd prefer something home-made? I'm pretty good at that kind of thing, but I'm not an expert."

"She'll be happy with either. She's not a big cake person." Ava caught her mistake too late. "I mean…"

"Should I get something else? A pie? A tort? Oh my goodness, it never even occurred to me she might like something else."

Marie was working herself into a tizzy, and Ava still didn't know what she really wanted from this call. "Cake will be fine. In fact, a bakery cake is the way to go." Someone needed to be decisive and save Marie from herself, Ava thought. And there was no use making a homemade cake when Mom wouldn't even notice.

"You think?"

"I know."

"Thank goodness I called. I wish you were flying out for the party. It's a shame you didn't think it was worth it."

Here it was, the real reason for the call. The guilt trip. Ava rolled her eyes, thinking of all the birthdays she'd had over the years that no one in her family had bothered to celebrate. That's what happened when your birthday fell right after your mother's in a family that hardly celebrated holidays to begin with. Mom hated a fuss about her birthday, which made it hard to demand one for her own. Besides, her family always traveled in the summer months. In fact, it was amazing her parents were in Bryn Mawr now. She knew they'd be leaving for West Sumatra in a matter of days.

"When is your birthday, by the way?" Marie asked. "Oliver is so lazy about these things. He doesn't even have the date on the calendar."

Ava laughed. She doubted Oliver even knew when it was. "Four days after Mom's, actually."

There was a silence on the other end of the phone. "Really? Why didn't I know that?"

"We don't make a big thing about birthdays in our family." Ava kept her tone light, despite the throb in her chest when she made that statement. She was far too old to care about such things and chastised herself inwardly for being sensitive about it still.

"Well, I think people should be celebrated," Marie said stiffly. "I don't know why the rest of you are so against that."

If Marie thought she could change her husband or in-laws, she had taken on a hopeless cause, but Ava figured she'd have to learn that for herself.

"I've got to go," she said. "I'm with a group of people shopping in San Francisco."

"That sounds lovely." Marie was wistful, and Ava wondered if she was a little bored. She wasn't working, and Ava had no idea what she did all day in the town house she and Oliver owned.

"I'll talk to you soon." Ava pocketed her phone just in time to hear Chloe's whistle. Everyone in the group made for the changing rooms. She went to find Sam.

"Where are your clothes to try on?" Chloe demanded when she spotted her.

"I don't have any. These aren't my style."

Chloe gave a little huff and turned away. Ava couldn't find Sam, so she waited by the entrance to the changing rooms. He came out a little while later looking sheepish.

"Found a shirt," he said, holding it up.

"Better get in line to buy that before the stampede."

Chloe's whistle sounded again, and Sam leaped toward the line for the cashiers, which soon extended into the racks of clothing as the rest of his friends joined him. Ava headed to the front of the store, stepped outside and took a deep breath. San Francisco's air wasn't exactly fresh, but it was better than the recycled air inside the store. One boutique down, how many to go?

Was she going to make it through this day?

She asked herself that question more than once as the afternoon continued. When they finally arrived home late that night, she couldn't help herself. Stepping out of the van, she sank to her knees and kissed the ground.

"Home. Glorious home," she moaned as if she'd trekked across the Sahara and back since she'd left this morning. It sure felt that way.

A few of her new acquaintances laughed as Sam pulled her back to her feet. "I know what you mean. I thought we'd never make it back."

"Nice," Chloe said sarcastically. "I worked hard to set up today's trip. Why is it that freeloaders think they can dump all over everything?"

Ava was immediately contrite. "Sorry, Chloe. It was an awesome day. I'm just done in."

"You're just rude, that's what you are." Chloe flounced inside, Ben hurrying after her.

Ava turned to Sam. "I really am sorry. She's right; that was rude." A familiar feeling took hold of her body. Shame. Once again, she'd missed the mark. All day she'd felt the way she used to when she was traveling with her family: rushed, overwhelmed and out of her depth. Todd had been a little easier to travel with. He made the final decisions, but he was laid back, and their travel days were never hurried. He liked to play the protective male, running interference for her when a situation got sticky. When he went off to do some extreme sport she wasn't comfortable with, he sometimes fussed when she didn't want to join in but usually didn't mind if she lolled on the beach with a novel as long as she oohed and aahed over his prowess when he was done.

"I think it's a miracle no one melted down before

now," Sam said. "That was a long day—and I feel like I barely saw you even though we spent it together."

She could tell he was about to invite her on a walk to the beach or to hang out on the deck, which meant he'd try again to entice her into bed. She'd have to fend him off—or give in, knowing it couldn't last. Suddenly she needed some time alone. "I'm going to call it a night," she forestalled him. "I'll see you in the morning for our walk, okay?"

He was obviously disappointed. "You never told me what you decided. About us," he clarified when she didn't answer. "I guess the answer is no, right?"

Ava still didn't have an answer to that question. Last night she'd told herself she had to end their budding relationship before it could really start, but after spending another day with Sam, she couldn't summon the stamina to do that. She desperately wanted to spend more time with him. If she was honest, she wanted a lot more than that. She was going to miss Sam so much when he was gone.

"Can you give me one more night?" she asked, knowing it was massively unfair to Sam. "I'm over-whelmed. I can't think straight, and I don't want to make a decision I'm going to regret." She held her breath, hoping he wouldn't be too angry or hurt. Before he could misunderstand, she went up on tiptoe and brushed a kiss over his cheek. "I really like you. I'm just con-fused."

Sam caught her hand and held it, searching her face as if he was trying to read her mind. "Yeah, I can give you one more night," he agreed, his voice husky.

Ava swayed in place, wishing she could kiss him again. Wishing he would reach for her and she could fall into his embrace without any thoughts or decisions at all.

That wasn't the way life worked, though. There would be consequences to whatever choice she made, so she had to think it through carefully—when she wasn't exhausted.

"Thank you." She kissed him again and darted away, around the side of the house to the stairs that led to her suite.

"Good night, Ava," Sam called after her.

"Good night."

THAT HADN'T GONE the way he'd hoped.

Sam let himself into his room, shut the door and locked it behind him, then kicked off his shoes, stripped down and pulled on a pair of worn-out sweatpants. He slid open the door to his balcony to let cool air blow in since his room had gotten stuffy during the time away. The moon was up, a crescent lighting a path of shining water across the surface of the ocean.

Maybe he should forget all about Ava. About Chloe and Ben, too. Head to the beach first thing tomorrow. Try surfing again. Spend the day in the waves, the way a vacation was meant to go. His life was slipping away operating on other people's itineraries and plans. What about him? What he wanted?

"It was nuts," he heard Ava say from somewhere above him. Her voice was muffled, but the exclamation carried through his open door.

Sam moved closer to it. She didn't sound like she was out on her balcony. Maybe she was in her suite with the sliding glass door open, the way his was? Was someone up there with her, or was she on her phone?

On her phone, he decided a moment later.

"Emma, you should have seen her bossing everyone around. She had a whistle."

Sam winced. Yeah, that was weird, he had to admit. He'd seen the way the other customers looked at them each time Chloe blew that whistle in one of the stores they'd visited. Like maybe they were a bunch of overgrown children needing to be carefully watched.

"They all went along with it like a pack of sheep. No one even questioned her. You should see her fiancé—he's terrified of her." There was a silence. "Sam? I think he's terrified of her, too."

Sam straightened. Like hell he was. Chloe didn't scare him; she just made life unpleasant when you didn't go along with her schemes. He supposed he'd gotten in the habit of appeasing her over the years, which was why things had gotten out of control. Thank God he'd stood up for himself when it counted. He wished Ben would grow a pair and stop letting her push him around.

"Her fiancé is Sam's business partner, and he follows her around like a whipped dog. Their employees don't know what's going on. It's obvious to everyone she's trying to take over, and it doesn't seem like Sam or Ben are going to do anything about it. I'm afraid Sam is going to lose his company if he doesn't watch out."

Sam gripped the handle of the sliding glass door, her words piercing him to the quick. She was right. He kept holding back, hoping Ben would fix the problem they were facing, but why would Ben do that when it was clear if he did, Chloe would leave him?

"I'd forgotten how much I dislike cities," Ava went on upstairs. "I mean, they're fine to visit now and then, but I need space. I need to see the ocean. The stars. I need forests close by. No matter where we went today, I could feel the walls closing in."

Something twisted in Sam's gut. There was no ocean near Chicago. No forests around his downtown condo. Would Lake Michigan and some local parks do the trick, or would Ava hate it there?

She'd probably hate it there, he decided.

It was already clear she didn't think much of his employees, even though he'd thought she'd gotten along well with them today. She'd probably turn him down flat if he asked her to join Scholar Central, an idea that had been growing in his mind over the past twenty-four hours.

"I get Sam's interest in online education, but Chloe's

obviously in it for the money. I can't get a read on Ben at all. I don't think Scholar Central is going to be the beacon of hope for disadvantaged kids Sam thinks it is." She was silent a minute. "Yeah, he's going back to Chicago at the end of next week. Can you imagine living there? I can't."

Each sentence she spoke hit him like a punch to his gut. Nothing about him was up to snuff in her eyes, was it? She thought he'd lost control of his business. She hated his hometown. In fact, she sounded a lot like Chloe had when they were together. Obstinate. Opinionated. Sure she was right and everyone else was wrong. He hadn't even asked Ava to be with him long-term, and she was already turning him down?

He didn't need someone like that around.

He ignored the little voice in his head that said Ava didn't know he was listening and it was unfair to judge her when she was venting to a friend after a very long day. As far as he was concerned, she'd made it very clear what she wanted and what she wouldn't accept.

There was no room for him in her life, and he wasn't going to waste any more time trying to change her mind.

"I GUESS HE'S not coming," Ava said the next morning when she, Emma and Penelope had waited in the Cliff Garden ten minutes past their usual time.

"Maybe he's sleeping in," Emma suggested. "Your trip to San Francisco sounded rough."

"Maybe." But Ava had an awful feeling there was more to it than that. When she returned to her house thirty minutes later, her fear grew even stronger when she spotted Sam milling about the parking area with the rest of his friends, preparing to leave.

"We're going to Santa Cruz," he said shortly when she asked where they were off to. "Boardwalk, beach, boutiques—and some surprise activity." It sounded like he was echoing what Chloe had announced as the itinerary for the day.

Ava waited a beat, but he issued no invitation to join them. She supposed she'd acted badly enough the previous day, he'd been told she wouldn't be welcome. Despite the warmth of the morning, a prickle of cold danced across her skin. Had he given up on her?

"I'm heading out pretty soon, too," she said. "I'm checking out a farm I might take my students to see this fall."

"Have fun."

"Would you like to come along?" she ventured.

"I'm going to stick with my friends today." Everyone was getting into the van, and he backed away from her. "Like, I said. Have fun." He turned and joined the line. A moment later he disappeared inside the vehicle, leaving her standing awkwardly in the parking area alone. Chloe was the last to get into the van. When the engine roared to life, Ava stepped out of the way and circled around it to reach the side of her home. She took the steps up to her apartment slowly.

What had just happened? Why was Sam so cold to her?

Because she hadn't invited him upstairs last night?

Because she'd refused to give him the answer she'd promised him?

Ava wondered if he'd lost patience with the whole affair and decided to wash his hands of it. After all, what were they accomplishing by trying to be with each other?

In her suite, Ava sat down on her bed, feeling defeated. This whole thing had been a setup from the start. From now on, she would never put herself in the position of falling for a guest. It was far too painful.

She picked up the photo album Aunt Laura had made for her so many years ago and leafed through its pages, trying to remember all the good things about her life. This house, for one thing, that provided enough income she could take this entire summer to explore the area. The job waiting for her in the fall. She couldn't wait to start and knew the combined income from guests and teaching would allow her to set aside a substantial amount for her retirement each year. Her friends were here for her and made each day special. So she didn't have a man in her life and she wasn't starting a family, despite edging closer to thirty each day. Those things would either come or they wouldn't. She had nothing to complain about.

So why did it feel so bad when Sam walked away?

Ava let out a frustrated groan, got to her feet, grabbed her things, locked up and clattered down the steps, determined to have a fabulous day without him. She drove to Heaven on Earth farm, a small operation run by three generations of women on a wedge-shaped property near the Castle. Colette Rainer was one of the people in Ava's aunt's photo album. It turned out she'd been a friend of Emma's grandmother and had overseen Brightview after Angela's death until it was time for Emma to inherit it. Ava had gotten to know Colette through Emma, and the woman had been delighted when she'd asked if her students could visit when school started. Today Colette would show her around the property so Ava knew what to expect when she brought her classes here.

"Good morning," Colette called out from the porch of her Victorian house when Ava parked in the driveway and got out of her car.

"Morning. Thank you so much for letting me come and take a tour of your farm."

"I'm so glad you did." Colette came down to meet her, gave her a grandmotherly hug and beamed at her. "I miss your aunt Laura terribly. She always pitched in at harvest time. Besides, we love having children visit the farm, so you have to promise you'll bring your students often once school is in session."

"Of course." Ava wished everyone was as welcoming of students. She tipped her head back to look at the house. "You have a wonderful home." It was a tradition-al "painted lady," all lilac and pale pink, with dashes of yellow in the ornate trim.

"Thank you. I have always loved to take care of the place. I paint her every five years. I have help, of course. My daughter, granddaughter and anyone else who can make themselves available. Normally, people hate painting houses, but there's something about a Victorian that brings the kid out in everyone."

"I bet." It was such a cheerful house you would feel privileged to spruce it up.

"Come around back. Julia is in one of the green-houses."

Ava could feel herself smiling ear to ear the minute they rounded the house. Heaven on Earth farm was about two or three acres large, she judged. Every square inch of it was in use. Vegetables were close-cropped in the gardens. Three neat greenhouses stood in a row. A flock of chickens was stepping and picking its way through a nearby bed of squash plants. Bees buzzed lazily around the flower border that edged the crops.

"This is amazing."

"Our own little patch of paradise," Colette agreed happily. She led the way to the greenhouses, where she introduced Ava to her daughter, Julia, who looked to be in her early fifties. She had her mother's smile but lacked her height. Julia's chestnut hair was tied up in a bun on top of her head, and the pockets of her green apron bulged with garden tools. "Julia makes sure we've got something growing year-round," Colette said.

"Welcome to Heaven on Earth," Julia said. "And don't let my mother fool you. She's as much of a work horse as I am in this operation." She took over the tour, however, leading Ava through the greenhouses and up and down the rows of the fields as they discussed the possibility of Ava's students planting fast-growing seeds in mini greenhouses they could take to the classroom and watch grow over the course of several months. Ava had a feeling she could talk gardening and plants with these women all day, but eventually Julia's daughter joined them near a row of carrots.

"This is my granddaughter, Chantelle," Colette said. "She runs the market on Wednesdays and Saturdays." Chantelle was as tall as her grandmother, thin as a whip and graceful, her hair in two thick braids.

"Nice to meet you," Ava said. "I'm Ava."

"Hi, Ava. Come up to the house for some tea when you three are ready. I've got some cinnamon rolls fresh from the oven."

"We'll be done in a minute," Julia assured her.

Chantelle joined them for the rest of the tour as they walked around the perimeter of the farm, taking a long route to the house so Julia and Colette could point out other features of their property.

"We practice permaculture principles whenever we can," Julia told her when Ava asked about the chickens roaming free in the garden. "You can't let them near seedlings, of course, but in an established patch of vegetables like legumes or squash they won't bother the plants, but they'll eat the bugs who love them."

"Of course what youngsters call permaculture, we called thriftiness in our time," Colette said. "Or common sense."

Julia rolled her eyes behind her mother's back.

"Does your husband work the farm, too?" Ava asked her.

Julia laughed heartily. "No husband," she said succinctly. "We Rainer women like our freedom too much for that."

"We Rainer women also don't have a good track record of choosing the kind of men who like to stick around," Colette said dryly.

They entered the house through a back door, and Colette led the way to a large, cheerful kitchen. The appliances were out of date, and Ava figured the room hadn't been renovated since the eighties or maybe earlier, but it was a welcoming place nonetheless. She joined the others at a wide table placed by windows that looked out over the fields as Chantelle served them rolls and mugs of steaming tea.

"This is wonderful," she moaned with delight after biting into the cinnamon roll.

"Chantelle does a brisk business on market days," Julia said with pride.

As Chantelle took her seat, Ava got a glimpse of a slight rounding of her belly. Chantelle caught her looking. "I'm due in November." She placed a hand on her abdomen. "Think it will be a girl?"

"It's always a girl at Heaven on Earth," Julia said with a laugh and a shake of her head.

"And no—its father isn't the sticking-around type, either," Chantelle told Ava. "Pass the butter?"

"Sure." Ava handed the butter to her and took in the comfortable cheerfulness of the women around the table. None of them seemed perturbed by Chantelle's situation. Colette was well into her seventies, if not older, Ava thought, but she rode her bike all over town. She was healthy enough she'd have time to watch her great-grandchild grow up. There'd be four generations of women tending one farm, if Julia's guess was right.

Ava had never thought of having children on her own. She didn't even know how she'd go about such a thing. It was possible, though, she supposed. She had financial security. A home. Community. Would she want to take such a journey alone?

She looked around the table again. Her family wouldn't be supportive like this. Besides, they lived two thousand miles away. Emma and Pen were great, but she would never want her friendship with them to be a burden.

It was something to think about, she told herself, but not something to take action on yet. She'd always imagined finding a partner first, then having children.

"Do you think your students will enjoy a visit here?" Chantelle asked.

"They'll love it." She was about to explain some of her ideas when the front doorbell rang.

"I bet that's Fee," Chantelle said, jumping up from her seat. "She said she'd come by today. I promised her a bunch of strawberry runners."

She went to open the door and came back with a woman about Ava's age. Ava immediately thought of the animated movie *Tangled*. Fee had a head of riotous red hair that fell past her shoulders in waves. As she entered the room, Fee was scooping it up, twisting it into a coil at the back of her head and sticking a pencil through it.

"Hi, Colette. Hi, Julia," Fee said.

"Hi," the two women chimed.

"This is Ava Ingerson," Chantelle told Fee, indicating a seat and taking her own again.

Fee settled in her chair and reached across the table to shake Ava's hand. "Nice to meet you."

"Nice to meet you, too." Ava was fascinated by Fee's hair. With every movement she made, it was working itself free again.

"Fee's the caretaker at the Castle," Colette explained.

Ava straightened. "What an interesting job."

"You'd think." Fee made a face. "It's not all that exciting, actually, since the place isn't open to the public and hasn't been for years. I keep busy keeping it up, though. This summer I'm trying to resuscitate the old kitchen garden. Sounds scintillating, doesn't it?" She shrugged.

"Don't let her fool you; she loves every moment of that job, and someday she'll get the place open again," Colette said.

"What's holding you back?" Ava had heard stories about Seahaven Castle, but she had no idea if they were true. Something about a family argument and no men allowed. Emma's husband, Noah, had accidentally photographed the heir to the property, James Kane, while he was surfing a while back. That was the picture *SurfWorld* had bought from him. Ava wasn't clear why James didn't have possession of the Castle.

"It's a long story."

"Ava's got time, don't you, Ava?" Chantelle asked with a wink.

"For a story about a castle? Of course," Ava said.

Fee took a sip from the glass of lemonade Julia set in front of her. "The Castle was built in the 1800s," she began. Her hair suddenly sprang free of its coil, sending the pencil flying. "Oh, for heaven's sake." Fee bent to fetch the pencil from the floor, looked at it, shook her head and tucked it away in her pocket, leaving her hair free.

Ava exchanged an amused glance with Chantelle.

"The Castle was built in the 1800s," Fee started again, "by Joseph Kane, who made his fortune in the goldmines up north. He got in early, before the true gold rush began, and amassed so much money he was able to buy enough property here to create his own town when California became a state. He married around that time and had two sons."

Ava was familiar with this part of the story. Joseph Kane figured on several historical markers around town.

"Kane's idea was to start a cannery to compete with the ones in Monterey, and he built plenty of company housing for the single men he lured here to work them. His older son, Henry, and his grandson, Richard, continued the operation, but ultimately Monterey won out, and Seahaven's canneries closed. Meanwhile, the single men who'd settled in Seahaven had found wives, started families, and the town had expanded. Times were tough for a while, especially during World War I, until Daniel Kane, the heir at the time, conceived of the idea of the Castle Watch."

Ava was enjoying the tale. Fee's face was expressive when she talked, and even though Ava was sure she'd explained this a thousand times before, she didn't feel like Fee was talking by rote.

"The Castle Watch was wonderful," Colette said wistfully. "All those handsome men."

"Nana, you're incorrigible," Chantelle scolded.

"I'm not dead yet. I can still enjoy a man in uniform."

"Daniel's son, Martin Kane, the heir to the Castle in

that generation, begged his father to open it to tourists and create a whole experience around it. His father agreed, but World War II broke out. Like many men in that era, Martin married his high school sweetheart, got her pregnant and went overseas to fight. He never returned. In honor of his memory, Daniel opened the Castle to the public when the war ended. There were food and craft stalls in the bailey, feasts, plays and medieval music in the great hall, jousting on the back field, and every summer solstice the Castle Watch took their places on the battlements and stayed there all night long. It was an honor to be chosen. Most of the town stayed up all night, too, with bonfires and parties. The positions on the walls were rotated through the public, but the four towers were special honors given to men who'd served the community in some way. Daniel thought the pageantry would keep families loyal to the town. The only problem was that Martin's only child was a girl—Bethany. No male heir," she added with a shrug.

"What happened?"

"Daniel worried a lot about the breach in tradition, but in the end he decided that as long as Bethany married early and produced a son, the tradition of passing the property down to the first male heir could be resumed and all would be well. He spent the rest of his life hammering that message into Bethany's head, and although he died when Bethany was twenty, she did what she was supposed to and married a man named Robert

Harper in 1963."

Fee took another drink of lemonade. Ava tried to be patient. It was obvious something had gone wrong after that wedding, and she was dying to know what it was.

"Bethany tried for a son," Fee went on, "but her marriage grew increasingly contentious, and she was getting increasingly angry about the way her father had made her feel like she wasn't good enough because she was a woman. Robert cheated on her several times. Meanwhile, Bethany had a string of miscarriages. In the end she carried only two pregnancies to term, both daughters, Lenore and Jeannette. When Robert left her, Bethany lost her mind a little. She shut the Castle down. Barred the gates, if you will. Decreed no man would ever enter it again."

Ava leaned forward. "What happened to the girls?"

"Lenore and Jeannette grew up on the castle grounds. Bethany was hugely protective of them. She brought tutors in. Female tutors. Tried to keep them away from boys and men altogether—from everyone, really. Told everyone who'd listen that Lenore was the heir."

"It would have been at least the seventies by then, right?" Ava tried to keep up. "Well after women's liberation. Who cared whether Lenore was a boy or a girl? I mean, she might have lived in a castle, but the Kanes weren't royalty. This is the United States."

"Tradition can be hard to overcome," Fee countered.

"As I'm sure you've guessed, Lenore and Jeannette both struggled as adults."

"Are they still alive?"

"No," Fee said unhappily. "They died together in an accident about seven years ago. Neither married or had children. Now it's my job to keep up the Castle until the heir meets Bethany's requirements to become 'king.'" She used finger-quotes when she said the word.

"Wait. I'm confused," Ava said. "I thought James Kane was the heir. Isn't he Lenore's son?" She remembered the way Noah talked about the surfer he'd photographed. He said all the locals treated James with awe for who he was.

"No, he's not. Lenore isn't the only direct descendent of the Kane lineage," Fee explained. "Old Joseph Kane, the man who started all this, had two sons. Lenore and Jeannette were descendants of Henry, the eldest. James Kane is a direct descendant of Joseph's younger son, Jonathan."

"If he's a direct descendant of Joseph Kane, why doesn't he take possession of the Castle now?"

"It's not that simple." Fee shrugged. Colette and Chantelle exchanged a glance Ava couldn't decipher.

"Fee is leaving out the most important part—as usual," Chantelle put in.

"What's that?" Despite her confusion, Ava was loving this. The tale was as complicated as a gothic novel. She looked from Fee to Chantelle, but neither of them answered for a long moment.

"If you don't spit it out, I will," Chantelle said.

Fee sighed heavily. "I'm Jeannette's ward. She took me in when I was a baby."

"Oh!" That was a surprising twist, but Ava supposed it made sense there was a connection since it was Fee's job to care for the Castle.

"You have to understand, I'm no blood relation. Jeannette didn't adopt me." She gave Chantelle a pointed look. "I have no claim to the Castle at all. I'm just a caretaker."

"She's the rightful heir, if you ask me," Chantelle said. "Jeannette treated her like a daughter all her life. She raised her. Fee has lived at the Castle since she was a few months old and is the one who's worked night and day to keep the property up. Meanwhile, James just runs around surfing. Why should it go to such a distant cousin? Lenore wanted you to be the heir. You know she did," she said to Fee.

"Hold on, back up," Ava said, her mind ticking over all the information she'd been given. "The same logic that says James should be the heir now would seem to say one of his forefathers should have gotten the Castle instead of Bethany, right? Why didn't it pass to that line when Martin Kane had no male children?"

"That side of the family was having troubles of its own. Alan Kane, who would have been the heir in that case, died young in the Vietnam War. His son, Scott, disappeared in his twenties and was never seen again. James is Scott's son. He showed up in Seahaven as a baby rather mysteriously, left on his aunt's doorstep. She was in her seventies, but Natalie Kane raised James like her own child and drilled it into his head he was the rightful heir. She's gone now, too."

"You're pulling my leg." Ava sat back. Fee's narrative had gone entirely off the rails, and Ava wondered how much of it was pure fabrication. Were these women having her on?

"Not at all," Fee assured her. "All of this really happened. We have no idea where Scott Kane went, or who James's mother is. A DNA test was done when he showed up. He's definitely his father's son, but no match was found for a mother. Of course, that was thirty years ago. If we checked today, a database might bring up all kinds of information. Unfortunately, James isn't interested in tracking her down."

Ava wondered why that was. Did he think his mother had deserted him?

"Anyway, I figured it was only a matter of time before James came looking for his inheritance when Bethany passed away, but he never has."

"Can you imagine walking away from something like that?" Chantelle asked. "You could fit four of our farms on the Castle grounds."

"You said you were keeping the place up for him, though," Ava said to Fee. "If Lenore wanted you to be

167

the heir, what changed? Why are you only the caretaker?"

"When Mom and Aunt Lenore died together in an accident, Bethany took it hard." Fee sighed. "There'd been too much loss. Too much sorrow in her life. She began to talk about a judgment against her. That she'd lost everything because she'd inherited the Castle instead of it going to a man. She began to lose her health. Got obsessed with the idea that everything was her fault. In the end she called for her lawyer and changed her will, in the hopes that I wouldn't be cursed, too. I get an allowance to take care of the place until James claims his inheritance, but technically once he meets a few requirements, it's all his."

"Which is just wrong," Chantelle said to her. "Accidents happen. It has nothing to do with who owned the Castle. You are Bethany's granddaughter, adoption certificate or no."

So the Castle had a curse, Ava mused. "What about your father? Is he still alive?" she asked Fee.

"I never knew him," Fee said. "I don't even know his last name. He was someone Mom knew for a single night."

"Wow." Fee had dealt with a lot during her short life.

"That's why I don't tell this story," Fee said to Chantelle, pointing at Ava's expression. "I hate that look of pity. I'm fine," she said to Ava. "I miss Mom, Lenore and Bethany, but I've had time to grieve and I've found peace. I live in a castle, and I have a yearly stipend that pays all my bills. Keeping it up takes a lot of work, but I have help. I have friends. I have a life."

"But you're just like Bethany," Chantelle said. "You keep far, far away from men."

"I haven't met the right guy!" Fee exclaimed.

"You're too picky."

"Sweetie," Julia said to her daughter. "It might possibly be that you're not picky enough." She gave Chantelle's slightly swollen belly a pointed look.

"Oh yeah? Like mother, like daughter, right?" Chantelle retorted. Julia rolled her eyes.

"Like I said, we Rainers have lousy taste in men," she told Ava, "which is why we aren't the best ones to come to for advice on relationships."

"All I'm saying is Fee might *try* having a relationship or two," Chantelle said.

"I'll keep that in mind." Fee stood up, twisted her hair into another knot and stabbed the pencil through it again. "I have to run. Do you have those plants for me?"

"That I do." Chantelle stood up, too.

"Nice to meet you, Ava. Good to see you again, Julia and Colette."

The other women said their goodbyes, and Fee left before Ava realized she'd squandered her chance to ask for a tour of the Castle.

At least she'd met Fee. Surely she'd see her again around town and then she'd take a chance. She knew Noah was dying to see inside it. Emma and Penelope, too.

"Are men really not allowed into the Castle even now?" she asked Julia.

"That's right," Julia said. "It's been over fifty years. James Kane has to meet Bethany's stipulations before there'll be an end to all that."

So Noah couldn't come, but the rest of them could.

"I HATE THIS. Why are we hiking this stupid trail again?" Elena hissed to her husband, Carter, as Sam passed them on the dirt path.

"I have no idea," Carter said. "Never thought Chloe was into nature."

She wasn't, Sam knew. He had a feeling she'd added this hike in direct response to Ava's criticism of her San Francisco itinerary. He wasn't sure what the point was, however, since Ava wasn't here to participate in it.

"What about surfing? What's the point of coming all the way to California if we're never going to go to the beach?" Elena asked.

Sam hurried on before they turned to him for an explanation. Let Chloe dig her own grave. It was to his benefit if she lost ground with her coworkers, and they saw her as fallible.

He wondered if Chloe had expected the hike to be this long. When she mentioned it, he figured she'd pick a trail like the redwood loop he'd walked with Ava a few days ago. Something short and flat. This path seemed to stretch through the woods forever. Not that he minded a good hike, but some members of their group were unprepared. One of the women was wearing sandals. Some of the others had grumbled about having to carry water, then had drunk it so quickly they wouldn't have any for the way back.

"We're going to follow the trail to the end," he heard Chloe saying ahead of him in response to someone's question. She was at the front of the line, of course, holding a folded map she consulted from time to time. "There wouldn't be a trail if it wasn't worth hiking."

"I've been on plenty of trails that weren't worth hiking," someone said behind him in a tone too low for Chloe to catch. Despite the grumbling, everyone kept walking, even though Sam had a feeling Elena was close to tears.

He looked up and down the line. Was anyone having fun? It didn't look like it. He could do this hike in his sleep, but some of the others tended more toward a sedentary lifestyle. When he met Hailey's gaze, she looked away. She'd done her best to avoid him since the incident in the nightclub. Gabe, her boyfriend, had been decidedly unfriendly. Sam didn't know how he could have handled the situation differently, but he hated how awkward things had become. He was going to have to work with these people for years.

"Remember our climb up Creststone Needle?" Ben said, coming up behind him. He'd been walking at the back of the line, ostensibly to keep the stragglers from falling too far behind, but Sam had a feeling he'd also wanted some space apart from Chloe. Something had happened during the morning that he hadn't witnessed, and ever since Chloe had been pretending not to see Ben. Usually when the two were arguing, Ben stuck close to Chloe, trying to get back on her good side, but not today. The whole thing was giving Sam the creeps.

"That was a great trip," Sam said. He and Ben had flown to Colorado and spent several days camping and bagging peaks over 14,000 feet, but Creststone Needle was the best. The climb itself was invigorating, and at the top they were rewarded with a jaw-dropping view.

"Wish we could go for it on a trail like that again. These days I always feel like I'm slowing down to match someone else's pace."

"If it was just the two of us on this hike, we'd already have reached the end and come back," Sam said. He wasn't going to touch the rest of what Ben had said. If his friend was slowing down to match anyone's pace, it was Chloe's.

Ben sighed. "Sucks not to be able to talk to you when things aren't going right."

Sam shrugged. He wasn't the one who'd stolen another man's fiancé, but he knew what Ben meant. They'd shared so much for years, and now it was like they were strangers.

"It's never going back to how it was between us, is

it?"

Sam swallowed down the pain that filled his chest. He didn't know how to answer that. How could it go back to how it was? But what were they going to do if it didn't? They were business partners. They spent most of their days together.

The last year had taken a toll on him he rarely admitted even to himself. He used to wake up excited to head to Scholar Central's modest offices and get to work. Every day there was a new problem to solve, new ideas to come up with. Ben had been his partner in crime.

Now when he woke up there came that moment when he remembered everything had changed. When he got to the office, Chloe would always be between him and Ben. There was no more laughter, no friendly competition to find the latest bug in the software, no brainstorming sessions.

"You wish you were still with her?" Ben jutted his chin at Chloe at the front of the line of hikers.

"No," Sam blurted. "I really don't. That doesn't change the fact you were in bed with my ex-fiancée days after she and I split up."

"I know," Ben said doggedly. "I don't have any excuse for that, except I saw my chance and took it. I always wanted her—right from the start. It killed me to see the two of you together. You weren't right for each other."

"You think you are?" Sam knew he was pushing it,

but he couldn't stop himself. Now that he knew who Chloe really was, it pained him to have wasted two years with her, but it was even worse seeing Ben make the same mistake.

"Yeah, I do." Ben made a face. "Most of the time," he added. Sam could tell he was thinking about whatever he and Chloe had fought about earlier. "Look, I know you think she's being ridiculous on this trip," he added, "but she's dreamed of a vacation like this with all her friends. What's the harm in it?"

Was Ben really so blind? "You don't think she has an ulterior motive?"

Ben didn't answer for a moment. When he did, there was an edge to his voice. "Fine. She's having fun ordering everyone around. Playing tour guide. Whatever."

"It's more than that."

"No, it isn't." Ben wouldn't meet his eyes. "She wants to be in charge for once in her life. Can you blame her for that?"

Sam walked a few paces, wondering if Ben was repeating something Chloe had said to him. She was obviously after a lot more than a chance to boss around her friends on vacation. He didn't want to have it out with Ben on a hiking trail surrounded by their coworkers, though. This was a conversation the two of them needed to have alone.

"I'm glad you're happy," he said stiffly to Ben.

"But you and I aren't going to go back to being friends."

"We're friends," Sam said, but he sounded unconvincing even to his own ears.

CHAPTER 8

*O*N THE WAY home from Heaven on Earth farm, Ava pulled into a parking area overlooking the ocean and called her brother. The Rainers' close family bond had made her a little homesick, and she hadn't talked to Oliver in ages. Of course, he ought to be the one calling her, since he'd been so eager to eject her from the family and adopt Todd instead. She'd decided she'd be the bigger person and overlook that. Maybe Oliver had come to his senses.

Oliver didn't answer. When she got his voice mail, she left a message and ended the call. Next she dialed her mom. She'd been putting off this call because she could guess how it would go. Ellen Ingerson was always cranky on her birthday.

"Ava? Something wrong?" her mother answered.

"No. Everything's fine. Why do you ask?"

"I'm short of time and thought I'd get to the heart of the matter if something was." Ava could tell her mother was moving as she talked. "Hold on." There was a moment of muffled noise. "Okay. Got my earbuds in."

"I just called to say happy birthday."

"Oh. That. Yes, all right."

"Did you get my gift certificate?" Ava repressed a smile. Good old Mom, always true to character.

"Yes. That was very thoughtful. We'll use it when we're home again."

"Home?"

"From West Sumatra?" Her mother's impatience was clear. "I'm packing as we speak."

"That's right." Ava had forgotten about their trip. "Do you have a plan for your field work this season?"

"Do I ever not have a plan?" Her mother sounded affronted at the idea.

Ava smiled. "No. Not you."

"That's how I get everything done. How are things in Seahaven?" Somehow her mother made the town's name sound like a second-rate destination.

"They're terrific. I just toured a small urban farm run by three generations of women. They're a fantastic family, and they're using intensive practices to get the most out of their small plot of land."

"Sounds fascinating." But her mother sounded more distracted than interested.

"I'm setting up the curriculum I'll be teaching this fall," Ava tried again. "I'll be doing a series of adventures with my students around town, teaching them scientific concepts as we go."

"I'm sure the children will love everything you organize for them," her mother broke in. "Ava, I have to go. I've got a meeting with the department chair in less than an hour. You know how it is before a trip."

"Of course." She did know since she'd accompanied her parents on many of their excursions. "Is Dad around?"

"He's at work, honey. He's just as busy as I am."

"Okay. I'll call again in a couple of days."

Her mother sighed. "Yes, I'm sure you will." She hung up, leaving Ava to stare at her phone, a twist of pain and shame tightening her gut. Did her mother not want her to call?

Did anyone want to hear from her?

Without thinking, she called Marie.

"Ava!" Marie answered before Ava could take a breath. "I'm so glad to hear from you. What's new?" She laughed. "Do you realize this is the first time you've ever called me? I've been married to your brother for over a year."

"Oh. No, I didn't realize that. I'm… sorry." Had she really never called her sister-in-law? Could that possibly be true? Shame pierced her all over again.

"Your family isn't very chatty, are they? No one calls anyone as far as I can tell. But I'm glad you got in touch. I wanted to ask your opinion about something to do with Mom's party tonight."

Not that again. Ava's heart sank, but she kept her mouth shut and listened to Marie talk, managing to insert "yes" or "no" at appropriate intervals through the conversation. Her mind was spinning. Marie was right. Her family wasn't chatty. They didn't want to hear about her problems—or her successes. They'd never been all that interested with what she was up to, and when she hadn't followed the family tradition and become a professor at a university, they'd simply lost interest in her.

How ironic that Marie was already doing a better job at being a family member than her parents or brother.

"You know what, Marie?" she said, interrupting her sister-in-law's flow of words.

"What?"

"I'm sorry I haven't called before. I'll make sure to do that more often from now on."

"Really?"

"Really. Now tell me more about your plans."

She sat looking at the ocean for a half an hour while Marie talked and she listened. She had to admit Marie had come up with some thoughtful ideas for Ava's mother's party, and Ava was able to make a few tactful suggestions about not going overboard. Her mother wouldn't appreciate too much of a fuss.

After they said goodbye, she drove the rest of the way home, changed into a bikini, packed a towel, a paperback and some sunscreen and spent a couple of hours at the beach. After all, it was summer vacation. She told herself she didn't miss Sam at all. When she was bored of reading, she returned to the house, showered, changed and passed the remainder of the afternoon working on curriculum plans, the sliding glass doors to her balcony wide open.

It was late at night by the time her guests came home. Ava was sitting on her balcony watching the stars. When she heard the sliding glass door open on the floor beneath her, she knew Sam must be out on his balcony, too.

"Ava? You up there?"

"Yes."

"Can we talk a minute?"

"Sure." She didn't get up and come to the railing, though. His treatment of her this morning had hurt.

He waited a minute, as if expecting to see her, then sighed. "Look, I'm sorry. I was out of sorts earlier. I… overheard you talking on the phone last night. As much as I hate to admit it, you're right about everything you said. I am in danger of losing my company. I've already lost my friend, even if neither Ben nor I want to admit it."

Ava drew in a breath. He'd heard her talking about him last night to Emma? She shut her eyes, shame coursing through her for the third time that day. Of course he had. She'd left the door open, hadn't she?

"I shouldn't have been talking about you. I'm sorry."

"It's okay. The thing is, I miss Ben. We've known each other forever. Long before Chloe came around. I can't believe we let her get in the middle of everything."

She got up and came to the railing. "Is there any way the two of you can patch things up?"

"I don't think so." He leaned back against the railing of his balcony and looked up at her. "Not if he wants to stay with Chloe. She won't stick around if he doesn't put her first."

"It's hard to lose a good friend."

He nodded. "It's more than that; I miss everything about my life from before. The things we did. The way we ran our company. Everything's different now, and I feel... stuck. I don't know what to do next."

The defeat in his voice tugged at her heart. From what she'd seen of Sam, he was a man who liked to set goals and achieve them. Now he was faced with a problem he couldn't solve.

"What if there was no such thing as Scholar Central and you never knew Ben or Chloe? What would you do then?" Ava asked, hoping her question could spark a new line of possibilities.

Sam paused a moment. "I have no idea."

"YOU HAVE NO idea?" Ava repeated.

Sam couldn't blame her for her disbelief. What kind of a man couldn't pivot when times got tough? The problem was he'd spent so much of the last decade racing toward one goal, he didn't know what to do now that everyone around him had changed the game they were playing.

"I want to help people," he said. "I thought that's what I was doing."

"By starting Scholar Central?"

Sam struggled to explain something he wasn't sure she'd experienced. "I haven't spent any time in Philadelphia, so I don't know if it's split into different neighborhoods the way Chicago is."

Ava nodded. "It's changed a little over my lifetime as areas get gentrified, especially around the university, but it's definitely split into areas that have a different feel to them."

"Exactly. In Chicago, those divisions are strong. I remember reading about the Berlin Wall when I was a kid and thinking we didn't need a wall where I lived. People sorted themselves into neighborhoods and followed unwritten rules about where they could and couldn't go. I became friends with a guy in college, and it turned out we'd lived three blocks apart when I was in elementary school, but we'd never met, or gone to the same stores, or hung out at the same places. The difference in our skin color meant we kept separate. Everyone in his neighborhood told him not to walk on my street or he'd get beaten up. Everyone in my neighborhood told me the same thing about his street. There was an invisible dividing line between us that we treated like it was made of concrete standing ten feet high."

"I grew up in the suburbs," Ava said. "It wasn't like that, although I knew there were parts of the city I was supposed to avoid."

"I moved away from that neighborhood in high school," Sam said, "but you don't forget things like that. Anyway, we got to talking about our grade schools. My friend told how few resources they had. How overcrowded the classrooms were. How their athletic teams had uniforms that were so old they shredded if you put them in the dryer. Both our neighborhoods were working class, and my grade school wasn't that hot, either, but it was better than that. It got me thinking. How is it right that three blocks can make such a difference between two people's lives?"

"It isn't right," Ava said.

"It got me wondering if there was a way to level the playing field. I decided I had to find out. We've pitched Scholar Central to schools that want to use our curriculum for students who live remotely or have health issues that prevent them from learning in person, but that's not what Scholar Central is intended for at its heart. It's for students who want to get the best instruction, no matter where they are."

She nodded. "You want to change things for people like your friend."

"It's not easy," he told her. "There are two parts to online education—giving the instruction and then measuring the work of the students. We've worked hard to make the first part bullet-proof, so a student can learn the material even if there isn't a teacher around to help them. It's the second part that turned out to be hard. There are a lot of ways to cheat when a student isn't in the same place as the teacher. We're figuring it out, though."

"It's a worthy goal." She ran her hand along the railing. "I'm sorry I gave you a hard time before. You were right. The kind of education I'm going to give my students this fall isn't available to everyone. When I was running my video channel with Todd, I liked that it was accessible to people around the world. We got comments from people in lots of different countries, and it made me feel like we were all learning together."

"Your video channel sounds pretty cool. Did you ever think about continuing it?"

"I'm not traveling anymore," she pointed out.

"You're going to be traveling all over Seahaven, sounds like."

"That's true." She thought about it. "Maybe I will. Hey, want to come up?"

AVA HELD HER breath while Sam scaled the balcony. When he landed on his feet in front of her, he hesitated only a moment before he stepped forward, cupped her chin with his hands and kissed her. His kiss went on and on, as if they were lovers who'd been apart for months. It had almost felt that way to Ava, she realized. The day had seemed endless without him.

Only when confronted with losing Sam had she realized how much she cared for him. It wasn't just his kisses. It was discussions like this one. Todd had never been someone who thought about goals or motivations, and he certainly couldn't put his in words. He just followed his impulses and assumed she'd want to follow them, too.

Sam thought about his past and his future. The things he did had meaning to him. He wanted to make the world a better place. The way he put his thoughts into words built a connection between them, one she wanted to weave back and forth until there was no pulling it apart again.

"I missed you today," he said when he finally pulled back.

"I missed you, too." She was aware of him in a way that kindled her senses, until being close to him became intoxicating.

Sam traced a hand down her arm until she shivered from the light touch of his fingers on her bare skin. "I know that it doesn't make sense for us to do this. I know I'm leaving soon."

Ava went up on tiptoe and caught him in another kiss. She didn't want to think about that anymore. She was tired of being rational all of the time. Who was she trying to impress with her desire to be sensible, anyway?

Her parents?

Ava broke away. "Ugh!"

"Ugh?" Sam drew back, his brows coming together.

"Not you. I was thinking about my Mom and Dad."

"While you kissed me?"

Ava laughed. She couldn't help it; Sam's bewildered disappointment was too endearing. "I was thinking I'm tired of trying to prove them wrong."

"About what?"

"About everything. That I'm not living up to my potential because I'm teaching kids rather than college-level students. That I give away my knowledge in fun videos rather than writing esoteric articles for magazines no one ever reads. Why do we all have to be the same, anyway?"

"I'm sorry it's like that for you. They should see what a wonderful daughter they have." He reached for her again.

"They should." She allowed herself to be drawn against him. She could hear his heart when they stood like this, beating strong and regularly. It felt good to rest in his arms, as if she could depend on him.

"I'm not like them," Sam whispered into her neck. "I see you, Ava Ingerson, and I like what I see."

Ava swallowed, knowing it was true. Sam seemed to like everything about her—except the way she kept holding him at arm's length.

She didn't want to do that anymore. She wanted to let him into her life, come what may. A week of being thoroughly understood—of being thoroughly liked just as she was—was better than nothing, even if her heart would be broken when it was over.

This time she forgot her parents and let him kiss her until she was clinging to him, every inch of her dying to be closer to him. When he began to maneuver her inside toward the bed, however, she dug in her heels.

"Ava." He sighed. "I want you."

"I want you, too. Out here. Not inside." She pulled away from his embrace, the night air cool against her flushed skin, and went to gather the covers off her bed. She brought them out with her and piled them on the deck, buzzing with anticipation of what would come next. After turning off both the interior and exterior lights, she took his hand, so large and strong within hers, and pulled him down into the nest she'd made out of her comforter and pillows. Here in the shadows, they'd be safe from observation.

Sam came willingly, his smile doing interesting things to her insides. "You're full of good ideas."

"I am." With anyone else, she'd be afraid of being made fun of. Some men would scorn her desire to be close to elements when they made love.

Not Sam. She knew without asking he felt the same way she did. He loved being outside. Loved movement and sensation. She'd found a soul mate, even if for only a few days.

Ava laid back, grateful for the stars overhead and the

susurration of the waves crashing on the shore far below them. As Sam began to undress her, she let all her worries go and surrendered utterly to the touch of his fingers brushing her skin. Bare to the night sky, she watched Sam tug his shirt up over his head and shuck off his pants and boxer briefs. He was all muscle and coiled strength. When he bent to explore her body, his hands caressing her, mouth tracing kisses all over her, heat rose within her despite the cool breeze blowing in from the sea.

Sam took his time getting to know her body, and Ava got to know his, too, each stroke of her hands over his skin stoking the fire of her craving for him. When he finally filled her, she closed her eyes, merging into pure sensation, and she knew that no matter what happened next, she'd remember this night, this sky—this man—forever.

EVERY MUSCLE IN his body ached when Sam woke up the following morning. He pushed himself up to a seated position on the hard deck, untangling himself from Ava's body. All the covers she'd piled up for them the previous night hadn't softened the cement surface of the balcony. He felt like he'd done back-to-back boot-camp training sessions.

He had gotten a workout of a sorts, he supposed.

Was he grinning? He was pretty sure he was grinning. Being with Ava was everything he'd hoped it would be.

They'd enjoyed each other's bodies for hours, making love several times. That's what anticipation got you— sweet, sweet release when you finally gave in and did what you wanted.

She was beautiful. She'd shared herself with him with an abandon he'd only dreamed of. Their bodies had merged as if made for each other, and he'd felt he could do no wrong. Now he felt as refreshed as a desert after a strong spring rain. He didn't know what the future would bring, but he was ready to face it.

"Ava?" The sun was up. She'd missed her walk with her friends, and she'd probably better move inside before she got a burn from the sunlight hitting the balcony. Besides, she'd be sore, too, sleeping on this hard surface.

"Mmm?" She opened her eyes. Sam was struck with a longing so powerful it took his breath away. He wanted to see those eyes looking at him every morning for the rest of his life.

He shook the thought away. Rest of his life? Who was he fooling? He hardly knew Ava, and the last time he'd fallen for a woman it had turned into a disaster.

That was Chloe, though, and Ava was different. Somehow he knew life with her would be anything but disastrous. She wouldn't pout if she didn't get the exact downtown Chicago condo she wanted. She'd be too busy creating some exciting opportunity of her own.

"Morning," Ava said, pushing up to her elbows. "Oh." She shut her eyes again. "Why do I feel like I climbed Mt. Everest last night?"

"Let's get you into bed."

She opened one eye, squinting at him. "You only have one objective in life, don't you?"

He laughed, the happiest he'd been in months, pulled her to her feet and wrapped her comforter around her. "You'll be more comfortable—"

A loud noise interrupted him: banging on a door somewhere below them. Both of them stiffened.

"Sam? Where the hell are you? We're going to be late!"

It was Chloe.

"What's on the itinerary today?" Ava whispered impishly.

"I don't know." He hurried them into her room, closing the sliding glass door behind them as the banging sounded again. "I'd better go, though, before she comes up here looking for me." He tugged on the rest of his clothes and drew her close to him. "I'm going with them today, because I need more time with Ben to try to sort things out, but I'll be back by dinner. I want to take you out tonight. Will you let me do that?"

"Okay."

"Don't overthink this while I'm gone." He put his hands on her shoulders. "I mean it, Ava. Don't think at all. Just be here when I come back."

She nodded, but he figured she was already thinking. The shine of the morning was gone, replaced by the same old problems that had haunted him for months. He was dreading this day with Chloe and the others the way he'd dreaded every workday for the last year.

Should he stay with Ava instead? He didn't care what they did together; anything was better than going on one of Chloe's dumb excursions.

"Go," Ava said. "Make sure Chloe doesn't steal your company. I'll be here when you get back."

He almost asked her to promise him she would be, but he knew there were no guarantees in life. He had to trust Ava or nothing they were doing would make sense.

He kissed her one last time instead, trying to let her know everything he was feeling. Judging by the expression on her face when they parted, he thought he'd done a good job.

CHAPTER 9

*W*HEN AVA TAPPED on Emma's door a half hour later, Emma answered it quickly.

"Ava! We missed you when we walked this morning. I hope you were doing something fun."

"I was."

Emma ushered her in and led the way to the large open room at the ocean end of the house that comprised the living room, kitchen and dining area.

"Oh, you have company," Ava said. She'd expected to find Emma alone, her bed-and-breakfast clients out for a day at the beach or something, but Kate Lindsey and Aurora Bentley were sitting at the kitchen counter, along with a young man Ava didn't recognize. Emma waved her into a seat and resumed mixing cookie dough in a large white bowl.

"Hi, Ava," Kate said. "We just stopped in to chat before our first job of the day. Have you met Connor Rexford?"

"Not formally." Ava shook her head. "Nice to meet you, Connor."

He nodded shyly. He was wiry, with a pleasant face and blue eyes.

"Connor has decided to become our newest employee," Aurora told her.

"Our only employee," Kate pointed out.

"He's taking my place so I can concentrate on billing and scheduling," Aurora went on. "It's time for me to take a break from any heavy lifting, but don't you two get comfortable," she told Kate and Connor, "because I'll be back out in the gardens before you know it. I'm not doing desk work forever."

"When you're ready, we'll hire someone else to do the desk work. I figure we're going to grow a lot over the next few years," Kate said happily.

Ava was glad Kate and Aurora had decided to give Connor a chance at a new start.

"Connor's a natural," Aurora told her. "He shadowed us yesterday and did great."

"Have you always wanted to be in landscaping?" Ava asked him.

He shrugged. "Not really, but yesterday was good." Ava decided not to grill him. He had the dazed look of someone who'd been inundated with information and wasn't on top of all of it yet, which made sense. Kate and Aurora must have had to teach him a lot if yesterday was his first day on the job.

"How are things going for you?" Emma asked her.

She filled them in on her trip to Heaven on Earth

farm and all the excursions she was setting up for her students. "It's an adventure school, so I have to set up a lot of adventures," she said.

"An adventure school?" Connor said. "I would have loved to go somewhere like that."

"I'm excited about teaching there," Ava told him. "Guess who I met while I was at the farm?" she asked Emma just as Noah wandered in and stole a finger-full of Emma's cookie dough, Winston trailing behind him. "Fee Harper."

"Really? You met her?" Noah asked, coming to lean on the counter nearby. Winston flopped down at his feet with a sigh.

She related the story Fee had told her. "I forgot to ask her for a tour," she finished, "but I can guarantee you I will next time I see her."

"So she would have gotten the Castle if Bethany hadn't changed her mind, huh?" Noah asked.

"I guess so," Ava said. "She doesn't seem bitter about it, though."

"I feel like I have more questions about the situation than I have answers now," Emma said. "Can you imagine growing up in a castle—and knowing someone was going to take it away from you sooner or later?"

"I wonder why James is holding back," Noah said.

"I wonder what Bethany's conditions are," Kate put in. "Maybe he's not able to meet them."

"I wish I could have seen the jousting in the old

days," Aurora said. "And the Castle Watch."

"I wouldn't mind being a knight," Connor put in, then went silent again.

They talked it all over some more and then Ava stood up. "I'd better go. I've got chores at home to do. My laundry situation is out of control, and my guests are gone for the day. I want to make hay while the sun shines."

"Don't be a stranger," Emma told her.

Ava was halfway home when her phone buzzed. She took the call before she'd read the name of the caller.

"The party was a disaster," Marie announced with no preamble, her voice thick with tears. "Your mother is... she's..."

"Not a party person," Ava filled in for her, knowing Marie was searching for a much stronger term. She rounded the house and started up the stairs, sympathy flooding her.

"She rolled her eyes when she opened my present!"

Ava could imagine that. Nothing Marie could buy in a store would be authentic enough for a woman who made personal relationships with craftsmen and women on multiple continents and spent her days studying every aspect of their lives.

"What about the cake?"

"She didn't eat a bite. She didn't even compliment it. She just sighed when I brought it out."

"Mom is... particular," Ava told her. She reached the

top of the stairs and let herself into her apartment.

"She's cold, that's what she is. I don't have the word Professor in front of my name, so I'm not good enough for her. You know, I thought when I married Oliver that I was getting a family along with a husband. I was so excited to have parents and a sister—" She broke down, sobbing.

Guilt flooded Ava. She hadn't known Marie was hoping for that type of close relationship. "You didn't get any of that, did you? You got a family, but it's a dysfunctional one." Ava wondered if there was any other kind. Maybe every family was strained in its own way.

She thought about the Rainers and decided there was definitely another kind. People who loved each other for who they were, mistakes and all.

She'd often felt like Marie did—that it was her parents and brother who made her family a cold and prickly place, but she wasn't any better than they were, was she? When had she extended any sympathy to Marie? She'd never called her sister-in-law before yesterday. Had done nothing to welcome her to the family. She had no idea when Marie's birthday was; she told herself she'd find out before she got off the phone.

"I'll be your family from now on," Ava promised Marie. "I'm sorry I've been a lousy sister. I didn't know how to be a good one before I got to Seahaven." She thought of Emma and Penelope. The way they were always there for her. The way they took her late-night calls, sent muffins and bottles of wine on the clothesline delivery system. Walked with her at sunrise, toasted the sunset. They never expected her to be someone she wasn't.

"I just want your mother to love me," Marie wailed.

Ava wished she could cry like that. She'd felt the same thing all her life—the same lack of connection. "She does in her own way," she assured Marie. "People are who they are. Instead of focusing on the ones who don't show up the way you want them to, concentrate on the ones who do. Someone in your life must be there for you."

Marie's sobs subsided as she thought about it. "My friends Sara and Bonnie show up like that," she said finally. "We went through school together. They're always willing to listen, but they're friends, not family."

"Sometimes we have to make our own families however we can get them," Ava said. "I'm not saying you should give up on Mom and Dad. I'm saying try to accept them, quirks and all, then fill in the rest of the spaces with people who actually fit the bill."

"That's good advice," Marie said. Ava could tell she was drying her eyes. "And you're a good sister-in-law."

"Not yet, but I'm going to be," Ava promised her. "How about this? You and I will talk once a week. We'll celebrate each other's birthdays and plan holidays when we can. We'll be the family we always wanted. Everyone else can join in on their own terms. You should come out to visit sometime. I'd love to show you around Seahaven."

"I'd like that," Marie said.

"Come anytime." She took a deep breath. "Like for your birthday."

"That's an idea," Marie said enthusiastically.

"When is that again?" Ava asked.

WHEN SAM REALIZED Chloe had finally planned a beach day, he kicked himself for not inviting Ava along, but as the hours passed, he realized coming by himself had been the right thing to do today. For once, Chloe had left things open-ended. Instead of going to the beach nearest to the Blue House, they drove across town in the passenger van to an area called the Leaf, where a wide beach favored by tourists spread along a shopping district full of boutiques and restaurants. They staked out a spot for themselves, spread towels and blankets on the sand, put up a couple of umbrellas Chloe had brought along and positioned coolers of provisions around the perimeter. They were able to claim a volleyball court for an hour, and Sam found himself laughing and diving for the ball along with the rest of them, all the tensions that had built up among them fading away in the bright sunshine.

When they got too hot, they all raced for the water, then shouted at how cold it was, splashing and dunking each other, trying to bodysurf when the waves crashed in.

The food Chloe picked up from a nearby restaurant tasted great after their morning's exertions. All afternoon, Sam alternately dozed in the sun and played in the waves with his friends. Ben had brought a football. Someone else had brought frisbees. They made up games they could play among the other beachgoers. When Sam crashed into Ben, vying to catch a football, they collapsed together in the sand.

"God, I've missed this kind of thing," Ben said. "Just playing. Know what I mean? Everything is so damn serious these days."

"You're right," Sam said. When had that happened? Was it Chloe's fault, or had they forgotten how to have a good time even before she came along? "Doing the whole start-up thing kind of takes it out of you after a while, I guess."

"Yeah." Ben heaved a sigh. They were still on their backs in the sand, and Sam knew they'd have to get up soon, but he didn't want to. From this position all he could see was an endless blue sky. "Do you ever wish we'd just gotten jobs in someone else's company?"

"Sometimes," Sam admitted. "But I don't know if that would have worked. You and I aren't exactly followers."

"But are we leaders? Good ones?"

Sam thought about that. "Not sure our behavior has been totally exemplary." He sat up. Helped Ben up, too.

"Too much fraternizing within the company all around, probably." Ben couldn't meet his eyes.

"You've got that right."

"I should have told you right away I wanted to date Chloe." Ben rubbed a hand through his hair. "Should have spoken up when she interviewed for the position. Bringing her on board under those circumstances was really unprofessional. If I'd said something, we all would have been better off."

"Life is messy." But Ben was right: Neither one of them should have dated a subordinate, and they should have faced the problem head-on right from the start.

"The longer the three of us work together, the worse it all gets," Ben said. "I've been thinking. Maybe I should ask Chloe to leave Scholar Central."

"You'd do that?" Sam was surprised. Ben had never wanted to entertain the notion before and seemed like he'd do anything to keep Chloe happy. Was that the reason he and Chloe had kept their distance from each other yesterday on their hike? Had Ben already alluded to the idea? Things seemed better between the two of them today, but Chloe mostly stuck close to her female friends, so maybe they were simply doing a better job hiding their problems.

Ben shrugged. "I don't want to ask her to leave," he admitted. "It seems unfair, given that Chloe—" He cut off. "Given what she brings to the company."

What had he been about to say? "If Chloe left Scholar Central, what do you think she'd do instead?"

"Start her own company, I guess. She's a smart woman. I'm sure she could do it, and I'd support her all the way, of course."

"You don't think she'd be mad?" Chloe was liable to bite off Ben's head, but as he was asking the question, Sam was wondering why he wasn't feeling more excited about the idea of things going back to the way they'd been. Never in a million years had he thought Ben would decide to take such a course. The plan was brilliant—if Chloe would go along with it.

So why did he feel flat?

"She might be mad," Ben admitted. "But when she got over it, she'd probably find it liberating. At Scholar Central she keeps on having to prove she's as good as we are. Even if we made her a partner, the two of us would always be the founders. She can't compete with that. Starting her own company puts her on equal footing in our marriage. We'd both have a sphere of influence all to ourselves."

"Sounds smart." Sam was still distracted by his own lack of enthusiasm, though. What was wrong with him?

"I'll tell her when we get back to the house. Are you coming to dinner with us tonight?"

"No, I'm taking Ava out."

"Good. I'll tell Chloe I want a meal alone with her. We can discuss everything together, and I'll see what she thinks. Everyone can go off and do their own thing for once tonight."

"Great."

"I need another dip. Coming in?"

"Sure."

The fun had gone out of the afternoon somehow, and for the life of him, Sam couldn't figure out why.

AVA HAD NEVER been to Surf Point before. It was one of the fancier restaurants in Seahaven with wonderful views of the ocean and was done up in neutral tones, understated yet elegant.

She appreciated the time alone with Sam. She'd spent much of the day catching up on chores around the house, grateful for some peace and quiet, but as the afternoon wore on, she'd gotten restless, excited about the chance to be with Sam again.

Now they were here. Whenever she looked his way, Sam was watching her, and his gaze stirred something deep inside her. He was thinking about being with her. She couldn't say how she knew that, but she did, and knowing it kindled her own desire.

They had hours to go before they could act on their impulses, and she resolved to enjoy the anticipation. When they'd ordered, Sam told her about his day and about Ben's unexpected offer.

"Chloe's going to leave Scholar Central? That will make things more comfortable for you and Ben, won't it?"

"I guess so—if it happens."

"You don't think it will?"

"I'm pretty sure she's been promising her friends at the company money if they support her in her bid to become a partner. That doesn't sound like someone who's going to walk away without a fuss."

She examined the man across the table. Worry lines creased his forehead as he buttered a slice of the homemade bread their waiter had left in a basket.

"What do you think Ben will do if she refuses to go?"

"I wish I could say he'd stand up to her, but I don't think he will."

"Still, he came up with the idea. Doesn't that count for something? He's putting his relationship with you first for a change."

"I guess."

She watched him take a bite of bread. "Will you miss Chloe if she leaves Scholar Central?" she asked softly. She told herself she'd known Sam only a few days. She couldn't be heartbroken if he discovered he still loved his ex-fiancée.

"Will I miss Chloe? No." His brows came together as he reached across the table to take her hand. "Ava, I don't feel anything for Chloe. It's you I…" He cut off and tried again. "You're the one making it hard for me to sleep at night," he said.

Had he been about to say something else? Something

that hinted he was becoming far more attached to her than she'd guessed? Ava didn't know how to ask him that. He was lost in thought, absently stroking his thumb across her skin. Each stroke raised her awareness of him. She didn't think he knew what his proximity did to her, and it killed her to think of Chloe at all when he was touching her.

"Maybe what's really going on is I feel like I've lost my way," he said.

"Mm?" It was hard to concentrate with him touching her like that.

"I didn't build Scholar Central to make money," he said. "I built it to reach kids who aren't getting a good education. Chloe and everyone else are putting money first."

"You want to give your service away?" The brush of his fingertips reminded her of the way it felt when he undressed her and caressed her body. Sam had a thorough interest in every part of her, and he made her feel more beautiful than she'd thought she was before.

He made a face. "No. I've got too many people working for me I've got to pay. So how do I get Scholar Central into the hands of the kids who need it while still turning enough profit to hire the best minds to work on it?"

"I don't know," Ava said. "What does Ben think?"

"That's just it. Since Chloe got with him, we don't talk about things like that. All we talk about are profits."

"Do you think Ben sees a different path for Scholar Central than you do?" Ava registered that this had become a serious discussion. She tried to push her amorous thoughts out of her mind.

"I think he sees Chloe's path," Sam said.

"But he's going to ask Chloe to leave," Ava pointed out.

Sam nodded slowly, then shut his eyes. "She's going to refuse."

He spoke as someone who knew what he was talking about, and Ava had no doubt he was right. She'd seen Chloe in action; the woman didn't strike her as someone who gave up easily, especially when money was involved.

"If Chloe won't leave and Ben won't make her, is there a way you can move forward on your own?"

Sam opened his eyes, stared at her, and after a moment his shoulders dropped. "Like leave Scholar Central myself?"

She shrugged. She didn't see what else he could do if the situation was making him this unhappy.

"I'd have to start over with a new idea. A new team. New funding. New everything."

"You don't have to make any decisions tonight," she said softly. "Maybe it's time to set the problem aside for a while. Have your dinner and let your subconscious work on it." She spotted their waiter coming toward them.

"I guess so," Sam said unhappily.

Once the waiter had placed their orders in front of them and was gone again, Ava steered the conversation to her friends and told Sam more about Emma's bed-and-breakfast and the boutique wedding business Penelope was developing. The food was heavenly, and soon Sam relaxed a little. They drank wine, gazed at the moonlit ocean and swapped stories of their childhood escapades. Whenever he could, Sam took her hand. Squeezed it. Stroked her skin with his thumb. The evening was everything she could have asked for, and yet... she could tell some part of Sam's mind was always somewhere else.

He was trying to solve the problem of what to do about Scholar Central. Despite his protestations, it seemed clear to Ava he couldn't get Chloe out of his head. And Ben, she supposed. Maybe he didn't want to return to the past, but he couldn't let it go, either.

All that changed, however, after dinner. It was as if Sam made a conscious decision to put his worries aside.

"I want to dance with you," he said as they stepped out of the restaurant onto the street. They were in Seahaven's tourist district and could hear live music coming from a club just a few buildings away.

"It's kind of late," Ava pointed out.

"Not for dancing." He laced his fingers through hers and led her to the nearby bar. Inside, the atmosphere was as raucous as Surf Point had been sedate. She forgot her concern for Sam's situation when they found the dance floor and Sam pulled her close. Just like before, he refused to follow the music's beat, instead swaying with her in a sensuous way as if a slow song was playing.

Ava didn't mind one bit. She was no longer worried he was thinking about Chloe. She couldn't mistake his interest in her, especially when he kissed the side of her neck as they swayed together and his hands slipped lower on her back.

They danced for hours. Had several more drinks. By the time they left the club, Ava was buzzing from the alcohol she'd consumed and from Sam's hands on her body. The way he touched her left no doubt in her mind what they'd do when they got home, and she couldn't wait.

They left her car behind and called a cab, since neither of them was in a condition to drive. The ride home couldn't have taken more than ten minutes, but it seemed like an hour to Ava, who was craving Sam's touch. Half in his lap in the back seat, she tried to keep her wits about her for the sake of their driver, but she was too far gone to be discreet.

"I'll be up in a minute," Sam promised when they parted outside the house.

"I'll be waiting. My door will be open. Both of them." She laughed, thinking about Sam's penchant for climbing her balcony. She hoped he took the safer route tonight, but when she reached her apartment, she threw her sliding glass doors open, needing the night air and the crash of the waves to accompany her mood.

It had been fun to make love to Sam on the balcony the other night, but this time she meant for them to share the comfort of her bed. Still buzzing from the drinks she'd had, she searched through her chest of drawers for something sexy to put on, found a tiny, silky thing and changed, hoping Sam would arrive soon and take it off. Even after she'd freshened up a little in the bathroom, though, he still wasn't there.

Ava turned on some music. Lit a couple of candles safely contained in glass jars. Everything was perfect.

Where was Sam?

She trailed out onto the balcony, breathing in the smell of the ocean, the breeze playing on her mostly bare skin. It was late, she was drunk and if she waited too long, she knew she'd be sleepy when Sam finally did arrive. She wanted to be wide awake for him.

She wanted him right now.

Ava looked over the balcony railing. He'd climbed up and come to no harm. Was there a way she could climb down?

TWO MINUTES. THAT'S all he needed before he raced upstairs and spent a night proving to Ava she couldn't do without him. Sam had decided he needed Ava to want him so badly she'd agree to extend their relationship past his vacation somehow. He'd never gone looking for something long distance, but that didn't matter now.

What mattered was being with Ava. Touching her—

"Where the hell have you been all night?"

"Hell, Chloe!" Hadn't he locked the door to his room when he came in? Maybe not; he'd been rushing. Had she been waiting for him to come back to the house?

She was dressed in soft pink outfit of shorts and a tank top obviously meant for sleeping in. She wasn't wearing a bra, and her hair was down. He hadn't seen Chloe like this since they were a couple.

"Have you been out with *her*?"

"With Ava?"

"Yes. Her."

"It's no business of yours if I have been." He didn't want to be having this conversation.

"It used to be my business."

Sam was bewildered. Why was Chloe here? Why was she dressed like that? She'd been buttoned up and professional every time he'd seen her since the day she'd come back from her trip to Cabo—with Ben. Now she was all soft curves and pouty looks.

Chloe stepped forward. "You and Ben had a little talk about me today, didn't you?"

He let out a breath. Of course. Ben had told her tonight that she would need to leave the company. She'd probably been hiding in some corner waiting for him ever since.

Sam thought of the empty bedroom across the hall.

Had she waited for him there? "Ben thought you'd be happier with your own business to run."

"Is that what Ben thought?" She put her hands on his chest. Leaned close. "What did you think?"

He caught her wrists, not knowing what she was up to but knowing he didn't like it one bit. He let go when she pulled her hands away from him, thinking she'd gotten the point, but she moved even closer.

"What did you think about Ben's idea?" she asked again, lifting her palm to caress his cheek. "You and I used to be so close. We used to work so well together. Do you think Ben is right? Should I leave Scholar Central? Go to work somewhere else? Or is Ben the one who should leave?"

Had Chloe been drinking? Suddenly Sam felt like he'd had one too many. She couldn't be serious—could she?

"But you and Ben…"

She silenced him with a finger to his lips. "Me and Ben. Ben and me. That's always been the problem, hasn't it?"

"Chloe."

She went up on tiptoe, braced her hands on Sam's shoulders and kissed him. Before he could even react, there was a sound behind him on the deck, a noise like something had dropped onto it from the third floor, knocking a chair sideways in the process. Still cradling his face, Chloe stiffened. Pulled away.

Looked over his shoulder and screamed.

Sam turned, but he already knew what he'd see—knew this was the end of everything he'd hoped for.

Ava stood on the balcony, every curve of her body visible through the tiny, silky item she wore, her knees scraped and bleeding, her hands outstretched as if to ward off the vision of him and Chloe in each other's arms. It was her gaze that cut him to the quick, though. The disappointment and betrayal clear in every slack line of her face.

"Ava." He pushed Chloe aside and started for her.

Chloe opened her mouth and screamed again.

CHAPTER 10

"SHE'S BEEN PEEKING in everyone's windows. Climbing from floor to floor like a peeping Tom. I bet there are cameras hidden in our rooms. I bet she'd been filming everything!" Chloe kept shrieking as the rest of their party came running. A knot of men and women crowded in the doorway, trying to see what was happening in the room. None of the men seemed to be able to keep their gazes off Ava, leaving her flustered and humiliated. There was no way through the room without pushing through them, though, and she was afraid Chloe wouldn't let her pass.

This had to be a nightmare, Ava thought, still standing on Sam's deck. The sliding glass doors were open, leaving no barrier between her and the others. She hugged her arms across her chest, knowing how exposed she was in this outfit. Sam grabbed a robe from his bed and thrust it at her. Ava struggled into it gratefully.

What the hell had she been thinking when she'd blown out her candles, climbed over the balcony and dropped down onto Sam's deck? She'd ended up tipping over a chair and becoming tangled in it as she crashed to the floor. Her knees ached. So did the palm of one hand and her shoulder, where she'd hit the concrete before scrambling up. She was lucky she wasn't more badly hurt.

"What are you doing in Sam's room?" Ben demanded of Chloe. He turned to Ava. "What are *you* doing out *there*?"

"I was coming to see Sam," she said faintly. "I didn't think he'd have company."

"I wasn't supposed to," Sam said firmly.

"She's a voyeur!" Chloe shrieked again, pointing at Ava. "She's probably filming all of us. I bet she's uploading it all to the internet." She turned to the crowd in the doorway for backup.

"I'm not filming anything!" Ava protested. It was bad enough she'd been humiliated in front of everyone. Every male guest had seen more of her body than any of them deserved. She was the one who should be screaming. "You were coming on to Sam, weren't you? You wanted to sleep with him. That's why you're here," she accused, forgetting Chloe was her guest, the one paying the bill for all these people.

"Why were you in Sam's room, Chloe?" Ben asked again in a quiet voice that somehow cut through everyone else's exclamations.

Chloe turned on her fiancé. "I'm not the one coming on to anyone. Sam's the one who dragged me in here.

He's the one who—"

She didn't get any further before Ben lunged for Sam. Ava shrieked. She wasn't the only one. Ben landed a punch on Sam's shoulder. Sam got him hard on the jaw. The two men crashed against the dresser together, grappled and fought and then lurched the other way.

Ava was afraid they'd go right through the glass. They'd already knocked everything off the dresser. "Stop them!" she shouted to the other men crowded in the doorway. A couple of them jumped into the fray, struggling to get the two men apart, without much luck. Sam landed another punch square on Ben's cheekbone. Ben retaliated with a blow to Sam's gut.

"If you touched Chloe, I will kill you!" Ben growled.

"I wouldn't touch her if she was the last woman on earth."

As SAM GRAPPLED with Ben and fought to land another punch, he knew there was no way this could end well. Fighting Ben, being caught alone with Chloe, took the tension between the three of them to a whole new level. Why the hell had Chloe come to his room in the first place? Did she really want him back? Or was this…?

"Hell." Sam let go. Ben, caught off balance, nearly knocked over the men trying to pull them apart before he caught himself, straightened and lunged at Sam again. Gabe and Carter followed after him, but this time Sam was ready for Ben. He stepped aside at the last moment, leaving Ben to crash into the wall, Gabe and Carter only just managing to avoid slamming against him. Muttering a curse as Carter extended him a hand, Ben got up, but before he could come at Sam, Gabe blocked his way. Sam took advantage of the pause. "Chloe's getting back at me because you told her to leave Scholar Central!"

Ben pulled up, breathing heavily. Some part of him must have realized it could be true, because he turned to face his fiancée. "Is he right?"

She shook her head vehemently. "That's ridiculous. But so is choosing him over me. He's the one who should leave, if anyone should. You know that."

Ben frowned. Uncurled his hands. "Sam is the one who came up with the idea for Scholar Central."

"Ideas are a dime a dozen. I'm the one making the kind of connections that will make the company profitable. You two would be lost without me." Chloe picked up speed. "And if I leave, you can be sure I'll take half the company with me."

"You're about to marry me," Ben pointed out. "Why would you do that?"

"Why would you choose your stupid friend over your future wife?" Chloe cried. "I'm the one you're sleeping with at the end of the day. I'm the one who deserves your loyalty. I'm the one who's about to—" She cut off. "The one who'll take this company to the next level."

Sam knew this confrontation was going to damage

company morale. This whole argument should have played out behind closed doors. He opened his mouth to say so, but Ben spoke up first.

"Listen, Chloe, you've done a terrific job laying the groundwork for a deal. I can carry it through. Meanwhile, I'll back you in your own company one hundred percent. I don't understand why you aren't jumping at the chance to start your own business."

"Are you kidding me?" Chloe clenched her hands into fists. "I do all the ground work, and you want to walk my deal across the finish line and take all the credit for it?"

"What deal?" Sam demanded. "What are you talking about?"

Chloe turned on him. "I've found a buyer for Scholar Central. One ready to pay top dollar for your stupid little company, and Ben here thinks I should quit so he can steal my glory."

"I think you should step away because it isn't appropriate for us to work together anymore," Ben said. "I'll make sure you get all the credit you deserve. You're going to be my wife—you're going to share all the proceeds I earn from Scholar Central's success."

"*My* success," she countered. "You won't earn anything without me, and you know it. I'm the one making the deal."

"What deal?" Sam asked again. "We never said anything about selling Scholar Central."

"What do you think we've all been working for?" Chloe cried.

Sam couldn't believe what she was saying. He looked to the others for backup, but they were no help. Gabe and Cooper had slinked away to the doorway. Julian and the women remained out in the hall. Was that really how they all felt about Scholar Central? "We've been working to solve a problem," Sam said. "To help people."

"Oh, spare me the theatrics. I am helping people. I'm helping all of us to a payday that will change our lives. Tell him, Ben."

Ben opened his mouth. Closed it again. "What... do you want me to say?"

"'What do you want me to say?'" Chloe mimicked in a falsetto voice. "I want you to tell your idiot friend to keep quiet and let the grown-ups get the job done. Tell him no one needs him anymore. Tell him I'm going to call the shots from now on, something everyone else in the company understands except him. Tell him to shut up, sign the paperwork to make me an equal partner and be grateful we're not kicking him out of the company altogether."

"Chloe." Ben straightened, his brow furrowing. "You're going too far." He darted a glance to their audience still clustered by the door. Sam wondered if he was really going to let her talk to him that way in front of his employees.

"Too far? Too far?" Chloe laughed disbelievingly.

"Are you kidding me? I'm not going far enough. I'm the only one in this operation with any brains or foresight. What did you think you were going to do with your software? Give it away? Why are you always so stupid?"

"Stop it, Chloe," Sam said. "You're way out of line." He couldn't stand still and listen to this, even if Ben had tried to beat him up a moment ago. The rest of the group retreated farther into the hall.

"I can say whatever I want," she said. "Because I'm this tight with the owner of the company who wants to buy Scholar Central." She crossed her fingers and held them up. "Ah, you didn't even think about that, did you?" she said to Ben. "You truly thought you could tell me to leave and I'd tuck my tail between my legs and run away, letting you be the big hero. You're so damn dumb it didn't even occur to you I'd take the deal with me. I set it up," she reminded him, "and I can shoot it in the head any time I want to."

"I'm not dumb," Ben said quietly.

"Baby, you are worse than dumb. You're the kind of dumb who doesn't even know you're dumb."

Sam wanted to throttle Chloe. Ben had gotten plenty of that talk from his dad when he was a kid; he didn't need it now from the woman who was supposed to love him. He felt rather than saw a couple of the women edge farther into the hall toward the stairs. He could tell the others wished they were anywhere but here.

Before he could say anything, Chloe turned on her

heel. "I'm not staying in this dump another night. I'm leaving. And I'm going to give this place a crappy rating—because it sucks."

Spurred into motion by her sudden retreat to the exit, the rest of the group backed down the hall to get away from her. Ben watched Chloe go, unmoving. Sam waited. Was he angry? Hurt?

Scared?

Just when he thought she was safely gone, Chloe reappeared in the doorway and pointed to Ben. "If you don't want me to leave you and take the deal of a lifetime with me, you'll pack your things and be in the van in ten minutes." She turned to call down the hall. "That goes for everyone. In the van in ten minutes!" she repeated and disappeared again.

There was a long pause before Ben faced Sam.

"I'm staying right here," Sam said to him, fury burning in his gut. He swallowed hard to steady his voice. "You should, too. We don't need her."

"I need her," Ben said. "She's the woman I'm going to marry."

"Are you serious?"

Ben cut him off. "I'm not walking out because things are hard. Chloe's right; it was wrong of me to ask her to leave when she's been working so hard to make a deal. She's got a right to be mad. When she calms down, we'll figure things out."

"She talked to you like you were a child."

"She talked to me like I chose an old friend over her," Ben countered. "She's going to be my wife," he said again. "I'm supposed to put her first." He walked out the door, leaving Sam alone with Ava.

Sick to his stomach, he turned to her. He wished he could pull her into his arms and erase what had happened from his mind, but he couldn't. He had to face it. "I'm sorry for all of this. I'll pay for any damage we caused." When she didn't answer him, his gut twisted with alarm. "Ava? What's wrong?"

She let out a disbelieving laugh. "What's wrong?" She lifted her hands. "Everything's wrong. You're fighting with your best friend. You're kissing your ex-fiancée. You tell me what's wrong."

Sam couldn't believe what he was hearing. "Chloe burst in here. I didn't invite her. She's the one who kissed me. You yourself said she was hitting on me."

"But you didn't stop her. I saw you, Sam."

"You saw me surprised. A moment later I'd have pushed her away. I didn't know what she was going to do until she did it."

Ava only stared at him. She dropped her hands to her sides. "You're going back to Chicago on Sunday, right?"

"Right." That's when the trip ended, but—

"Then what the hell are we doing anyway?"

"We're figuring it out as we go along. Forget Ben and Chloe. I'll stay here tonight. We'll talk this out."

"What is there to talk about?" When he didn't answer, she laughed again. "Really, Sam? What could we possibly have to talk about?" She turned to go.

"We could talk about the fact I care about you."

Ava stopped, but only for a moment. Then she walked right out the door.

THEY WERE GONE.

Ava could tell by the complete silence in the house that her guests had all left, but she snuck down the stairs, took in the empty spot where the passenger van had been parked, let herself into the main house and walked the rooms to be sure. No one remained. Not even Sam.

She'd told him to go. Not in so many words, maybe, but she'd made it clear enough she was done with their relationship. Maybe he hadn't kissed Chloe, but he hadn't stopped her, either. Even if everything that had just happened had been Chloe's doing, he was still leaving in a matter of days. It was madness to hope they could be together.

She locked up and wearily climbed the stairs to her apartment. She'd already changed into sweatpants and a T-shirt, disgusted by the sexy lingerie she'd put on to seduce Sam, but now her head was pounding and her mouth was dry from the combination of alcohol and fear. She wrapped a blanket around her shoulders and went out onto her deck.

"Ava?" Penelope called from next door. "Are you

okay? I heard shouting a while back."

"I'm okay." But she wasn't, and she didn't know when she would be. If this was what a fling felt like, she wanted no part of it. Of course, she hadn't done much better with a long-term relationship. She bent her head and began to cry.

"Ava?" Penelope called again. "I'm coming over. Let me in when I knock, okay?"

Ava did so a minute later when Penelope knocked softly on her door. She was surprised to see Emma with her. "It's so late. You have guests, don't you?" she asked them. She'd dried her eyes, but they still burned.

"Friendship trumps sleep," Penelope said. "Sit down. Tell us what happened. I'm going to make us some chamomile tea." She bustled around Ava's tiny kitchen while Emma got her settled on her bed, tucked under the covers. She shut the doors to the deck almost all the way, letting in just a touch of the breeze.

"There are more blankets in the closet," Ava said. Emma fetched a couple of them. Penelope brought tea, and they wrapped themselves up and sat in chairs they brought close.

"What happened?" Penelope asked when she was settled in her seat.

Ava told them everything, including her fall from the upper deck and Sam kissing Chloe.

"He was kissing her?" Emma asked. "Are you sure? Or was she kissing him? It makes a world of difference, you know."

Ava lifted her shoulders. "I couldn't really tell. Sam's back was to me, but they were definitely kissing." She wanted to believe it was all Chloe's doing, but she'd never forget the look of triumph on Chloe's face before she opened her mouth and screamed.

When Penelope began to protest she couldn't possibly be sure, Ava set her tea down on her bedside table. "It doesn't matter. Sam's leaving in a week. One way or another, it's over. So's my business, probably. Chloe said she was going to leave a terrible review, and she can probably make the rest of her friends do the same. No one's going to want to rent the Blue House after that."

"You have dozens of wonderful reviews," Emma assured her. "A couple of bad ones won't change that."

"Bad ones that say I was spying on them late at night? Peeking in windows? Sneaking onto their balconies? I think that will change a lot." A tear slid down her cheek. "What on earth am I going to do?"

Penelope and Emma exchanged a look. "I don't know," Emma said slowly.

Ava's heart sank because it was clear Emma had an idea but was afraid to voice it. "Yes, you do. Tell me."

Emma chewed her lower lip, but it was Penelope who finally answered. "You could apologize to Chloe. Ask her to come back. Give her a break on the cost of renting the place."

"Give it to her for free," Emma said.

More tears slid from Ava's eyes because she knew they were right. She had to stop thinking about Sam—or her pride—and think about her business.

"She's going to gloat," she said.

"I know," Emma said. "It's going to suck. But then it will be over and life will go on." She came to sit on the bed as Ava's tears kept coming. Suddenly Ava was exhausted. She didn't think she could face any of this.

Penelope came to sit on her other side. "We'll help you in any way we can," she promised. "We'll send care packages on the pulley system every hour on the hour."

"You'll get through this," Emma said. "Someday it will be a funny story."

"I don't think so," Ava said, but it didn't matter, did it? She'd live through it, and that was all that counted.

AVA HADN'T ANSWERED her phone for two days. Sam had called and texted her a dozen times at least from the hotel to which he and the others had retreated, and he wondered if she'd blocked him. He'd tried to explain again that Chloe was the one who'd hit on him, but if she wasn't even looking at her messages, they couldn't do any good. He'd confirmed that she'd managed to retrieve her car from the pier, and he knew she'd spoken with Chloe and had offered to deduct 50 percent of the cost of the accommodation if the party returned to the Blue House and let her make it up to them. Chloe had refused, despite everyone trying to change her mind.

The vacation had gone on, however, taking on a surreal quality in which everyone pretended that what had happened hadn't happened at all. Ben was the ringleader of the new normal, all cheery greetings and encouragement even though Chloe refused to speak to him. The first day after the incident, they'd driven to San Jose and toured a museum that housed Egyptian artifacts. It should have been interesting. Instead it was miserable. Chloe rattled out orders in a too-bright, too-sharp tone of voice, and the others were terrified of coming under one of her attacks.

When Sam broached the topic of heading home to Chicago early, Ben shut him down. "We need to see this through," he'd snapped. "We owe it to Chloe."

"Chloe said she wanted to kick me out of the company," Sam reminded him.

"She was overwrought. She didn't mean it," Ben said.

Sam had decided to let sleeping dogs lie for the time being. At least he knew where Chloe stood now and why Ben was going along with her bid for power. He knew Chloe would leave him if he didn't. He kept talking about the deal she claimed to have made. How selling Scholar Central would set them up for life.

Sam wasn't buying it for a minute. The more he thought about it, the less he believed Chloe meant to share more of that money than she needed to. Would she even marry Ben? Or would she figure out a way to claim the lion's share of the profits and then take off?

He wished they could fire her, but he had a feeling Chloe had them over a barrel there. She could launch a lawsuit if they didn't follow the rules to the letter, and it could take months to force her out. He needed to convince Ben to tell her she couldn't represent Scholar Central in talks with anyone. He couldn't fathom how she'd convinced Ben that he wanted to sell something he'd worked so hard to make a success.

Whenever he tried to get Ben alone to talk to him, though, there was Chloe, making it impossible for them to have any privacy. He was afraid to push it. Afraid to rouse Chloe's suspicions before he made sure Ben would back him up.

It didn't seem likely Ben would. He was always watching Chloe. Always placating her. It was making Sam sick.

Meanwhile, time was ticking by and he couldn't get through to Ava.

Which meant he needed to try something different.

He slipped out of the hotel early and walked to the Blue House. One thing he'd learned about Ava was she constantly forgot to lock her car. He tried the handle of the back seat, sighing in satisfaction when it opened. He got in and hid under the blankets she always had piled there. Now he'd have to wait. She frequently went on excursions to plan for the school year. If she didn't today, she'd at least go out to run an errand or something, right?

Two hours later Sam was bitterly regretting drinking his morning cup of coffee when he finally heard footsteps. The front door of the RAV4 suddenly opened and someone got in. The door closed, the engine started and soon they were on their way.

Sam would have waited ten minutes or so if it wasn't for that cup of coffee.

"Hi, Ava," he said, sitting up.

Ava shrieked, swerved, got control of the car again, met his gaze in the rearview mirror and pulled right off the road. "What are you doing?" she demanded, her voice high and tight.

"Sorry I scared you. I didn't think you'd talk to me unless I cornered you."

"You could have gotten us both killed!"

"I wasn't thinking about that. Look, can we go somewhere to talk?"

Ava rolled her eyes. "Fine. I was going to pick up coffee anyway." She looked over her shoulder, pulled back out onto the road and a minute later they were at Cups & Waves. Sam excused himself, made a trip to the bathroom and met her at the counter a few minutes later, just when it was their turn to order. Kamirah nodded at him.

"Hello again."

"Hello."

Kamirah took their orders and got busy making their drinks. Sam struggled to think of small talk but couldn't come up with anything with Ava glaring at him. "Caramel macchiato," Kamirah said to him, handing him his beverage, "and a mocha for the lady, extra whipped cream."

"I didn't ask for extra whipped cream," Ava said.

"Figured it might help make up for whatever this one has done." She cocked her head at Sam.

"I didn't say—" Ava broke off. "Is it that obvious?"

"It's that obvious," Kamirah confirmed. "Have a good day, you two." She shooed them away and greeted her next customers.

Sam followed Ava to a table in the corner by the windows.

"You've got five minutes. I've wasted enough time on you," she said ungraciously.

Not an auspicious beginning, Sam thought. He wanted to reiterate his innocence and tell her how Chloe was the one who'd instigated the kiss she'd seen, but he knew that wouldn't go over well. He needed to make her understand who he really was. Maybe the best way was to tell her a little more about his life.

"I met Ben in second grade," he started. "We lived next door to each other in row houses on the southside. We walked to school with each other sometimes, but we didn't really talk or anything. I could hardly get a word out of him when I tried, so pretty soon I gave up trying."

"Okay." She didn't soften at all.

"Then one day I found him on his hands and knees

on the sidewalk outside his house. I thought he'd been in a fight and gotten knocked down. I didn't like him much, but he lived on my block, which meant we were linked, friends or not. Chicago is a pretty territorial city."

Ava blew on her coffee and took a tentative sip. She didn't seem to be giving his story any special attention, but he had a feeling he'd hooked her.

"I tried to pull him to his feet, but he refused to budge. I ended up on the sidewalk beside him. He was looking at this beetle. One of its legs was hurt, and it wasn't running away, even though both of us were looming over it. It was clear the thing wasn't doing well. 'I'm going to save it,' Ben said and then stiffened, like he thought I was going to hit him." Sam swallowed, remembering that day. "I don't know how I knew, because I was pretty young and stupid back then, but I understood in that moment that he got hit—a lot. I had been about to laugh at him, the way I'd have laughed at anyone interested in a stupid bug, but instead I froze. I didn't know what to do. 'It's a stag beetle,' Ben said. He started telling me all about it. He thought I was interested because there I was on my knees beside him on the sidewalk and I guess because I wasn't hitting him after all."

He hadn't realized he'd stopped talking until Ava lifted her gaze to him. "What happened?"

"He told me the sidewalk wasn't the ideal habitat for a stag beetle. He said we needed to take it to where it could heal. There was an empty lot a few streets over he thought would do. We were already going to be late for school, and I knew I'd catch hell if I didn't make it by the bell, but I also knew I was going to save that damn beetle because what else could I do? Ben lived on my block. He was my responsibility. Someone had been beating on him, that was clear, and they weren't going to do it again that day if I could help it. I told him I'd go with him and I did. He spent the whole time filling me in on every detail about stag beetles, and when we got to the empty lot, and we let it go, he kept finding other bugs to talk about. And plants. And pigeons." Sam laughed. "God, that kid could talk. I don't think anyone had ever simply listened to him before. He must have said out loud everything he'd been holding inside until then."

"You became friends."

Sam rubbed a hand over the back of his neck. "We did. Once he relaxed around me, it turned out he was funny. He had a hell of an imagination. And he was a history buff. We re-enacted the Peloponnesian Wars all over the south side of Chicago. Then we spent about a year pretending we were Louis and Clark. I started bringing him home after school. His best bet was not to be around his own home very much. He started eating dinner with us most days. Became part of the family, basically."

"He was lucky to find you."

"I was lucky to find him, too. I was a bit of a screw-up as a kid. Everyone in my family was so bent on academic achievement, I rebelled against it right from the start. I was the youngest in the family, which meant my sisters always knew more than me. I acted like a clown because I never got to be right. Ben was an excellent student, though, and I'm competitive enough I couldn't let him get better grades than me. He did," Sam confessed, "but not by much."

"Did you go to the same college?" Ava wasn't pretending not to find this interesting anymore.

Sam hesitated. He didn't usually talk about this part. "In the end we did," he said. "My parents did well for themselves. When I was fourteen, we moved away from the southside."

Ava, who was about to take a sip of her coffee, put the cup down. "Oh, no."

Sam nodded. "When I broke the news to Ben, I found out what people mean when they say the color drained from someone's face. It literally did. I thought he was going to faint. I told him he could still come over all the time, but when we checked, it turned out he would need to take two buses to get there. We wouldn't be going to the same school anymore. The look in his eyes…" Sam would never forget it. "I knew damn well by then it was his dad who beat him and it was getting more and more out of control. His mom wasn't in the picture. I kept telling Ben he had to learn to fight back—

231

he's a big guy, but his dad was bigger, and he wouldn't do it."

"What happened?"

"We moved," Sam said helplessly. "I invited Ben over all the time, but he didn't come. I don't know where he was spending his afternoons and evenings. At the library, maybe. He had a part-time job there on weekends and a couple of nights a week. He was trying to save for school, but his dad was after that money morning, noon and night. He told Ben if he was old enough to work, he was old enough to pay his way. I had this feeling in my stomach all the time, like something awful was going to happen. I didn't know what."

"Did you think Ben might kill himself?"

Sam sucked in a breath. He'd never admitted that to himself. He nodded, finding his throat too clogged to allow him to speak for a moment. "Yeah," he said finally. "I think I did—if his dad didn't kill him first. One day I decided enough was enough. I went over to his house after school. Knocked on the door. His dad opened it. He was drunk. Just… wasted. He didn't even recognize me, even though I'd lived next door to him for most of my life. 'What the hell do you want?' he asked. Ben came down the stairs behind him. Halfway—just far enough for me to see that the side of his face was black and blue. I've never been so mad. I wanted to beat the shit out of his father, but Ben was back there shaking his head, telling me not to try it. I learned later his dad had put more than one person in the hospital."

"What did you do?"

"I stood there for a second. I didn't know what to do. And then I said, 'Ben's coming to live with us. With my family. We live in a better school district.' I think I confused him." Sam shook his head. "He kind of scratched his head and said, 'Fine. Do whatever the hell you want, but if you take him, you pay for him.' I went in, followed Ben up the stairs to his bedroom, had him packed up in five minutes and took him home. I told my folks Ben was living with us now. I have to give them credit. They didn't fight it. Didn't even ask any questions. Just set him up in the spare room and finished raising him. I don't know how they squared it with Ben's dad, or how they registered him for school, but they did. He started there with me the next week. When it came time for college, my folks helped him there, too."

"I'm so glad you were there for him," Ava said softly.

"Me, too."

"So what are you going to do about Chloe?"

"I don't know," Sam said miserably. "But I can't give in. She's trying to walk away with everything I've worked to build."

Ava nodded slowly. "You should be at the hotel with them. You shouldn't leave Ben alone with her."

"I didn't want to lose you." He took her hand. "Ava, I'm falling in love with you. I can't let you go. Not now. Would you come to Chicago to be with me?"

CHAPTER 11

*C*OME TO CHICAGO?

Ava's heart lurched in her chest when Sam asked the question. He'd said he loved her.

Loved her.

And she thought she might love him back. But leave Seahaven? The Blue House? The life she'd made here?

Pain clogged her throat as she searched for an answer that wouldn't break his heart—or hers. She accepted Sam's explanation of what had happened. After all, Ava had seen Chloe's triumphant look when she'd crashed onto Sam's balcony, and her gut had told her all along Sam was a man who valued other people's feelings. She remembered gliding with him silently around Sunset Slough in their kayaks—the way he'd honored all the living things around them. The way he'd let her set the pace. She knew she could trust him.

No one had made her pulse quicken like he did. Sam listened to her. He was interested in the things that interested her. The great outdoors was a classroom and playground for them both. When she thought of the life they could build together, it took her breath away.

Which made what she needed to say that much harder.

After Todd left, Ava had wondered if she'd squandered her one chance for happiness with a man in her life, but now she'd learned all that a relationship could be. Sam was everything she'd ever wanted—

But she couldn't have him.

And that hurt like hell.

Sam was waiting for an answer. She knew he deserved a real explanation, not just a yes or no. She took a deep breath, summoning the strength to be as real with him as he'd been with her.

"I met Todd the summer after I graduated from Penn," she said, her voice rough as rocks in a grinder. She cleared her throat, pushing down the ache that threatened to overcome her ability to speak. She had to tell her story, like he'd told her his, or he'd never understand. "Even though I'm not a professor there now, the way my family wishes I was, I did go to school there to get my bachelor's degree. Todd was one of Oliver's friends. He was funny and loved to hike and camp, like I did. We hit it off right away, went on a couple of dates and then started hanging out together all the time, which annoyed Oliver quite a lot," she added.

Sam nodded, his gaze never leaving hers.

"Todd always talked about wanting to travel," she went on, "but at the time, I was starting a teaching job and he was an associate professor at Penn. We worked and saved money for two years before he convinced me to take a year off to set out on a grand adventure. I thought I loved him, so I said yes. That's what you're supposed to do for the person you love, right? Make their dreams come true? He said we'd take one year to see everything, then come home and settle down. I believed him."

She took a sip of her drink, hoping to steady the tremor in her voice. Sam sat back, his expression wary.

"The trip started out all right. We travelled well together, mostly because I always gave him his own way, and because we were both old hands at it. I missed my classroom almost immediately, so I started making science videos and uploading them to the internet. Meanwhile, every time I started filming, there was Todd doing crazy stunts to get my attention. I found that if I added his antics to my videos, the kids loved it."

"You're not answering my question," Sam pointed out.

"I'm trying to," she assured him, hearing the strain in his voice. "The videos took off, and pretty soon Todd began to feel like a star. He was the one riding dirt bikes, hang gliding, surfing, you name it. I identified flowers and trees. He demonstrated the theory of gravity by jumping off cliffs. People loved him, and he began to have fans. He was already a self-confident guy, but as time went on, it went to his head. When it came time to decide where we'd go next, his vote counted more than mine. If I wanted to stay somewhere and he wanted to leave, we left. He was the star, so he figured he should get to call the shots. When the year was up and I said it was time to go home, he didn't want to. He needed one more year. Then he needed another. Then another. We ended up traveling for five. I always thought we'd get married someday. Settle down. Raise kids. Have a different kind of adventure. When I inherited the Blue House, it seemed like the time was right."

She shrugged, not needing to go on. Sam already knew the rest of it.

"He left you. I wouldn't do that."

He hadn't understood what she was trying to say. "You're asking me to leave the home I've created for myself. I've got a better idea. Why don't you stay here in Seahaven?"

He paused a beat too long before scrambling to answer. "My work is in Chicago. All my contacts. I own a home there. I grew up there. My family—"

"I've got all that here if you substitute friends for family, but you think it's fine to ask me to walk away from it." She wasn't going to give an inch on that point.

"It's different."

"How?"

She could tell he was searching for an answer and struggling to find one, but she could also tell he thought the reason should be self-evident.

He was the man. Which meant his work was more important than hers, his friends more important. His preferences more important. Just like Todd had.

"My business is here in Seahaven," she said evenly, not waiting any longer. "So are my teaching job and my friends. I put a man first for a long time. I let Todd take the wheel and control my life because I thought he would provide me with the family I wanted, and that would make my sacrifices worthwhile."

"I want a family," Sam said.

"But I'm not willing to sacrifice myself anymore. I've planted myself here," she said. "I'm staying here, Sam. I'm putting my needs first. I like you—a lot. I might love you. Maybe I could marry you. Maybe you're the one." She shrugged. "I'll never find out if it means I have to leave my home again."

She held her breath. Every fibre of her being wanted to take it all back and do anything it took to see if what she had with Sam was really all that it seemed to be. She didn't want to be single anymore. She wanted the family she'd always dreamed of.

She wasn't going to give in to that desire, though. Maybe she would spend the rest of her life alone.

At least it would be her life she was living.

WAS HAPPINESS TOO much to ask for? Sam's chest burned with the bitter taste of Ava's refusal and the knowledge that another man had poisoned her against him. If she'd never met Todd, if he'd never dragged her around the world for years on end, she wouldn't have thought twice about the small adventure of moving from California to Chicago. He wasn't going to feel bad about asking her to move, though. His start-up was bound to out-earn her teaching job—by a lot, which made it practical to choose Chicago over California. He had a whole family close by there who would help if and when he had children. Wasn't that important?

Or did Ava think she'd earn enough from her vacation rental to cover costs when her kids were little? Would she miss her friends as much if she moved away as he would miss his family if he did?

Ava was watching him. Waiting patiently, one eyebrow cocked as if saying, "Yes, it's complicated, isn't it?"

Sam didn't know what to think. Ava had said she liked him—maybe could love him. Then she'd put her foot down. Here she was and here she'd stay. It wasn't very romantic. If he was honest, he felt like the ground was shifting right out from under his feet. He hadn't thought through his invitation very well, had he? He'd thought he was offering Ava something special, but she already had a home of her own. She had a job and a business, too. She could provide for herself.

So what did she even need him for, anyway?

"I don't know what to say," he finally managed.

"Maybe there isn't anything to say." Ava smiled sadly. "Maybe there's no such thing as finding 'the one.'

Maybe there's only the one who's convenient, and we're not convenient to each other."

"But—"

"I need to go, Sam. I think you do, too. Go talk to Ben and Chloe. Sort things out."

She didn't even want to spend the day with him. True regret washed through Sam. Would he ever have another shot at what he and Ava could have had together?

"Ava." He couldn't seem to get his footing in this conversation. She was wrapping it up too fast. They hadn't said the important things.

Or maybe they had.

Hopelessness washed through him. When Chloe had finally showed her true colors in their relationship, Sam had felt hurt but also empty, as if their final fight was only proof of what he'd already known. This was different. The pain in his heart was so searing he wasn't sure he could stand up, let alone watch Ava walk away.

"You want a ride?" She gathered her cup and stood.

"I think I'll walk." He stayed where he was. How could she be so matter of fact about this? Had he been wrong in thinking she cared for him?

She nodded and shut her eyes for a second, holding on to the back of her chair. Her knuckles were white, her lips pinched together. Sam made to rise—he wanted to go to her, take her in his arms and make the pain so clear on her face disappear, but before he could, she got a hold of herself again. She opened her eyes. Blinked a few times. Drew her shoulders back. "Good luck with everything."

"I'll see you again before I go," he said so sharply a few of the other customers turned their way. He wasn't ready to say goodbye, and he needed her to know this wasn't over. Not yet.

He thought she'd say something then, but in the end she shook her head and hurried out the door, leaving him wanting to flip the table over and go after her. With difficulty, he kept his seat and forced himself to finish his cup of coffee. She needed time to think and so did he.

There had to be a way to be with Ava, without losing everything he'd spent his life to build.

A half hour later, when he'd finally found the strength to walk to the hotel, he was so caught up in trying to solve this puzzle he didn't hear Ben calling out to him before they met on the sidewalk.

"I was wondering where you'd got to." Ben turned to walk with him. He was pretending to be cheerful again, which meant something was wrong.

"Did Chloe send you? Because I'm not going on some excursion." Sam could barely breathe. He knew the day was warm, the sun shining, but everything seemed distant, the light all wrong.

"No excursions today. Everyone is doing their own thing."

"Chloe's allowing that?"

Ben shot him a look.

"What?" Sam demanded, fighting to get the words out past the pain in his throat. "Come on, she's run this whole vacation like a drill sergeant." He had no patience for any of this right now. He was losing Ava. Had lost her already, maybe.

"That's not what I'm here to talk about."

"What are you here to talk about?" In another minute he was going to lose what little control he had left over his temper. He had to figure out how to change Ava's mind.

"I was wrong the other day when I said Chloe should start her own business, especially when she's close to bringing us a buyer."

"I don't want to sell the company."

"I think we have to. It isn't fair to everyone else if we don't."

"How is it not fair?" Sam stopped short and faced him. "We hired these people—including Chloe—to do jobs. We pay them salaries. There's no reason for that to stop."

"But Chloe—"

"Chloe is an employee!" Sam burst out. "She doesn't call the shots. She wasn't here when we founded the company. She didn't put in sixty- to seventy-hour workweeks like the rest of us did. So why the hell is she dictating anything we do?" He held his hands out wide. "Who even told her she could look for a buyer or negotiate on our behalf if she found one? Huh? That's not in her job description. She's supposed to be looking for school districts to partner with. In fact, that's going to be the first mark against her in her file. If you won't ask her to leave, then I'm going to fire her just as soon as I've got the paper trail that will let me do it."

"That's my future wife you're talking about."

"I wouldn't count on that," Sam shot back. "You're not married yet. But already you're acting like she gets to make all the decisions in your life. A couple of days ago you knew as well as I did that having her in the company was bad for everyone. You and I didn't build Scholar Central to hand it off to someone else to run; we built our dream career. Why would we give it away?"

"Because Chloe and I want to buy a house in the suburbs."

"What?" The sentence was so incongruous, Sam couldn't follow Ben's train of thought at all. "What does that have to do with anything?"

"We need money, lots of it, right now," Ben said doggedly. "And Scholar Central doesn't pay me enough." He waved away Sam's protests. "I know it will in the future, but we can't wait that long."

"Why not?"

Ben looked at the ground.

"Well?" Sam pressed.

"There is a reason," Ben admitted. "We weren't going to tell anyone yet."

Sam swallowed, suddenly cold, knowing already what Ben would say next but not believing it. Could this day get any worse?

"Looks like I'm going to be a dad sooner than I expected," Ben said quietly.

Sam shook his head. "No way."

"I wouldn't lie about that."

"Chloe doesn't want kids," Sam said flatly, his mind whirling at the possibility he was wrong. That's what she'd told him every time he'd mentioned his interest in having a family. She hadn't wanted to put them off or even think about it. She hadn't wanted kids at all.

Or did she simply not want to have kids with him?

"Sure she does, but it's early days," Ben said. "She'll be really pissed if she finds out I told you."

Because she wasn't pregnant. Sam would stake his life on it. After all, it was common enough for a woman to lose a baby early on. As soon as Chloe had Scholar Central's shares in her hands, she'd fake a miscarriage and keep right on going. The alternative was impossible to think about—that she'd played him right from the start. That she'd never meant to marry him at all—but she did love Ben enough to make a real future with him.

"Let's go talk to her," Sam said. He didn't care about Chloe, he told himself. He cared about Ben. A little voice in his mind told him that wasn't exactly true, though. He might not love Chloe, but he needed to think she'd cared for him, at least a little, while they were together. Because if Chloe hadn't, and Ava was able to walk away from him—

Maybe he wasn't half the man he thought he was.

Ben reared back in alarm. "I just said—"

"I won't breathe a word about her pregnancy." Her fake pregnancy. Luckily Chloe wasn't the only one with a devious mind. He was grateful now for the arguments about education he'd had with Ava during his visit. They'd just given him an idea. "I need to run a new possibility by both of you." He strode toward the hotel, forcing Ben to hurry to keep up with him. Maybe he was crazy to push things this far, but he had to know the truth.

"What new possibility?" Ben followed him, frowning.

"Something I want to add to Scholar Central."

"It's probably too late for that, but you can always create a new company. You'll have a lot of cash if we sell." Ben kept shooting glances his way. Sam could tell he didn't know whether to be pleased at this progress or afraid this was some kind of trick.

It was definitely a trick. Chloe had held the reins for too long. It was time for him to step in.

"You know damn well whatever company wants to buy us is going to shackle us to Scholar Central for five years at least," Sam said, "and we won't have creative control anymore. We'll be working stiffs like everyone else, with a middle-management boss to answer to.

When our five years are up, we'll have non-compete clauses in our contracts that guarantee we'll never work in the educational software industry again." He was overstating it, but those were all the kinds of things Ben hated.

"What's your idea?" Ben asked, his frown deeper. Chloe's sugar-plum fantasy about being pregnant, starting a family and moving to the suburbs must be irresistible to him. His childhood had been a nightmare, and Sam couldn't blame him for wanting something that sounded so sweet, but he had to expose the lies behind Chloe's promises.

"I don't want to explain it twice." He didn't want to show his hand yet. His plan might not work, but it was the only way Sam could think of to demonstrate to his friend what the future would really look like if he let Chloe take control.

He remained silent until they reached the hotel. Ben led the way to the room he was sharing with Chloe, who was sitting on the tiny balcony, fingers racing over her laptop. She shut it quickly when they came near.

"What's all this?" she asked, standing up and coming into the room. She folded her arms over her chest and looked from one to the other of them.

"I had an idea," Sam said. "I want to add a whole new suite of options to our program."

"You've got to be kidding. We're not starting any-thing new. We're about to sell Scholar Central to a company that can take the product all the way to the end zone. They're not asking us for complexity," she added. "If anything, right now we need to tie up all the loose ends."

"We've left out a whole branch of opportunities," Sam went on, ignoring her. When they started out, he and Ben spent weeks of sleepless nights banging out a list of features and possibilities for their service. He knew Ben wouldn't be able to help himself once he heard the idea. "Place-based tailored curriculum," he said, gesturing with his hands as if to encompass the enormity of the concept. "We give kids the information they need to be better citizens of the towns or cities where they live. We combine history, reading, art, natural sciences. Everything they need to know to truly understand their homes."

Ben's eyes lit up. "You could tie that into every subject in the curriculum," he said. "Civics, ecology, environmentalism, scientific research."

"It's the kind of spin that would make our product stand out head and shoulders above everywhere else," Sam said.

"We could get so many people involved," Ben said. "Local naturalists and scientists. Historians."

"It's a story that writes itself. Think of the publicity. Think about local papers and news channels. Think about the articles they'll write and the stories they'll run about a curriculum that ties into everything that makes their area special."

"There's so much you could do with the idea." Ben had that look—the one that said he was ready to brainstorm. In the old days, this would be the signal for them to order a couple of pizzas, commandeer a whiteboard or two and spend the rest of the night batting around ideas.

Right on cue, Chloe let out an exasperated noise. "I can't believe the two of you. Look at you getting so excited about such a lousy plan!"

Ben blinked. He didn't do well with being interrupted at times like these. "What?"

"It's a terrible idea," she repeated. "It would add way too much complexity. How would we come up with the curriculum for thousands of different towns and cities? How would we grade the assignments? We can't automate that."

Ben shook his head. Once he got started thinking about possibilities, he didn't want to stop. His brain worked quickly, ticking over all the permutations until he understood them inside and out. Sam had learned to leave him alone for a while in situations like this. Sooner or later those ideas started spilling out.

"Maybe some things shouldn't be automated," Sam told her. Ava would be proud of him, unless she guessed he was mostly trying to rile up Chloe.

It was working.

"You want to screw up our payday? Is that it? For

god's sake, Sam, even you have to see this isn't the time to add anything new!"

"Even if it makes the product better?" Sam goaded her. "After all, our aim is to reach students—to improve the quality of education they're getting access to, right?"

"The idea is to make money." Chloe's voice rose. "You're talking about doubling or tripling the need for staff. Bloating a company that right now looks like a cash cow. No one is going to want to buy Scholar Central if you do that."

"Money isn't our primary object." He nearly laughed at her reaction to that, but he kept a straight face as he turned to Ben. "We can't back away from an idea as explosive as this one is. I think we should put it on the agenda for our next full-company meeting. We need focus groups. See what they think. It might push back our launch date for a year or two, but..."

"No one is pushing back the launch date." Chloe was beside herself. "My buyers want Scholar Central because it's so close to being profitable."

Sam could tell Ben was still thinking over the initial proposal. Rubbing his chin with his hand, rocking back and forth slightly, he was deep in thought, but his gaze was focused on his future wife.

"We need to shoot this idea in the head right now," Chloe said. "It's ridiculous. Ben, tell him the answer is no."

Ben didn't say anything. Sam could tell he was agitated. Chloe's repeated interruptions were interfering with his analysis, and from experience Sam knew he couldn't handle an emotional situation when he was in full-on analytical mode.

"I say the answer is yes." Sam kept going. He had to push Chloe to the breaking point if he wanted this gambit to succeed. He thought he knew how. He faced Chloe and looked her dead in the eyes. "You know, when you think about it, you really have no say in this, Chloe."

Her eyes widened. Her mouth dropped open. "Of course I have a say. I have the final say!" she exploded. "Ben is going to be my husband, which means Ben's opinion is the same as mine. That's our deal, and there's nothing you can do about it. You lost, Sam. Face it. You should have given me the shares when I asked you for them in the first place. Then you and I would still be engaged."

Ben stopped rocking.

Almost there, Sam thought. "Would you really ask us to stop development before Scholar Central was the best it could be?" he asked Chloe.

"I don't give a damn about being the best. I don't care if Scholar Central is good or bad or stupid beyond all belief. What I care about is the money!"

"What are you going to do with your millions?"

"Get the hell out of Chicago, for starters," she snapped. "I'll go to Europe. Monaco, maybe. I want beaches. A fast boat. Fashion. Parties. A real life."

"What about kids?"

"Kids?" Caught off guard, her face wrinkled in disgust before she remembered herself a second too late. "Kids can come to Monaco," she said hurriedly. "Ben and I deserve to be happy, whether or not we have children."

"Whether or not?" He turned to Ben, hating himself for betraying his friend's confidence, even if his intentions were good. "I was under the impression there was a child on the way already."

Chloe's cheeks suffused with color, something that didn't happen often. She turned on Ben. "I told you not to tell anyone."

"So you are pregnant? When are you due?" Sam caught her gaze again and held it. Two pink spots of color bloomed high on her cheeks. As soon as she looked away, he knew he was right. She was lying.

"I might have spoken too soon," she stammered. "Ben… I… I got my period. I was late, so I got excited, but I was wrong…"

"So you're not pregnant," Sam said mercilessly. If Chloe had wanted a child and lost it, she would have let everyone know how devastated she was. This pregnancy had been a fabrication from the start, pure and simple. "And you're not buying a house in the suburbs of Chicago. In fact, you're not going to live in Chicago at all. Is that the way you want to spend your life?" he asked Ben. "Parties and cruises in Monaco?"

Ben came out of his reverie looking so wretched, Sam almost regretted doing any of this. "You're not pregnant?" he asked Chloe.

"No, I'm not. But so what? I can always get pregnant some other time," she snapped. "What's the damn hurry?" When Ben didn't answer, she scowled at both of them. "You know what? I didn't come here to discuss the terms of my marriage or to add some new idiotic feature to our curriculum. I'm here to get our ducks in a row so we can sell Scholar Central and all be rich. Why is that so hard?"

"Ben?" Sam asked. "Chloe isn't a partner in this business. It's for you and me to decide what we should do with our company next. Do we want to hold on to our curriculum and expand it, or sell it to the highest bidder?"

"I don't know." Ben's voice was husky as he stared at Chloe.

"Of course you know," Chloe said. "We're going to sell. We talked about it. That's what's best for us—for you and me. I'm the one you're marrying, Benjamin. Not him." She pointed at Sam. "And I'm not marrying any man who chooses his friend over me."

When Ben's gaze dropped to the carpet, Sam swallowed the bile that rose in his throat and fought down a sense of suffocation. Ben used to look just like this when he was a kid living with his dad: shoulders hunched, head bowed, eyes on the ground.

Suddenly Sam needed to get out of this room. Wanted to drag Ben with him away from Chloe, but Chloe moved to place her hand on her fiancé's shoulder, and Ben didn't shrug it off.

He still wanted her. Wanted Chloe so badly he'd put up with anything.

But Sam didn't have to.

"Guess we're at a stalemate," he said.

And walked out the door.

WHEN THE KNOCK came on her door, Ava's heart leaped, but she instantly crushed the surge of happiness that swooped through her. Even if it was Sam, and somehow she knew it was, that meant nothing. They'd discussed all the reasons she couldn't be with him, and she hadn't changed her mind.

After they'd parted at the coffee shop, it had been all she could do to drive home, climb the stairs to her apartment and stagger out onto her deck, where she sat on one of her chairs and cried so hard she ended up with a headache. Her eyes were puffy, her throat sore. She knew she'd made the right decision, but it felt so wrong. Without Sam, the sunshine was dimmer. The sparkle of the ocean flat.

She'd questioned her decision—to the extent she'd actually pulled out her phone and looked to see if there was a school like the Seahaven Outdoor Adventure

Academy where she could teach in Chicago. There wasn't, and even if there was she would have hated to leave her home. The Blue House felt as comfortable as a warm hug. Seahaven was the community she'd always longed for. If she allowed her life to be uprooted again, she knew she'd never find this level of contentment again.

She'd asked herself if that meant she really didn't care that much for Sam, but that wasn't true, either. She did care for him—a lot. Every time she thought about his arms around her, or about making love to him, a new wave of pain crashed over her.

She'd been telling herself she'd get over him in time and there'd be someone else for her, since she couldn't be with Sam, but she didn't believe it. No man she'd ever met felt so right.

Which made saying goodbye almost impossible. She'd done it once. Could she do it again?

"Hi," Sam said when she finally opened the door. "Can I come in?"

Ava wanted to throw herself into his arms, but instead she stepped back. "Of course." She led him to the deck, where he took a seat across from her.

She couldn't stop drinking in the sight of him, storing up memories she could replay when he was gone for good. She wished she could take his hand. If he kissed her, she'd—

No. She wouldn't say yes to moving to Chicago to be

with him.

But god, she wanted to.

"I know I shouldn't have come here," Sam said. He ran a hand through his thick dark hair, and she thought it wasn't the first time he'd done that. Something had riled him up. Was it their conversation? "I didn't know where else to go," he went on. "I was going to call my sisters, but I could guess what they'd say. Chitra would tell me Ben and Chloe weren't worth my time. Priya would tell me I had to keep them happy, at least until we launch our product and get some kind of return on our investment. Leena would tell me to ask the universe for a sign."

"A sign about what?" Ava wished she could meet Sam's sisters. She thought she'd like them, which made her sad all over again.

"What to do about Scholar Central," he said.

Ava couldn't keep up. "Scholar Central? What happened?"

"Ben demanded we make Chloe an equal partner, and she's already throwing her weight around."

"You can handle her, can't you?"

"I don't think Ben can." He braced his elbows on his knees and rested his face in the palms of his hands.

Something was bothering him. Something he hadn't admitted yet. "Why do you say that?"

"We all have hurt places, right?" He looked up again. "Vulnerable points in our armor, I guess you could say.

255

Chloe's found his, and she's taking advantage of it."

"She bullies people," Ava said. She'd seen it every day Chloe had spent at her house.

Sam stared at her. Nodded slowly. "It's not always the bigger guy who wins the fight," he said.

Ava wanted to ask him more questions, but she wasn't sure if it was her place to pry or if she was in too emotional a place to be much help. Every time she looked at Sam, her longing for him overrode everything else. The longer they were alone together, the less chance she had of sticking to her resolution. "Would you take a walk with me?" she asked him. "A short walk."

He straightened up and looked around, as if just taking in where he was.

"Sure."

She led the way through her apartment and took him down to the street level, evading him when he reached for her hand. If she touched him, she would be lost. Out on the sidewalk they passed Brightview, then veered through the gate in the white picket fence to the Cliff Garden.

"It's a nice night," Sam said, taking in the ocean, but his heart wasn't in it. That was okay; they weren't here for the view. Ava led him to the Trouble Bench, a scarred, old wooden bench that faced the water.

She decided she wouldn't even tell him that people came here from all over the neighborhood to find answers to their problems. Instead, she sat down and patted the bench beside her. "Take a load off. Sometimes looking at the horizon gives you a new perspective on problems."

"We were looking at the horizon from your place." He was watching her with that way he had of seeming like he could peer into her soul. "Ava, we should talk more about us, too."

"One problem at a time. Sit for a minute. Take a couple of deep breaths," she added to buy a little time. She sat back on the seat and demonstrated what she meant. Sam settled in with a sigh beside her.

They hadn't been contemplating the ocean long before Emma showed up with a covered plate and two glasses of water, just as Ava had hoped she would. Emma was in charge of the Trouble Bench and kept an eye on it when she was at home. She had a knack for sensing when someone needed comforting.

"I thought you could use refreshments," she said.

"Thanks. Refreshments always help." Ava returned Emma's smile gratefully but smoothed her expression before Sam noticed. Emma handed each of them their glass, then passed the plate to Ava. "Would you join us?" Ava asked her. "We're trying to sort out a friend's problem." She hoped Emma's presence would keep her from giving in to the lure of Sam's offer.

"Sure." Emma sat down. She took one of the cookies from the plate when Ava offered it to her. Sam, too, took one absently, bit into it and moaned.

"This is good."

"Everything Emma makes is phenomenal," Ava said. "She's creating online cooking classes and holds real-time ones at Brightview. We should go to one." Too late she remembered Sam was disappearing from her life in a few days.

"What's wrong with your friend?" Emma asked him.

Ava waited for Sam to explain, and after a long moment, he did. "He thinks his fiancée will leave him if he doesn't let her call the shots," he said shortly. "He needs to toughen up or she'll control everything he does."

"Why do you think he doesn't stick up for himself?"

He hesitated again. "Ben's early years were... rough."

Ava remembered what he'd told her about them and realized what Sam's real fear was. "Do you think Chloe's going to take his dad's place?" she asked.

"I don't think she'll beat him, if that's what you mean," Sam said heavily. "I don't think she'll have to."

Ava looked to Emma, who often had good advice when people needed it.

"Here's the thing," Emma said gently. "You can't control what Ben does, or what his fiancée does, either, and if you try you'll end up on the outs with both of them."

"I'm pretty much there already."

"When you find yourself tied up in knots about someone else's life, it's a clear indication there's something in your own life that needs tending," Emma went on. "So what's going wrong in your life?"

Sam didn't answer for a long time. He balanced his glass on his knee and stared at the ocean. Ava ate a cookie and drained her glass of water, grateful for the reprieve. Her emotions had gotten a workout over the past few days, and she had a feeling she wasn't in the clear yet. He cast a glance her way, and Ava wondered if he'd bring up her refusal to follow him back to Chicago.

Instead, he said, "I'm beginning to hate my job."

"Why?" Emma asked.

"Because my business partner—Ben—isn't treating me with respect. He hooked up with my ex-fiancée, and the two of them keep ganging up on me. Now they want to sell our company, when I thought we were building something we'd work on for a lifetime. I dread going to work. I'm not excited about my future anymore."

"So you're worried that your friend's fiancée isn't treating him with respect, but you've been letting him disrespect you?" Emma summarized for him.

Sam put down the cookie he'd picked up absently and stared at her.

"Hell, Ava was right—you are good at this. I never thought about it that way. I gave him a chance today to take my side and keep our partnership an equal one. He chose to side with his fiancée. The woman I used to be engaged to. He's never apologized for what he did, and he sees no issue with forcing me to accept Chloe as an equal partner. If he was setting out to try to humiliate me, he couldn't do any better."

As his words hung in the air, Ava wondered how it had felt to say them out loud. Did he know how brave it was to admit Ben's actions had hurt him? In her experience, men liked to pretend they were invincible.

"We're good at shifting our own problems onto other people. Not that Ben might not have problems to solve, too," Emma added.

"I need to leave Scholar Central," Sam said and straightened, his shoulders relaxing for the first time since he arrived at Ava's door. "I think I've known that for a long time but I didn't want to admit it. I kept hoping somehow it would all go back to the way it was before Chloe came around."

"You love what you do," Ava told him. "It's clear when you talk about it. You've put heart and soul into your start-up. No wonder you don't want to turn your back on it."

"I love how it used to be," he corrected her. "Not what it's become."

"Is there a way to extricate yourself from the company?" Emma asked.

"I don't know, but I guess it's time to find out."

A COUPLE OF weeks ago, the idea of leaving Scholar Central would have crushed him, but now all Sam felt was relief. No more struggling to maintain his vision against Chloe's incursions against it. No more resentments seething inside him when Ben chose her side instead of his. It saddened him to see Ben fall for a woman who so clearly didn't mind using or hurting him, but Ben was a grown-up now. It wasn't his job to try to rescue someone who didn't think he needed rescuing.

Staying at Scholar Central had clearly become untenable. Leaving opened all kinds of possibilities.

Maybe even a future that included Ava.

"I think you two should come to Brightview for lunch." Emma stood up before he had time to consider the notion fully. "Ashley and Andrew will be there, and Noah, of course. You need a break from all the angst. We're cooking hamburgers, and I've got plenty to share."

"That sounds like a good idea." Ava stood, too.

"You sure?" Sam asked Emma. "I don't want to crash your party." Hamburgers sounded good, though. He'd been thinking over his problems for too long and suddenly wanted to be among people. Especially Ava. Maybe she'd relax if there was a crowd.

"I'm sure. You can run the grill while Ava and I get the rest of the meal together."

A half hour later, Emma's picnic table on her back deck was full of people. Her husband, Noah, was there when they arrived and welcomed Sam's help. Emma's sister, Ashley, and Ashley's fiancé, Andrew, who was also Noah's brother, came bearing chips and dip. Penelope came over, too. Now they were munching on burgers, laughing and chatting happily.

When Andrew asked him what he did for a living, Sam explained he was about to be unemployed. "I'm thinking of starting something new," he told them, feeling a rush of excitement for the first time in months. "I'm not sure what, though. It'll have to be different from Scholar Central. I'm sure Ben and Chloe will demand a non-compete clause."

"You should help Ava get her science channel back up and running," Penelope said. "Have you ever seen her videos? They're awesome. As wonderful as it is that she's going to teach locally, I think it's a shame everyone else is going to lose out on her work. You should read the comments people leave on her videos. There are teachers saying how they used them in the classroom and students showing how they tried the experiments. You need a forum," Penelope said to Ava. "It's fine to load your videos on the big websites, but you need a site of your own where people can come and talk to each other about ways to use your information."

"That could be fun," Sam mused.

"It would be hard, considering you're going to be in Chicago," Ava said. Her tone was light, but he caught the undercurrent. She was reminding him that when push came to shove, he hadn't budged an inch. He'd thought she should move to be with him, but he'd never considered moving to be with her.

Why hadn't he done so? Was Chicago a part of his identity?

Was he afraid he couldn't make a go of anything without Ben by his side?

The idea floored him, and he set his burger down on his plate. He was the strong one, after all. The one who'd saved Ben from his abusive homelife. The one who'd connected him to other friends, showed him the ropes after they moved to a new school. The bolder, brasher, more popular one. The one with a supportive family and prospects for a bright future.

Things had changed over the years, though, hadn't they? Ben was the one who'd been brash lately, making his play for Chloe, even though he knew it would mean a break between him and his staunchest ally. Ben was a competent, employable adult, who was as much a part of Scholar Central as Sam was. Sam realized that for some time his vision and drive hadn't been as important to Scholar Central as they were at the beginning of the project. Ben's slow but steady work ethic and Chloe's ability to make connections with potential clients were important, too. If he was honest with himself, ever since Chloe had hooked up with Ben, his performance had suffered.

He was still passionate about education and helping children who deserved a better curriculum, but the time for big ideas was over. Now it was down to execution. Scholar Central would be just fine without him. So would Ben.

The thought of leaving either behind left him feeling

off-balance, though. Sam knew it was only a matter of time before he got a new job or created a new opportunity for himself. Losing Ben was a different matter. As a boy Ben had shadowed him. Now Sam realized he'd leaned on his friend in recent years. Ben backed him up. Steadied him. He'd never had to feel like he was facing a challenge alone.

He studied Ava. She deserved a man who stood on his own two feet. Who made friends with equals rather than those who needed him. Who was he without Scholar Central and Ben's presence in his life?

Someone who loved motion and activity, he thought as he remembered how good it felt to be hiking the other day. Someone who loved nature. The hours he'd spent kayaking with Ava at the slough had been one of his best afternoons in years. Chicago was his home, but now he found himself craving a more physically challenging, outdoor life for himself. He was still driven to succeed. He still needed a way to earn an income, but if he loved a woman who lived in California, there was nothing stopping him from moving to be with her.

The realization was like the sun burning off the coastal marine layer that shrouded the beaches here in the early morning hours. Suddenly he could see more clearly. His horizons were limitless.

He imagined a life spent surfing, kayaking, hiking, exploring, climbing and more. Ava loved all those things, and he'd already met Noah and Andrew, who enjoyed active pursuits. Seahaven was in easy driving range of Silicon Valley, home to a slew of start-ups and large tech ventures. If he couldn't come up with his own ideas, he could always join someone else's company for a while.

"What?" Ava asked when the moment stretched too long.

"Know of a room I can rent if I move here?"

She met his gaze. The corners of her mouth turned up. "I might know of an apartment. It's a shared situation, though."

He knew he was grinning. "That sounds perfect."

"You'd really consider staying?" she asked.

"I'm past considering it. I've decided."

He edged closer to her on the bench seat, leaned in and brushed a kiss over her cheek. How could he ever have thought he could go home to Chicago without her?

"What changed your mind?"

"I kept thinking I had to finish what I'd started at Scholar Central, and I realized that's not true. Ben can do the rest without me. He's made it clear Chloe's the person he's putting first in his life, as he should if he's going to marry her. I don't like his choices, but at the end of the day, it's none of my business. I need to make my own decisions, based on what I need—and that's you, Ava Ingerson." He drew her close, tipped her chin up and kissed her, this time taking his time to show her exactly how he felt.

"Whew, it's getting hot in here," Ashley exclaimed,

fanning herself.

When they broke apart, Sam took Ava's hand and squeezed it. "Should we go back to your place?" he asked in a low tone as the others laughed at Ashley's joke.

"Our place, you mean?" She nodded. "Sounds like a good idea."

They said their goodbyes and hurried back to the Blue House, laughing like teenagers at their own haste to get up the stairs and into her apartment. Once inside with the door closed, Ava's hands tugged at his shirt, and he pulled it up over his head and tossed it away. He made short work of her shirt, reached around to unclasp her bra and palmed one of her breasts when she shrugged out of it.

He traced kisses down her neck and shoulders as she worked to undo his jeans. It was a struggle to get out of the rest of their clothes and stay upright, but as soon as they'd managed it, he led her to her bed and they climbed on top of it, already intertwined. "God, I missed you," he told her, running his hands over her curves. "I couldn't stand the thought of leaving you behind."

"I couldn't stand it either," she confessed. "I wasn't sure how much longer I could stick to my guns on staying."

"I'm glad you did."

"Are you sure?" Half underneath him, she clung to him, her worry plain.

"I'm positive. This is where I want to be—right here

with you in Seahaven. I'm ready for a new adventure."

"With me?" She kissed the underside of his chin.

"With you," he confirmed and settled into the task of showing her he meant it.

CHAPTER 12

"*H*EY, BEAUTIFUL."

Ava woke up in Sam's arms the following morning and basked in the memory of the night they'd shared. Sam was going to stay in Seahaven. They'd agreed it was much too early to promise each other anything more than that, and she decided not to worry about the future. She was going to enjoy the present—especially this time together with Sam, who looked altogether delicious lounging in her bed.

A knock on her door startled both of them into sitting positions, however.

"I bet it's Chloe," Ava hissed, clutching the bed-clothes to her chest. "What do we do?"

"Ava? Yoo-hoo! Are you in there?" a woman's voice called from outside.

"That's not Chloe," Sam said.

Ava couldn't think who it was. It wasn't Emma or Penelope, yet the voice was definitely familiar. She got up and grabbed a robe. Sam got out of bed, too, and pulled on his jeans from the night before.

The knocking came again. Ava hurried to the door and opened it a crack.

"Marie?" Astonishment had her stepping back.

"Happy birthday!" Marie said, bouncing up and down on her toes. "Are you surprised? I wanted to surprise you."

"I'm definitely surprised."

Marie hooted. "Victory! This is going to be your best birthday ever. I've got a whole plan. Come on, everyone."

"Everyone?" Ava sucked in a breath of surprise when Marie pushed past her into the room and Oliver and her parents trouped in after her.

"Happy birthday," Oliver told her heartily. Ava couldn't tell if he was happy to be there or not, but he looked around her apartment with an appraising eye. She tried to see the place the way he did and doubted it appealed to him much. Oliver liked large spaces, concrete and exposed beams. The Blue House was comfortable and eclectic—just what a beach house should be in her opinion.

"Happy birthday." Her mother gave her a shrug and then a quick hug. "It is good to see you."

"Happy birthday, pumpkin," her dad said, tousling her hair.

Only then did Ava remember Sam. He'd managed to put most of his clothes on, but her family stopped when they spotted him, grouping together in a little knot of confusion. Her unmade bed and his tousled hair were all the evidence they needed as to what kind of relationship they were in.

"Um… Mom, Dad, Oliver, Marie—this is Samuel Cross. My… friend."

"Hi, everyone." Sam gave them a little wave.

"Oh, we're interrupting something." Marie put her hand to her heart. "I'm so sorry, Ava."

"You're not interrupting anything," Sam said. "It's Ava's birthday. Of course you've come to celebrate!" He sent Ava a look, and she knew he was wondering why she hadn't told him this was a special day. The truth was, she hadn't even thought about it. Like she'd told Marie once, her family didn't make a fuss about birthdays. Todd forgot hers most years, so she'd learned to put it out of her mind.

There was an awkward pause until Marie rallied. "We brought food and our bathing suits so we can all go to the beach. We're here only for the day."

"We still have a plane to catch to West Sumatra tomorrow," her mother explained.

"We're taking the red-eye home tonight," her father said.

Ava realized they must have flown overnight to get here. "You haven't had any sleep," she exclaimed. She turned to Marie. "I can't believe you pulled this off. I haven't celebrated my birthday with my family in years."

Marie beamed. "I know. I thought that should

change."

Ava glanced out the window. "It's awfully early. Why don't I open up the main house for you, and you all can have a quick nap while I take a shower and make some breakfast. We can reconvene in an hour and spend the day at the beach."

"You don't have guests?" Oliver asked.

"Not at the moment." She didn't feel the need to explain. She could almost see Oliver making another check mark on his mental list about the place. Not a lucrative venture.

Let him think what he wanted. Ava suspected the real reason Aunt Laura had left her the Blue House was because she knew no one else in the family would settle in Seahaven. Her parents and brother were tied to the University of Pennsylvania. In their free time, they traveled the world. Aunt Laura had known Ava was dying to make a home somewhere and stay put for once. Her aunt had wanted the Blue House to stay in the family.

She escorted her unexpected guests downstairs, leaving Sam to use the shower first. It was fun to show them the changes she'd made to the house. When they were all settled in their rooms, she returned upstairs for her turn in the shower.

"You didn't know they were coming?" Sam asked her, toweling off when she came into her apartment. She wished she could climb right back in bed with him, but there'd be plenty of time for that when her family was gone.

"Not at all. Marie must have forced them to come. They would never have made the effort otherwise."

"She's a good sister-in-law."

Ava was starting to appreciate that.

"Do you want me to go?" Sam asked.

"Of course not! I want my family to get to know you. If that's okay."

"That's terrific."

It turned out to be one of the best days she'd spent with her family since leaving home. Marie insisted that Ava call Emma, Penelope and anyone else she wanted and let them know there'd be a party at the Blue House that afternoon. In the meantime, they went on a hike through the redwoods, the whole family appreciating the beauty of the enormous trees. Ava couldn't believe how well Sam was hitting it off with her parents. He even had Oliver laughing at a joke. They arrived at the Blue House in time to receive an enormous order of food from a local catering company, something Marie had planned ahead of time. She set it all up on the deck, and soon they were joined by Emma and Noah, Ashley and Andrew, Penelope, Kate and Aurora. Winston settled in the shade nearby and soon fell asleep.

"I haven't had a party like this for my birthday since I was a kid," she confessed to Emma and Penelope during a lull in the proceedings. "Todd never remembered birthdays."

"Sam seems like the type who might stay on top of things like that," Penelope said.

"That would be nice," Ava admitted.

"More to the point, now we know when your birthday is," Emma pointed out, "and *we'll* never forget it."

Ava hugged her—and then hugged Penelope. "I'm so lucky to have met both of you."

"Where's my hug?" Marie demanded.

Ava hugged her, too. "You're amazing," she told her sister-in-law.

"I've been trying to tell you that for ages." Marie grinned at her. "Come on, everyone," she called out. "Time to eat!"

After they'd filled themselves with gourmet food and cake, Marie declared it was time for presents. Ava couldn't understand how her friends had managed to find gifts with such short notice, but Emma gave her a beautiful journal in which to record her sightings during her outdoor adventures, and Penelope gave her a blue tablecloth embroidered with seashells that went perfectly with her decor.

Her parents gave her a woven wall hanging they'd been gifted in Peru by villagers high in the Andes mountains. Her brother presented her with a wooden bowl hand-carved by an artisan in Tanzania.

"Thank you," she said to him, touched by the gesture.

"I remember you always were more interested in nature than people," he said. "I thought you'd like something made out of wood."

"You're right. I mean, I like people, but I adore nature. It will go perfectly with the rest of my things."

He nodded. "This place suits you. I see why Aunt Laura left it to you."

Ava sucked in a breath, but he didn't seem angry. "I wish she'd left you something more."

"She left me what she could, and I've got everything I need, anyway," he said with a shrug. "It bothered me at first, but Marie said you and Aunt Laura were in constant contact ever since you were little. She said you kept her from being lonely. I didn't bother to do that."

Ava told herself she'd thank Marie when they were alone. She doubted her brother would ever have understood all that without her input.

"Here's my present," Marie said, handing her one last package. It felt like a book. Ava was prepared to smile and give thanks no matter what title Marie had chosen, but when she unwrapped a photo album and saw that it documented her family's life during the time period her sister-in-law had been a part of it, real appreciation made her eyes mist over.

"Oh, Marie, this is so thoughtful."

"I know it must be hard to be so far away from your family, and I remembered that album you said your aunt Laura made for you. I thought we should make you one, too," Marie said.

Her parents and brother suddenly looked as sheepish as she felt. She barely remembered telling Marie about Aunt Laura's album and she'd rarely shared photos with her family, even though she'd spent so much time away from them since she left home. They'd all taken each other for granted, hadn't they?

"It is hard," Ava said. "I miss all of you. I'm glad you got to come here and meet my friends and get a glimpse of my life. I've wanted you to know me better."

"We haven't seen your school yet," Oliver said suddenly. "Where you're going to teach this fall."

Ava was surprised all over again. Was Oliver trying to extend an olive branch? She had a feeling his visit had satisfied some question in his mind. He'd needed to put to rest the idea that maybe he'd have preferred living in the Blue House to his life in Bryn Mawr. Now he was at ease.

She was certainly willing to forgive him for wondering.

"We're not leaving until after dinner," Marie said. "We could drive over there later this afternoon. After we go to the beach."

"I'd love to show you where I'm going to teach. You, too," she told Sam.

"Sounds like a good plan," her father said.

After cleaning up their meal, they all walked to the beach and lazed in the sunshine for several hours,

275

heading into the water when they got too hot, lying out on their beach towels to dry off and then doing it all over again. Sam got Oliver, Noah and Andrew to toss a football around. Marie made Ava and the other women try boogie boarding. They trooped back up to the house, where her family cleaned up and piled into Ava's RAV4 and Marie's rental car for the drive to the Seahaven Outdoor Adventure Academy late in the afternoon. Ava's stomach grew jittery on the way over. Sam, sitting in the passenger seat, touched her hand.

"You okay?" he asked.

She nodded, but she appreciated his quiet presence when they arrived at the empty campus and parked their cars. Since school wasn't in session, there wasn't a lot to see, but she showed them around as best she could. Each discipline was housed in its own little building, and she led them to the science center, where she'd be based. Through the windows they could see that one part of it resembled a tiny natural history museum and another space was set up as a laboratory.

"Of course, we'll be out in the field as much as possible." Ava braced for derision, but her family only nodded their heads and murmured approvingly. "I've been going on local adventures all summer, taking notes and making plans for the school year. Sam's been helping."

Sam moved to put his arm around her. "Can't wait to help even more," he said.

"Where are you working again?" Ava's mother asked him.

"At the moment I'm part of Scholar Central, an online educational start-up, but I'll be leaving that company and starting something new."

"You should get a job here, too," Ava's father said. "The combination of classroom and real-world experiences is a commendable way to impart knowledge to children. You know what I'd do if I were you?" he asked Ava. "I'd involve my students in my research. Make sure you publish now and then," he added. "It's the only way to command respect in academia."

Ava opened her mouth to object, then closed it again. Why shouldn't she do research and get published? Involving her students in the process could be fun.

"Maybe I should take a job here," Sam said, surprising her. "At least until I figure out what to do next. I told Ava I could help her with her science videos, if she wants."

Her family turned her way. "Are you going to start those again?" her brother asked.

Ava found herself shaking her head. "I keep talking about it, but the truth is, I don't really want to. I made those videos because I couldn't teach while I was traveling with Todd. Now I want to teach the kids who are present with me rather than ones I never actually see."

"That's understandable," her father said.

"You don't mind, do you?" Ava asked Sam.

"No. I guess if I feel like making videos, I can do it myself. I don't think I'm ready to make any decisions about my future today. Not until Scholar Central wraps up."

"That's fair."

As the others wandered the grounds, Ava found herself near her mother. "Well?" Ava asked her. "What do you really think?" She braced herself. Her mother liked to tell it as she saw it.

"I think you're right where you belong." Her mother faced her. "I think Laura understood you in a way I never did, but then I never understood her, either. She was always looking for a settled home. I couldn't wait to be untethered."

"You made a home in Bryn Mawr," Ava said.

Her mother considered that. "Our house there is just a stopping place in between trips. My home is wherever my research takes me. You're more like Laura. You want roots. That's okay, you know."

"It is?"

"Oh, Ava. I'm sorry if I made you feel that it wasn't." She touched Ava's arm. "I've had this feeling since I was a little girl—this hunger to understand people who live differently from us. I'm never satisfied at home. I feel… caged. Growing up, I got a lot of pushback for that. There was a certain expectation from my parents that I'd settle down sooner or later." She shook her head.

"I had to fight for what I wanted. After I had children, it would have been so easy for me to get caught in a life that wouldn't have allowed for the research and adventure I crave. Can you understand that?"

Ava thought she could. She felt like she'd had to fight as hard to be allowed to plant her feet in one place and stay there.

"Do you remember that year when you refused to make friends? You spent all your time lying in the dirt, drawing. And then all the local children started copying you instead of playing the games they normally did. You were changing the dynamics of the very group I was trying to study!"

"I'm sorry."

"You shouldn't be. That's not why I brought it up. You were being you. For all my concern about my research, that wasn't what was upsetting me. It was guilt."

"Guilt?" Ava couldn't imagine that. Her mother was so driven. So focused on achieving her goals.

"You always wanted something different from what I was providing for you, and I never changed to accommodate you. Mothers are supposed to put their children first." Her mother hugged her arms across her chest and kept her chin high, but her eyes were moist with unshed tears.

"I didn't want you to change," Ava rushed to tell her. "I just wanted you to love me."

Her mother blinked. "I loved you. I've always loved you. Ava, that's why I brought you along on all my research trips to begin with. I wanted to share my whole world with you."

Ava had never looked at it that way. Remorse sent prickles over her skin. "And I rejected the world you shared," she said softly. "I'm sorry."

Her mother waved that away. "It hurt when you weren't interested and it confused me, too. It felt so good when Oliver took to that life like a fish to water. I thought I was the one who'd made him curious and resilient. Then you came along and proved me to be the bad mother my parents always said I'd be if I didn't quit my job and settle down."

"Mom." It killed Ava to think of how unhappy they'd made each other. "I wish I'd known all of that. I wish I could have read your mind."

"I wish I could have read yours. I'm sorry, honey. I really am." Her mother rubbed a hand across her cheek, wiping away the tears that had escaped. She gave a little laugh. "You know what's the damnedest thing?"

"What?"

"I got a book delivered to me last month—from West Sumatra."

"Really?"

"It was a field guide of insects. Written and illustrated by one of the boys you had lying around the place on his stomach that year, drawing pictures of what he saw in the dirt. Turns out he grew up to be an entomologist."

"You're kidding."

"When I find another copy, I'll send you one. I'm keeping mine," she said with a smile.

"So I'm not useless?" Ava joked, but her voice wobbled.

"You're wonderful." Her mother opened her arms, and Ava flung herself into them.

"No more guilt for either of us. We want what we want, and that's perfectly fine. Right?"

Her mother hugged her tighter. "You don't hate me deep down for not being the mother you wanted? The one who stayed home baking cookies?"

Ava had wanted a mother like that, but she'd gotten someone else. A mom who'd fought for the life she wanted. A mom who was true to herself, which allowed Ava to be the same. "I don't hate you," she said truthfully. "And from now on you're going to hear a lot from me. I will celebrate your adventures while I settle in right here."

"I can't wait."

THERE WAS SO much food left over from the party, they invited their lunch guests to reconvene for dinner that night on the deck. Sam had enjoyed the afternoon and was happy to have met Ava's family. He'd been watching all day as Marie maneuvered her husband and in-laws into getting to know Ava better. At the start of the day,

Ava's parents were a little stiff with her. So was her brother. From things she'd said during the short time he'd known her, he had the feeling she thought her family disapproved of her, but now he was beginning to think her parents and brother had been laboring under the mistaken impression she didn't like them.

All of them relaxed as the day progressed, and by dinner Ava was joking around with her brother and filling her parents in on details of her life.

"Someone's knocking," Penelope announced when the meal was winding down. "Want me to get the door?"

"I'll get it," Ava assured her. Sam got up and walked with her to see who it was, wanting a moment alone with her. He detained her in the entryway, stealing a long, slow kiss until the knocking came again.

"Guess we'd better answer that," he said.

"Guess so." Ava was smiling as she opened the door, but her smile disappeared at once. Sam nearly groaned when he saw Ben and Chloe standing outside.

"Where have you been?" Ben asked. "We haven't seen you since yesterday. We still need to sort things out."

"I've been right here." Suddenly Sam was tired of these confrontations, but before he could tell the two of them he'd see them later, Chloe stormed right inside.

"Are you having a party? In the house we're still renting from you?" She pushed past Ava.

"You left," Ava reminded her, following her to the

great room. "You said you weren't coming back even after I offered you a huge discount. It's my birthday, and my family surprised me by coming to visit."

"Chloe, settle down," Ben said, coming after them. "We just need to talk to Sam for a minute. We can do that outside."

"We can do it right here." Chloe turned on her heel. "While you get these people out of here," she added to Ava.

"Are you coming back to stay?" Ava said.

"Of course not."

"Then I'm going to enjoy my birthday party." She crossed her arms, defying Chloe to do something about it.

Chloe looked from her to Ben. "Are you going to stand there and let her talk to me like that?"

"We're here to talk to Sam," Ben said again.

Sam waved Ava toward the deck. "Enjoy your party. I'll deal with this and be there in a couple of minutes."

"You sure?"

"Positive." He nodded to let her know he had it under control. He could tell she was reluctant to leave him, but in the end she did.

"We can talk at the hotel later," Sam told the others, herding them back toward the door.

"You need to get your ass over there right now," Chloe said. Sam could tell she wasn't only furious that he had so far refused to give in to her demands but also that he was enjoying himself so much with Ava after she'd tried to destroy their relationship.

"Why?" Sam challenged her.

"Because… because you came on this trip to celebrate our upcoming marriage, and that's what you should be doing."

"Is that why you came to talk to me?" he asked Ben. "Because I'm not properly celebrating your upcoming marriage?"

"No. We came to talk about Scholar Central. About the shares you're being so stubborn about."

"Good," Sam said. "Because I've made a decision about those shares. If you want them, you can buy me out."

Ben gaped at him. Chloe lifted her chin. "Buy you out? Why? I don't want to buy anything—you're supposed to give me those shares. Ben, tell him. It's supposed to be your wedding present to us," she added to Sam. "And Ben will give me some of his shares, too. We'll each end up with about a third of the company."

About a third? Sam was more determined than ever to get out of Scholar Central. He just bet somehow Chloe would end up with a share or two more than either Ben or him.

"I don't like your vision for the company," he told her. "You two will do better without me."

Frustration contorted Chloe's face. "You can't do that."

"Why not? I thought you'd be thrilled to see the back side of me."

"Because you're the reason the buyer—" She snapped her mouth shut, but Sam had already heard enough to guess at the rest of it.

"The buyer wants me, huh? I'm part of the deal?"

"Of course you are," she hissed. "You designed the program."

"Some of it," he corrected her, but she was right; he'd been the main driver of the company in the early days.

"You're staying," Chloe said, "and that's that."

"No." Sam held his ground. "I'm going one way or the other. I can't work with you for another day. I was trying to build something special, but you don't share that vision, and I won't stick around to see you trash it." He turned to Ben. As usual Ben looked miserable, and again Sam thought of the day he'd met his friend. "Remember that bug?" he asked. "The one on the sidewalk. The one we rescued?"

Ben's brows pushed together in confusion, then he must have understood. His forehead smoothed, and for the first time, he met Sam's gaze. Nodded.

"Remember how hard we worked to get it to safety and make sure it had a chance for a better life?"

"Yeah," Ben said huskily.

"What the hell are you talking about?" Chloe asked.

Sam ignored her. "Remember what happened after

that? Coming to my house? Eating dinner? Moving in?"

Ben watched him as if he suspected a trap. Sam's chest was tight with the knowledge of how they'd lost each other.

"Nothing's changed on my side." He fought to keep his voice even. "You don't need me anymore. You've got this, Ben. I know you do. But no matter what's going on, or how many years pass by, remember I'm always down to rescue more bugs." He hoped his meaning was clear. Chloe might not be beating on Ben with her fists, but she'd managed to destroy Ben's self-esteem almost as thoroughly as his dad had done in grade school. It hurt like hell to turn his back on Ben now, but Ben was a grown-up. He had to make his own choices.

He saw a flicker of understanding in Ben's eyes. His friend nodded.

"What are you talking about?" Chloe half shrieked in her fury at being left out of the conversation.

Sam turned to her. "We're talking about the fact that I'm done. With you. With Scholar Central. With all of it. Get the hell out of this house, Chloe, and don't come back."

WHEN AVA'S FAMILY left that night, she could honestly say she hoped to see them again soon. Somehow the good food, the presence of her friends and the magic of a sunny afternoon spent at the beach among other places combined to bring out the best in her family. She so rarely saw her parents relax, but today they'd let go of their ever-present need to accomplish something and seemed to simply enjoy themselves. Oliver had even apologized for taking Todd's side before.

"It pissed me off for years that you stole my friend," he'd told her, "and then you tossed him away."

"It wasn't quite like that," she'd pointed out.

"We didn't talk for a while after you broke up. Now he keeps sending me videos about cheesemaking," Oliver had said with a shudder. "It's like, dude… No."

Ava couldn't imagine Todd making cheese, but maybe something about her had hampered him from getting in touch with his more domestic side when they were together. Before she met Sam, that idea would have sent her into a tailspin of self-reproach, but she couldn't be bothered anymore. Todd had his life. She had hers, and she liked it just fine.

"Are you okay?" Sam asked her when they'd shut the door on the last of their guests. He followed her out to the back deck and helped carry in dishes.

"I'm fine. A little sad, maybe. I'm going to miss my folks." She scraped the dishes into a compost container and loaded the dishwasher. It was nice to work in this larger kitchen, and she took a moment to enjoy the view. "I've spent a long time being angry with my parents and brother for not being who I wanted them to be."

"Who did you want them to be?"

"The kind of people who paid attention to me, I

guess. I wanted my mom to make a fuss over me when I got hurt or was feeling sad. I wanted more hugs and fewer how-tos. Mom always pushed me to be independent, which is a good thing, but I wanted more hand-holding."

"What was it like, going on research trips with them?"

She told him about the endless flights halfway across the world. Arriving in the middle of the night in a strange country that smelled different, sounded different, tasted different on her tongue, fighting to stay awake as a cab or cart or whatever conveyance they could find got them to their destination. The long negotiations it sometimes took before they were allowed to settle in at the site of her parents' field work. The curious stares— or hostile ones—from the people they'd arrived to study.

Sometimes Ava had wondered if her parents realized those people were studying them right back and wondered how they categorized the Ingersons. Bossy mother. Scholarly father. Older brother who tries too hard. Younger sister who barely tries at all. Did they recognize the dysfunction? Did they applaud her family's efforts to understand their culture?

Or did they think her family was nosy as hell?

"My childhood was beautiful and strange and uncomfortable and transcendent and very, very lonely," she summed it up. "If I made a friend one year, I rarely ever saw them again. Because both my parents had research projects, we didn't go to the same place every year. I was gone for so much of the summers, my school friends at home were always better friends with each other than they were with me. I grew up on the edge of everything both in Bryn Mawr and abroad. Now I want to be in the center. I want connections that last."

"I can understand that."

"What about you?" she asked. "How are you doing?" He'd told her about the confrontation with Chloe and Ben. She could understand him turning his back on his ex-fiancée, but leaving Scholar Central and his best friend behind had to hurt. She wondered if he'd soon regret it.

"I'm all right."

She could tell he really wasn't. "What do you think Ben will do when he gets back to Chicago?" she asked cautiously. "Will he and Chloe really buy you out?"

"I guess so."

"But if they're selling the company, shouldn't you hold out for your share?"

"Will it make a difference to you if I don't cash out big?"

"No," she said honestly. She'd had years of experience living on a shoestring, and now she had both a business and a full-time job starting in September. She didn't need financial assistance; she just wanted Sam's companionship.

She ached to smooth the worry out of his forehead,

but it was clear to her Sam was struggling. He might not want her to make a fuss about it, but that didn't mean it wasn't real.

"It's hard to leave a friend behind," she pointed out. She didn't understand why Ben would choose Chloe over someone as loyal as Sam, but love made people do strange things.

"I'm worried about Ben," Sam said, as if he'd read her mind. "Chloe could take him for everything he's got and leave him broken-hearted. I feel guilty that I'm not forcing him to see that. I've tried, but he won't listen."

"Ben gets to make his own decisions, even if they're bad ones."

"That's what I keep telling myself, but he's got a rough past," Sam said. "Maybe he's not capable of making this kind of call."

"You can't live his life. Only he can do that. You can't get in his head and see things from his perspective, so you have to trust he can make up his own mind. I know it had to be hard to walk away, but I think you did the right thing. If you'd stayed and let Chloe manipulate both of you, it would be twice as bad."

"It's galling to think of her reaping the benefits of all my hard work."

"I know. I'm sorry it worked out this way." When he remained lost in thought, she moved closer to him and touched his arm. "You know, I don't expect you to stay, Sam."

"What?" Sam's bewilderment hardened into something else. "Ava—I'm staying. I already told you that."

"Your back was up against a wall. Hear me out," she went on when he tried to interrupt. "I'm glad you want to stay. I want you here—very much. I also know how close you are with your family and how much you care for Ben and your work. I think you should give it a test run before you commit to anything. Stay with me a while, or get your own place—whichever suits you best. See if you like Seahaven. See if you like me. There's plenty of time for commitments later, don't you think?"

"I know what I want," he assured her, drawing her into his arms and bending to brush a kiss over her mouth. "I'm here to stay, Ava."

"Good." But she told herself she'd believe it when she saw it.

"YOU MADE THE right choice," Chitra said later that night. "You couldn't stay at Scholar Central and let Chloe run roughshod over you."

"But she's ending up with the profits either way," Priya protested. "He needs to come home and buy out Ben. That would teach her."

"He doesn't want to come home," Chitra said. "He wants to stay in Seahaven with the woman he loves. I think it's romantic."

"I think he's got his priorities all wrong," Priya said.

"I think he finally followed his heart," Leena put in.

"Sam, I'm proud of you."

He waited, keeping one eye on Ava, who was out on the deck, toasting the sunset with Emma and Penelope. He made sure he was actually going to manage to get a word in edgewise before saying, "Thanks. This feels right. I think Ava is the one."

Silence greeted this pronunciation before all three of his sisters began to speak at once.

"When will we meet her?" Chitra asked.

"Do Mom and Dad know?" Priya asked.

"We're going to miss you," Leena said.

"Miss him? Why would we miss him?" Priya demanded.

"Because I'm staying here in Seahaven," Sam said, grateful for the lead-in Leena had given to this thorny topic.

"Staying in Seahaven?" Priya couldn't seem to get anything else out. Her normally cultured alto careened into soprano territory.

"I had a feeling you would," Chitra said wistfully. "Who can say no to a beach house on the Pacific Ocean?"

"Plenty of people!" Priya shrieked. "You can't move away from the rest of us. You need to bring Ava here, where you belong. You said yourself she doesn't have family there."

"She has friends, a job, a business. That's more than I can say about Chicago right now," Sam pointed out.

"What about us?" Priya demanded.

"You can come and stay anytime you want to."

"I'll be there every other month," Chitra said. "I wonder if anyone is hiring in the area."

"Don't you dare move to California," Priya told her.

"Maybe we all should," Leena mused. "Aren't you getting sick of these brutal winters? I know I am. Besides, if Sam found love in Seahaven, maybe we could, too."

Sam decided to step in before Priya really lost control. "You should visit me at least. Why don't you all come in a couple of weeks and meet Ava, check out Seahaven and take a little vacation? I'll see if Ava has any breaks in her bookings coming up. We can hash out the pros and cons of Chicago and Seahaven together while we sit on her back deck and look at the ocean."

"No contest," Chitra laughed.

"Sounds lovely," Leena said.

"I do have some vacation time to use up," Priya said.

"Gotta run," Sam told them as Ava let herself back into the apartment. "Hope to see you soon."

CHAPTER 13

"*I*SN'T THAT BEN?" Ava asked the following morning. She pointed to the Trouble Bench as she and Sam came through the gate to the Cliff Garden. They were a few minutes early to meet Emma and Penelope and had intended to wander the garden paths and see what was blooming. Ashley wasn't in sight this morning; Ava wondered if she'd already been and gone.

In the foggy gloom, Ben was a lone figure against the backdrop of the silent ocean. He was facing away from them, motionless, hunched a bit as if he were shouldering the weight of the world.

"Ben?" Sam called softly as they approached.

When Ben turned, his face was haggard, and dark circles under his eyes hinted he'd been up all night.

"What happened?" Sam sat beside him. Ava waited a few paces away, unsure if she should sit on his other side or fade away so the men could talk.

"Chloe's gone," Ben said.

Ava stepped nearer.

"After we talked, we went back to the hotel, and I

told her I couldn't keep going with Scholar Central if you weren't a part of it. I told her she needed to leave the company so that you and I could work things out. I said I wasn't going to change my mind. She didn't take it very well. She smashed up the hotel room…" He trailed off, shaking his head. "Broke the TV. Cracked a mirror. She was totally out of control. They've asked us all to leave by checkout time this morning."

Ava exchanged a surprised look with Sam. Chloe was bossy and critical, but she hadn't thought the woman capable of violence.

"I didn't see it coming," Ben said, still shaking his head. "I knew she liked her own way, but I told myself she was just a modern woman sticking up for herself. Then it got—worse." He lifted his head to look at Sam. "Did she call you stupid when you two were together?"

Sam shook his head. "No, but she'd say things like, 'You don't know what you're talking about.'"

"She used to say that to me, too, but lately… I didn't like the name calling."

Ava didn't imagine anyone would like that.

"I laughed it all off. I'm a lot bigger than her—she couldn't hurt me," Ben said, lifting his hands, "so I put up with everything. The comments. The insults. She escalated things slowly enough I didn't notice how bad it was getting. I didn't want to lose her, you know?"

"I know," Sam said.

"Then she hit on you."

Ava bit her lip. So Ben realized that's what had happened the night she crashed onto Sam's balcony to find Chloe kissing him. She remembered the way she'd blamed Sam that night and was glad that hadn't been the end of their relationship.

"I hoped you'd realize that wasn't my doing," Sam said.

"At first I thought it might be. I guess that's what I wanted to believe because the alternative was so much worse, but when we settled into our hotel room and went to bed that night, she was… triumphant. And really turned on. She liked being the center of attention. Every time she orchestrated a fight between you and me, she wanted to sleep with me afterward." He shook his head. "Last night when I told her I wasn't giving her any shares of Scholar Central, it was a whole different ballgame. She lost her mind. Started screaming at me and wouldn't stop no matter what. When she started throwing things, I got out of there. The only other choice was to restrain her, and I didn't want to land in jail."

"I'm glad you left," Sam said.

"When I went back, the room was trashed, the police and hotel management there." Ben shook his head. "I haven't seen something like that since I left home. At least Dad had the excuse of alcohol."

Ava heard soft footsteps behind her and turned to see Emma coming through the gate, a covered plate and a glass of water in her hands. Ava went to meet her.

"Is everything all right?" Emma asked.

"It's Sam's friend—Ben. The one he told you about before," Ava said in a low voice. "I'm sure he'd be glad of some food and water. I think he's been up all night."

Emma approached the bench and talked quietly to the men, handing Ben the glass and the plate. When she removed the cover, Ava saw slices of fruit and several generous scones. Ben took a bite and washed it down with a long swallow of water.

"Chloe left my ring behind, so she knows there's no coming back from this," Ben went on.

"I'm sorry," Sam said again. Emma sat down on the end of the bench. Ava waited nearby, ready to be of service but keeping out of the way.

"I'm not," Ben said. "I feel like I've just woken up from a really bad dream. What the hell was I doing with her?"

"Was she... familiar?" Emma spoke up. "Sometimes we have to re-enact old relationships we haven't quite come to terms with before we can move on to something healthier."

Ben digested this. "She was familiar," he finally agreed. "She's just like my dad. Maybe I do have unfinished business with him. I never stood up to him. If Sam hadn't gotten his family to take me in, I would have finished growing up at home. I would have had to confront what he was doing sooner or later. Maybe I needed the chance to stand up for myself."

Sam nodded. "I can see that."

"You'll come back to Scholar Central?" Ben asked him. "I know I messed up—I know you'll never trust me."

"I trust you," Sam said.

"I don't know how you can," Ben said. "I jumped at the chance to be with your fiancée. She nearly convinced me to give her shares so we could outvote you in your own company."

"But you won't do it again, will you? The next time you fall for a woman, she's going to be amazing. From now on, no one's going to be able to get anything past you."

Ben snorted. "You got that right. From now on, cynical and suspicious are my new middle names."

"I've got a whole lot of new ideas for Scholar Central, you know."

With a laugh, Ben shoved his shoulder with his own. "Watch it, or I'll have to bring Chloe back to reel you in."

"We can brainstorm them together. Make our product even better."

"Now you're talking."

"There's only one problem." Sam sobered up. "I told Ava I intend to stay in Seahaven. We'll have to figure out a way to work virtually. I can fly back and forth a couple of times a month."

"Or I can move to Seahaven, too," Ben offered. "Seems like a change of scenery could do me good."

"Really?" Sam asked.

"Really," Ben said.

Penelope entered the garden, came to meet them and looked at the gathered group. "Am I late to the party?"

"Nope," Sam said. "It's just getting started."

As Emma took the plate and glass to her house, Ava touched Sam's hand.

"Happy?"

"Very," he confirmed. "I guess I'd better skip the walk and go to the hotel with Ben to get the rest of my things. Should I meet you at the Blue House later?"

"Of course."

"Speaking of the Blue House," Ben said. "Any chance the rest of us could come and stay until Sunday? We've lost our hotel reservations."

"Chloe paid for two weeks," Ava said. "Of course you can come back. You might be my last clients, anyway, after Chloe leaves her evaluation of her stay. I don't think she'll have much positive to say."

"If she says anything bad, I'll leave my own review explaining everything that happened," Sam assured her.

"Me, too," Ben said. "I'm not going to let my mistakes ruin your business."

"I appreciate that." Ava beamed at them. She hadn't been letting herself think about the future, but fear of what Chloe could do to her reputation was eating away at the back of her mind. One bad review could kill a vacation rental's profits.

"I appreciate you letting us come back." Ben's relief was palpable. "Maybe we can salvage something of this trip. Have a couple of days at the beach. Brainstorm your ideas, Sam. Get a bunch of sun before it's time to go home."

"Would you and your friends be up for testing out my next cooking class?" Emma asked. "It's always a fun time, and I'm trying some new recipes and techniques. I wouldn't mind having friends try them first before I take them public. Some of the recipes are from my cookbook. Noah and I are making good progress on it."

"You really should try it," Ava told them. "Emma's cooking is phenomenal, and you should see the photos Noah has been taking of the results."

"Sure," Sam said. "That's a great idea."

They walked together to the garden gate. Once they reached the sidewalk they separated, Ava and her friends to do their usual morning walk, Sam and Ben to head to the hotel.

"You sure you're okay with all this?" Sam asked him.

"I'm better than okay. I feel like I just got my life back."

CHAPTER 14

September

"*H*OW IS THE best teacher ever doing today?"

Ava dropped her oversized bag in the entryway of their suite and stepped into Sam's embrace. These days her apartment felt a little crowded with two desks lined up against the wall across from their bed, one for each of them. Sam was still working from home, but that would change when Scholar Central officially moved to Seahaven next spring. He and Ben had started scouting office space in some of the commercial buildings, and she was sure they'd find something suitable.

For now, she enjoyed coming home to find Sam there, on a video call with his fellow workers, or leaning back in his chair trying to solve some coding problem in his head, or typing furiously at his keyboard, getting a new idea down before it escaped him. He always broke off what he was doing when she came in and greeted her with a hug and kiss.

They both had work hours that stretched beyond dinner, but they made it a point to put everything away by eight and cover their workstations with the decorative weaving Ava's parents had given her on her birthday, before they went out on the balcony, wrapped themselves in blankets if the night was cool and talked for an hour to wind down. Today was a Friday, which meant she didn't need to rush to get any more work done tonight. Sam had promised to order food so they could simply relax.

"I'm really good," Ava told him, still in his embrace. "I took my students to Shelbridge Heights today. Remember that place?"

"How could I forget our picnic amid the devastation?" Sam joked. "It was very romantic."

"Until we got into an argument," she reminded him. She was grateful they'd found their way to a place where disagreements were few and far between. They had found ways to fit in fun and adventure around their jobs. They got up early for walks and surfing now that they'd both had lessons with the Surf Dads and Moms, hiked and camped on weekends, had bonfires on the beach with friends.

"An argument about whether or not I could do more than kiss you," he said. "Glad you came to see my side of things."

"Me, too." They exchanged a grin that promised all sorts of fun later, but Ava was tired from her day at work—and thirsty. She went to look in the refrigerator. "We talked about forest fires and patterns of regrowth. It was great."

"I'll bet the kids loved it."

"They're so happy outside," Ava said. "So am I. I have the perfect career."

"I have the perfect girlfriend." Sam followed her into the kitchen area and kissed her neck just under her ear. Ava felt the sensation down to her toes.

"I'm glad you think so."

"Our food should be here in ten minutes," Sam pulled back.

"Wonderful." Ava poured some juice, put her things away, changed into more comfortable clothes and freshened up. When the food arrived, they took it out on the deck since the evening was warm.

"I was thinking," Sam said when they were comfortably situated, "about kids of our own."

Ava, her fork halfway to her mouth, stilled, then set it down on her place. "Kids of our own?" she repeated.

Sam nodded and reached over to take her hand. "Is it possible to time things so a baby arrives over summer vacation?"

Ava found herself counting months. "I'd need to get pregnant next month to line that up right."

"Exactly." He squeezed her fingers. "And I want to marry you first."

Ava stared at him. "What are you asking me?"

"Ava Ingerson." He put his plate down and came to kneel before her, still holding her hand. "Would you do me the honor of becoming my wife?"

Love and joy and wonder welled up inside her and other things she couldn't even name. They'd fit into each other's lives so easily since Sam had moved in, she wondered if he'd grown too comfortable to want anything to change. "You want to get married—by next month?" She wasn't sure how she felt about that. On the one hand, it was so close. On the other, she didn't want to wait another minute to join her life to Sam's for all time. She was ready. Was he?

"I know it's crazy, but I don't want to wait any longer," he said, echoing her thoughts. "I want to know I'm going to spend the rest of my life with you. I want to start our family. I want to cherish you forever. Can you understand that?"

She nodded. It was the same way she felt about him. And to have a baby—she wanted that, too, but she was almost afraid to admit it. Starting a family meant they really would settle down.

"Say yes," he urged her. "We'll start the wedding plans today. Everyone will help us."

"Yes." She leaned forward and kissed him, almost dumping her plate of food on his lap in the process. "Yes, I will marry you, and yes, I want to have a baby. I really want that, Sam."

"I do, too. I love you." He took her plate and placed it on the floor of the deck, then pulled her to her feet, rising with her. "Ava, I'm going to spend my life making you the happiest woman on earth."

"I already am." Could she really be getting everything she wanted? Ava found herself braced for the next shoe to drop, but maybe it wouldn't. Maybe it was perfectly fine to want a husband, children—a community she loved.

"We could start now," Sam suggested. "After you're done with your dinner."

"I'm done." Ava laughed at her own eagerness. She was already unbuttoning her blouse, neighbors be damned. She backed up to the sliding doors and inside, leading Sam to their bed. Once she'd tossed her blouse aside, he took over undressing her. Moments later they were under the covers. "This will only be practice, though. I'm on birth control," she reminded him. "I'll have to go off it."

"Practice is just fine," Sam said as they joined together. Ava sighed as he filled her, knowing she'd remember this the rest of her life.

"I'm sure I'll enjoy every minute of it."

SAM COULDN'T GET enough of Ava. Lost in the feel of her, he let pure sensation guide him. Every curve of her body under his hands made him want her even more. When he was with Ava, he felt like his only purpose was to worship her. He didn't know how making her feel good made him feel so turned on, but it did, and tonight he wanted to show her what she meant to him.

He took his time, showering every part of her with his attention. Ava moaned as he touched her, urging him closer, but he held off until he knew she was as close as he was to losing control.

Knowing soon they would try for a baby made him hungrier for her than he'd ever felt before, something he wouldn't have thought possible. When their first throes of passion were over, Sam found himself unable to stop touching her. Their second round of lovemaking was slow and thorough. Their third, sometime later that night, was fast and hard and hot.

He couldn't sleep even after Ava had been softly breathing beside him for quite some time, so he got out of bed slowly, crept through the still-open door onto the balcony and allowed the moonlight to bathe him.

I'll be a good husband and a good father, he vowed to the ocean and the stars. *I'll never leave her. I'll protect and provide for my family.*

He didn't feel like he was making any promises he couldn't keep. Sam hadn't felt this sense of purpose since the day he and Ben came up with the idea of Scholar Central. Energized, he wanted to pace the deck, or sneak out to run on the beach, but instead he kept watch over his sleeping wife-to-be and whispered more promises as the night slowly passed.

Early in the morning, he slid back beneath the covers, ready to kiss Ava when she woke.

"Morning," she murmured sleepily sometime later.

"Morning."

"Sleep well?" She pushed up onto her elbows and blinked in the sunlight streaming in.

"Best night I've ever had."

"I WISH YOU two could be my trial customers," Penelope said when they gathered for their predawn walk. It was a Saturday. The men had gone surfing; it was just Emma and Penelope with Ava today. "Unfortunately, Fisherman's Point—I mean, EdgeCliff Manor—won't be done by then. I'll still be waiting for the delivery of all my appliances."

"I know," Ava told her. "But I hope you'll help me hold the wedding at the Blue House."

"Of course! I'm so excited." Penelope bounced on her toes. "I'm so happy for you. Sam is a great guy."

"He really is, and he and Noah get along so well. What are the chances of that?" Emma said.

"We're really lucky." Ava linked arms with her friends. "I'm so glad he agreed to stay here. I don't know what I would have done if he'd gone back to Chicago."

"I'm glad he didn't figure out a way to change your mind about going with him."

"No way. I'm staying right here." She turned to Penelope. "Meanwhile, you're getting closer and closer to being ready for business. Aren't you thrilled?"

"Thrilled—and scared. I need to get a bunch of bookings, fast. I wonder if you would mind doing a bridal photo shoot at my place in the next few weeks? We could get flowers, and you and Sam could dress up so I can get some good shots up on my website. I've had an idea. I thought if I could get someone kind of famous to have their wedding at Edgecliff Manor—someone like a minor celebrity—then that might drum up a lot of business. I need some beautiful photos to entice a person like that to book their wedding with me."

"I'm game. Anything to help a friend." She couldn't wait to buy her wedding gown. Searching for one would be so much fun. "You two will come along to help pick out my dress, won't you?"

"Of course," Emma said. "And I'm sure Noah would be glad to take some photos."

"Awesome." Penelope hugged them both. "Maybe I won't have to sell my boat, after all."

"You'd better not. You deserve that boat," Ava said. "Someday you'll have to take us out on it."

"Someday," Penelope promised.

"WHAT DO YOU think about a picnic?" Sam asked when he returned from surfing.

"That sounds nice. What should we pack for lunch?" She was already heading for the refrigerator to see what she had on hand when Sam snagged her fingers in his and stopped her.

"Emma's already making a basket for us. I asked her when I picked up Noah to go surfing."

"Really? I was just there and she didn't say a word."

"It was a surprise."

"You pulled it off. You've put some thought into this."

"Yes, I have." He stole a kiss. "I think about you all the time. Didn't you know that?"

"I had a feeling." Ava let him gather her close and enjoyed the comfort of being in his arms. "It's kind of more exciting to go on a picnic when someone else packs the basket."

"It's the mystery of what it will contain."

"And where we're going."

"You'll see soon enough. Come here." He led her to the bed. "We've got an hour before it's time to pick up the basket."

"How ever will we pass the time?" Ava wondered dramatically.

"I can think of a few ways."

They were a little late getting to Emma's house, but she greeted them with a broad smile.

"Have fun, you two. I think I outdid myself with this lunch."

"Everything you make is incredible," Ava told her.

They took the RAV4, Ava content to be the passenger today. She daydreamed about the future as they drove along the ocean, but when they circled through the Leaf to the shopping district by the main tourist beach in town, she sat up straight to get a better look around.

"Are we going to Seahaven Castle?"

"You guessed it. We'll picnic on the bluffs in front of its entrance. There's just one quick stop we need to make first."

Ava got out of the car and joined him on the sidewalk. Sam had parked in front of Ashbury Jewelers. He took her hand and led her to its door.

"Sam?"

"Time you had a ring, don't you think?" He ushered her inside, and Ava let him, dazed by the idea. She hadn't even thought of a ring. "Noah said this is where he and Emma found theirs. I figured it was the best place to look."

"Of course." She felt a little shy as they approached the counter. A broad-shouldered man, whose name tag read "Lance," looked up and greeted them from where he was sketching on a piece of paper.

"Be with you in a minute." His pencil flashed across the paper, and Ava saw he was drawing a ring.

"Lance designs most of the jewelry we sell." A smaller man came out of the back of the shop. "Hi, I'm Gary. Can I show you anything?"

"We're looking for an engagement ring," Sam told him.

"How wonderful to be able to design any piece of jewelry you want," Ava said, still fascinated by Lance's sketch.

"If you can't find what you want in one of the trays,

we could always design a ring together," Lance offered.

"We're kind of in a hurry," Ava told him, "but someday I'd love to do that."

"Well, why don't you take a look at some of these," Gary said. "We have loads of rings to choose from."

Sam made a game of handing her five or six rings at a time and making her choose the best one from each lot until they had five finalists lined up on the counter. She liked one in particular, a platinum swoop that reminded her of an ocean wave, set with five diamonds of cascading size, but she played the game until the end, finally holding up the one she'd decided on, secure in the knowledge it really was the one for her.

"Let's try that on." Gary handed the ring to Sam, who slid it on her ring finger. "That's not bad," he said approvingly. "Is it too loose?"

"Actually, I think it's just right."

Gary checked to be sure and nodded. "That's a coincidence. Usually we'd have to resize it for you."

"I guess it really must be the right ring," Sam said.

Ava slid it off and handed it back to Gary, who took Sam to the till to wrap up the transaction.

"Onward to the Castle," Sam said when they were done, taking her hand again. She liked how much he liked to touch her. He was never overbearing—just present. He enjoyed being connected to her, she thought, and she enjoyed it, too.

They got into her car, drove onto the bluffs and

turned into the large parking lot beside the Castle.

"The view here is fantastic," Sam said as they got out.

"The view everywhere in Seahaven is fantastic." Ava laughed. "But it's very romantic to have a castle in the background."

"I sure hope so."

Ava carried a blanket, Sam hefted the basket and together they made their way to the grassy area between the Castle and the bluffs. Once they were seated, Ava opened the basket and began to lift things out. There was a bottle of wine, two glasses, a baguette, a platter of sliced cheese and salami, several salads, crudites and dip.

"We'll never be able to eat all this," she said, laughing.

"I bet we can make a pretty good dent in it."

They spent the next half hour doing just that. When they were done eating, Ava leaned against Sam, her head on his shoulder, lifting it only to take a sip of wine now and then.

"I never want to leave," she murmured. "This is perfect."

"I'm glad to hear it because I never want to leave, either." He pulled a little box from his pocket and opened it. "You sure you still want to marry me?" he asked.

"Positive." Sam slid the ring on her finger and kissed her until she was breathless. She held up her hand to get a look at it. "I love it. I love you, too." Ava thought she had to be glowing. She couldn't remember ever being this happy before.

"Good." Sam kissed her again. "I can't wait for the wedding."

"Do you think we'll feel different after it?"

"I think so. Don't you?"

She nodded. "There's something special about making a commitment in front of your family and friends," she said. "Especially when the person you're making it with believes in commitment."

"I do believe in commitments. You know that, right?"

She nodded again. "It's something I love about you."

He wrapped an arm around her. "I love everything about you."

"I GET THAT you and Ben have been through a lot and of course you want him as your best man at your wedding," Chitra said when Sam called his sisters to tell them the news, "but I don't see why it can't be best sister instead."

"If it was, I'd be the one filling that role," Priya said.

"Nonsense, I would," Leena said, stunning them all into silence. Leena wasn't usually one to put herself forward.

"What happened to peace and love and putting yourself last?" Chitra asked her.

"I never said anyone should put themselves last. One of the most important things you can do is acknowledge the best parts of yourself. And I'm the best sister. So there."

"There's no way I could choose between you three," Sam said before a fight could break out. "You're all fabulous sisters. I wouldn't have made it this far without you."

There was another pause.

"Who are you and what have you done with Sam?" Priya asked, laughing.

"Are you feeling all right?" Chitra asked him. "You never admit you need our help."

"My work here is done," Leena said. "You are a fully realized human being now."

Sam groaned. "Don't let a little praise go to your heads. You'll need to be good sisters to Ava from now on, too."

"We will," Chitra assured him.

"Can't wait to meet her," Priya said.

"I wouldn't have encouraged you to fall for her if I didn't like the sound of her," Leena said. "I'm sure she'll be a wonderful addition to the family."

"Speaking of additions to the family," Chitra said. "Are you thinking of having kids?"

"We'll see," Sam said, wanting to maintain a little mystery. If he wasn't careful, his sisters would think they could run his life.

"You're right, Chitra," Priya sighed. "If Sam has babies, we're all going to have to move to California. I can't live far from my nieces and nephews."

"At least he picked somewhere sunny," Leena said.

"When we come out for the wedding, we can look around at real estate," Priya said.

"Real estate?" Sam repeated. Would his whole family really uproot to join him here?

"Let's focus on one thing at a time," Leena intervened. "First let's get Sam married. Then we can worry about the rest of our lives."

CHAPTER 15

October

"*Y*OU LOOK BEAUTIFUL," Marie exclaimed when Ava turned from the mirror and let all the women who'd come to help her prepare for her wedding get a good look at her gown.

"You really do, even if marriage is an outdated construct of a patriarchal society," Ava's mother said.

"You're married," Ava pointed out.

"Tax breaks," her mother said. "I'd hoped that would change by the time my children grew up."

"Ellen, where's your sense of romance?" Marie exclaimed. "Marriage is a wonderful institution, and I'm glad Ava found a man she loves and admires enough to share her life with."

"I am, too," Ava said, determined for once not to let her mother's pronouncements throw her off. "And I love my dress." It was a crepe sheath dress with a low neckline that skimmed her body perfectly and flared at the hemline. If it was any other color than white, she'd feel right at home walking a red carpet in this gown. She knew she looked stunning in it and couldn't wait to see the look on Sam's face when she walked down the aisle.

She'd asked Emma, Penelope and Marie to be her bridesmaids. They wore mulberry-colored gowns that were just as elegant as her dress. Both mothers wore mauve, her own sporting a chic number she'd bought in Paris on her way home from West Sumatra and Sam's in a traditional sari. Everyone looked beautiful in Ava's eyes, and the Blue House was at its best.

They were to be married on the back deck, which Emma and Penelope had helped to decorate. Kate, Aurora and Connor made sure the lawn beyond it was in fantastic shape. A catering company was providing the appetizers and dinner after the ceremony, but Emma had made them the most wonderful wedding cake.

"This place is growing on me," her mother remarked as she got ready to go downstairs and take her seat. "I always thought California was a little too obvious in its charms, but your home has real character and so do your friends."

"Thank you." Tears stung Ava's eyes. From her mother that was a hell of a compliment.

"Your father is proud of you," her mother went on. "We both are." She dropped a kiss on Ava's cheek and made for the door before Ava could entirely take that in.

Proud of her?

That meant a lot.

"I'm so happy Sam found you," Divya said, coming

to give her a hug, careful not to crush Ava's dress or smear her makeup. "You've made my son so happy. He's needed a good woman to center his world."

"I'm glad he found me," Ava said. "You've raised a wonderful son."

Divya beamed at her, pressed her hands and followed Ava's mother out the door.

Ava turned to the mirror to check her makeup one last time.

"Excited?" Penelope asked her.

"My heart is beating a mile a minute," Ava admitted.

"That means you're exactly where you should be."

Ava nodded. She didn't have any doubts about that. She loved Sam and knew he'd be a good partner. He'd already become her best friend.

"Time to take our places," Penelope said. She handed Ava her bouquet, and the four of them went to the door.

"Ready?" Emma asked.

"Ready," Ava said.

"YOU LOOK SO handsome," Chitra said as she followed Sam from the room where he'd gotten ready, Priya and Leena close behind.

"Thank you." Sam's palms were damp as he headed for the stairs. It was time to take his place under the flowering arch they'd installed on the back deck.

"Do us proud," Priya told him as she hurried past to

take her seat.

"You've found your destiny," Leena said as she edged around him.

"We all love you." Chitra touched his arm and then she was gone, too.

Sam's father waited for him at the bottom of the stairs. Ben was standing at a respectful distance near the wide-open door leading to the deck.

"You've done very well for yourself," his father said. "I want you to know how proud we are of you and how happy we are to welcome Ava to our family."

"Thanks."

"Your sisters think we should sell the house and buy something out here."

Chitra had already found a job in San Jose. Priya was interviewing at a hospital in San Francisco later this week. Leena had taken a more philosophical stance. "I'm sure an opportunity will present itself if I'm meant to live in California," she'd told him a week ago.

"You should live where you want to live," he told his father, "although of course we'd love to have you nearby."

"It's a conversation for another time," his father said. "Now, let's get you married." He shook Sam's hand. "See you on the other side."

When Sam reached the doors to the deck, Ben joined him and led him to the arch.

"Ready?"

319

"I think so." Sam took a deep breath. "I can't believe this is happening."

"But you're happy, right?"

"You bet I am. This is what I wanted. A wife. A family. Working with my best friend."

Ben brightened. "It's what I want, too. Think there's any chance I meet someone in Seahaven? It's not that big a place."

"I think there's every chance you could meet someone here. Just be yourself. Tell people who you are and what you want. Make sure the women who are attracted to you know the kind of man you are, so you weed out the ones who aren't compatible."

"Is that what you were doing when you met Ava?"

"Not exactly," Sam admitted. "But somehow it all worked out."

"Guess that's what counts," Ben said. "I suppose I've got to be patient. Not sure I want to be, though."

Sam patted him on the back. "Soon as I'm married and back from my honeymoon, I'll get to work on finding you a woman."

"Deal," Ben said. "I think the ceremony is about to start." The strains of Wagner's "Bridal Chorus" started up. Ava must be close to walking down the aisle.

Sam took another deep breath and let it out. He couldn't wait to see his bride.

WHEN AVA STEPPED out of the house onto the back

deck on her father's arm, she was gratified by the number of friends and family who were there to witness the vows she was making to Sam, but she barely registered their faces. Her gaze was drawn inexorably to the man she was about to marry. Sam was gazing back at her, so much love shining in his eyes that it took her breath away.

She'd never thought it possible that a man could build his life around hers the way Sam was doing. He was so strong and so loving, their time together was always a joy. Since he'd moved in, she'd grown in confidence with both her teaching and her business. He never butted in, but he was a resource for her when times got hard, always ready to listen when she needed to air her frustrations, ready to pitch in when there was a job to do, and ready to back her up, a strong, solid presence in her corner when she needed his help.

Together was a word she hadn't really understood before. Growing up, she was on the fringes of her family. With Todd, she was more like an audience for the show he put on daily. Being with Sam was different. They were present for each other. Able to discuss things and hammer out common ground. When Sam took her hand, it wasn't to hurry her along or dictate the direction she should head, it was to make that connection between them tangible. They faced troubles together, talked together, laughed together, made love together.

And she never wanted to be apart from him again.

She reached the flower archway Kate and Aurora had constructed with Connor's help. Her father kissed her on the cheek and passed her over to Sam. Ava smiled up at her fiancé as he took her hand. There they were again— connected—just the way she liked it.

Throughout their vows, he kept his gaze on hers, and she hoped he could read just how much he meant to her in his eyes.

"You may now kiss the bride," the officiant said.

Ava went up on tiptoe as Sam bent down. Their kiss went on and on until the whoops and cheers of their guests rained down around them.

When they finally pulled apart, Ava's heart was full. This was the life she'd always wanted, and now she had the man she wanted to spend it with.

"Happy?" Sam asked.

"Happy," she confirmed.

SAM NEVER WANTED to let Ava go again, but they were thronged as they walked up the aisle. Soon everyone was moving the folding chairs aside so tables could be set up on the deck and lawn. The caterers began to carry platters of food out from the kitchen, and the hubbub of voices and laughter filled the air.

When they'd shaken everyone's hands and gotten hugs and kisses from enthusiastic friends and family, he drew Ava to the side.

"Let everyone else get things set up. I want a minute

with you."

"You're going to get a whole lifetime with me."

"Good." He kissed her again, even longer than they had before, and felt his whole body stirring with want, the way it always did when she was near.

"I love you," he told her. "I always will."

"I love you, too."

"Can't wait to be alone with you. It's time for us to really start working on that baby."

"I'm looking forward to it. But I think this party is going to go on for a while."

"Guess that's okay." He lost himself in kissing her some more. All too soon it was time for them to take their places at the head table, which had been set up on the deck.

"Guess what?" Penelope asked when they were seated with their meals. "I got confirmation this morning. My first guests are coming next month. I'm going to host a celebrity wedding!"

"That's fantastic!" Ava said. Sam had a feeling she wanted everyone to be as happy as they were.

"Who is it?" he asked.

"Olivia Raquette. She's marrying Vincent Chadwick."

"The actor?"

"That's right. Olivia is a social media personality, and together the two of them will garner a lot of attention. If I can pull this off, I should get plenty of bookings!"

Ava beamed at her. Emma popped up from her chair

and hugged Penelope. "I'm so proud of you."

"I'm proud of all of us," Ava said. "All of our dreams coming true."

"I hope so," Penelope said wistfully.

Later, when the deck was cleared for their first dance together, Sam gladly took Ava in his arms again.

"Have all your dreams come true?" he murmured, drawing her close and swaying with her.

"They have," she confirmed. "What about you?"

"Every single one."

To find out more about Emma, Noah, Ava, Penelope and the other inhabitants of Seahaven, look for Beach House Wedding, volume 3 in the Beach House series.

About the Author

With over one-and-a-half million books sold, NYT, USA Today and WSJ bestselling author Cora Seton writes contemporary women's fiction and romance. She has thirty-nine novels and novellas currently set in the fictional towns of Seahaven, California and Chance Creek, Montana, with many more in the works. Cora loves the ocean, kayaking, gardening, reading, binge-watching Jane Austen movies, keeping up with the latest technology and indulging in old-fashioned pursuits. She lives on beautiful Vancouver Island with her husband, children and two cats.

Visit **www.coraseton.com** to read about new releases, contests and other cool events!

Made in United States
North Haven, CT
20 April 2022

18418797R10200